SHRINE OF STARS

SOUL COURT ASCENSION BOOK THREE

MEL HARDING-SHAW

CORUSCATE PRESS

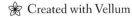

For everyone who hasn't found their City of Souls yet.

You deserve a place to belong.

CHAPTER 1

BAST

"Fuck!"

The despair and frustration of Bast's cry was absorbed by the shadowed limestone of the cave system as he stared at the writhing mass of darkness filling the tunnel ahead. It was blocking him from reaching the last place Hel had been before she'd disappeared—dragged through a portal to her homicidal father after a lifetime running from him.

The contagion outbreak on the edge of the Earth Court council chamber was the fastest growing he'd ever seen, strengthened by feeding on the sentience of the stronghold itself as its deadly absence stretched toward the large population of elementals residing there. For the first time ever, Bast was grateful he couldn't communicate with the being that embodied the caves surrounding him like the rest of his kind could. The slumped unconscious bodies of the Earth Lord Mica and the other elemental rulers nearby spoke to the dangerous psychic feedback the damaged stronghold must be projecting.

1

He didn't have time to deal with them.

They'd taken Hel. His mate. His everything. If Hel was right about her father's intentions, she wouldn't last long and their mating bond would take him right along with her when she died.

But it wasn't just that. He'd lost little Kaia as well. The girl's kidnappers had disappeared by the time he'd recovered from the shock of Hel's capture that sent him tumbling from the sky mid-flight in pursuit. Guilt screamed in him for the decision to race back to the Earth Stronghold. There was nothing he could do about Kaia until he had more information, though. The Air Court scouts who'd grabbed her had too much of a head start now.

With Hel out of his reach, he needed to make sure Kaia was safe before he followed his mate to his death, but none of that could happen before he sorted out the contagion he thought they'd permanently eliminated from the Melded Earths. The portal that had taken Hel from him must have let it back in from her father's world.

Bast's body thrummed with fear and rage as he forced himself to focus on the problem before him. One wingbeat at a time. That was the only way he'd be able to keep functioning.

Dragging his power around himself, he channelled his pain into a vast sphere of sparking silver energy that tightened around the ravenous absence like a noose. His phone was vibrating in his pocket, but he couldn't spare it any attention. The mindless taint on reality was fighting him harder than it ever had before. He refused to relent. He needed to finish this already so he could find a way to get to Hel. Every cell in his body was screaming for her.

As he tightened his sphere around the darkness, each

shuddering contraction sent shots of agony through him. He didn't let up until the containment sphere's radius was no wider than his wingspan. There was no point making it any smaller. No one would be using this side tunnel to the chamber again. Even with the contagion now pulled clear, the tunnel that surrounded it showed the effects of its taint. Pale limestone walls that once reflected the magical lights still hanging in the council chamber as they shone with veins of glittering mica were simply gone. In their place was a dark void—the absence of existence. That was what this contagion did. Removing reality and leaving nothing in its place. Just like if someone removed Hel from his soul, there would be nothing left of him.

With so much distance between them, his connection to Hel was no more than gossamer thread where before it had wrapped through every part of him. Bast couldn't access enough of her power to get to her so many worlds away, but now he'd dealt with the contagion he could sense with the dregs of her power that the portal she'd been taken through was gone. There was no way to follow her path. He swallowed another scream of frustration. Now was not the time to show weakness.

A scrape of cloth on stone behind him and a muffled moan had him turning toward the elementals at his back in time to watch Lord Mica stumble to his feet, his copper wings dragging behind him as he clutched his head.

"You need to anchor my construct and have the stronghold grow walls around it so no one touches the void," Bast said, voice curt.

He was too exhausted and desperate to be polite. His people had been taken in the heart of this man's territory. Mica had promised them the safety of guest right, and, in return, the niece of his heart and the woman who was a piece of his soul had been torn from him.

Mica blinked and for the first time Bast could remember, he saw anger on the usually temperate ruler's face. "Look what you've done to my stronghold! I told you your mate was a liability."

Bast took a deep breath and tried to remind himself that Mica would be half-crazed from feeling the stronghold's pain as his own. The loss of part of its structure so deep in its core and the deaths of Mica's people where the contagion had spread would be like torture to the Earth Lord. The reminder didn't help. He was too raw. Bast took a single threatening step toward Mica, his black wings flared wide.

"Now is not the time to argue," a much calmer voice said from his left.

Bast glanced over at Kairon, one of the vampyr whose reality had been melded with theirs by Hel's father. It seemed like an age since he'd first walked into the council room with Kairon and Hel at his side, but it had probably only been an hour. Kairon was crouched next to Lady Nerida, his pale hand glowing red with his magic where it cupped her cheek. A circle of matching red light encircled each of his pupils as he watched Bast.

"What are you doing?" Bast asked, ignoring the still fuming Earth Lord who'd turned his back on him to finish entombing the contagion behind the living rock of the stronghold.

"I'm a healer. It took me a little while to synch with your elemental physiology, otherwise I would've had Lord Mica up sooner. I've got it now. I'll have them all conscious soon," Kairon replied.

His words proved true as Nerida, the Water Lady he was

healing, shot up into a sitting position. Drawing her blade in a blur of motion, she pressed it to the pale white skin of Kairon's neck. The man didn't even flinch as he kept his hand where it was and let the red glow of his magic slowly fade. A smirk spread across his face revealing a flash of sharp fangs as Nerida dug the dagger in a little harder and sent a tiny trickle of his blood running down to the leather of his collar.

"You elementals move so fast. We should at least hunt together first," he joked, the sexual innuendo in his voice clear even through the translation spell that was allowing them to communicate.

Nerida quirked an eyebrow in response but sheathed her blade and pulled away from him to stand. "Thank you," she murmured, quietly enough that Bast almost missed it.

Kairon just nodded and moved to the still prone Fire Lord nearby. Now that he wasn't distracted by the contagion, Bast looked around the space more carefully. It didn't take long to realise who was missing and what it likely meant. Aliya, the Lady of Air, was nowhere to be seen. She'd been working with Hel's father for who knew how long, but this was a new low even for her. As ruthless as the elemental rulers were, they still had rules. It was unheard of to damage one of their precious sentient strongholds this way, even if it was by recklessness rather than design. How had she even opened a portal when it wasn't an elemental magic?

Bast staggered as the ground beneath him trembled and a deep rumble carried through the surrounding limestone. He fought the urge to run as the sound grew and dust filled the space when the nearby tunnel crumpled in on itself, the stronghold responding to its Lord's call to seal away the damage. The movement of its walls should have been smooth and controlled, the benefits of a living home that could reshape itself at will, but instead the rock formed in fits and bursts of jagged motion and a high-pitched whine almost out of hearing range echoed beneath the grinding of the caves.

"Is the stronghold okay?" Bast asked, momentarily focusing on a pain outside the ache in his soul at Hel and Kaia's absence.

"No," Mica snapped, the same tension running through his voice as had echoed from the cave moments before.

Bast nodded once, unsure what else could be said between them, before striding further from the still waking rulers to make a call to Ra. Given how many times it'd rung, his righthand man must know something was wrong. The call barely had a chance to ring before Ra answered.

"What the fuck's going on there? Tijmen said Kaia's been taken?" Ra asked.

The question in his friend's so-familiar voice almost undid him. He hadn't had time to really process any of it. Now that he had a moment to breathe, the full weight of his failure to protect the one he loved hit him.

"They're both gone," he said, voice cracking.

"Wait, *both* of them? Who else was taken?"

"The kidnapping was a distraction so Aliya could grab Hel. Her father has her," Bast said, his voice flat with despair.

"But Aliya can't portal," Ra said, confused.

"Apparently, she found a way. Opened a rift up right in the heart of the Earth Stronghold and let in the contagion. We've only just got it under control."

"Oh, fuck," Ra gasped.

Their City of Souls might not be a stronghold like the other courts, but after co-ordinating Bast's efforts to contain the contagion over the previous months, Ra was familiar with what an outbreak like that meant for Mica's home.

"I need you to track Kaia. They were ten minutes east of the stronghold when I collapsed. They must be heading toward Aliya's territory. Find them," Bast said.

"Will do. But if they're screening their passage with magic, we won't be able to pick them up by satellite. What about Hel?"

"She's not on this world anymore. We need to find Tir. They're the only chance of reaching her." And who knew how long that would take. Bast hadn't seen the Archivist since the day Tir had portalled them away from the arachdryn swarming them and their attackers in the Spider-hive in exchange for a 'life-debt'.

"We don't have any way to contact them—unless you can use Hel's power to portal to them like you did before?" Ra asked.

"I can't use her power when she's so far away. Reach out to our separatist contacts. They must have a way of contacting Tir. We don't have time to delay. If Hel's father kills her..."

"We won't let that happen. And I won't ever let you go, brother," Ra said.

"You might not have a choice."

Bast ended the call and turned back to the council table. He'd been speaking quietly enough to mask his conversation from the other rulers, but Kairon was watching him closely, his ears flicking independently from each other. The vampyr had such sensitive hearing he'd probably heard everything they'd said. Behind him, Ty had revived enough to sit slouched at the table. Nerida and Mica had joined him there.

Between one blink and the next, Kairon was suddenly

beside him, voice soft as he spoke for Bast's ears alone. "I can help you find the child. My kind are trackers as well as healers. If you have something of hers, I can use it to trace her blood once we're within a certain radius of her location."

"In exchange for what?" Bast asked.

"My immediate clan is scattered and hiding here. We're not used to your predators and the elemental cities won't let us inside their boundaries. Nor do we have currency to purchase anything from your people. Give us a home."

"How many people are we talking?" Bast asked.

It wouldn't be the first time they'd taken in refugees or outcasts. That was the founding principle of the elemental free city that had existed there before the first melding, and it had only grown stronger when the realities merged and they became the City of Souls. That was how Bast came to live there in the first place.

"Initially, only as many as I can call to me quickly as we travel back. A dozen, perhaps. But more would follow," Kairon said.

"I can't carry you safely right now. The flight is too long and if something happens to Hel and I ... collapse ... you'd be stuck in the middle of the ocean. But if Ra can get hold of our archivist, we may be able to transport you. We'll take your twelve, but I won't commit to more until we find Kaia."

Kairon inclined his head. "That will give us time to sound each other out, yes? See if our worldviews align. I agree to your terms."

"Are you making a deal with the enemy behind our back, Bastion?" Ty sneered from across the room.

"Kairon is a neutral party. Unlike the man you helped tip off to my mate's location who has caused literally millions of deaths on our Earths not once, but *twice* now," Bast growled back.

Ty, surprisingly, looked uncomfortable at that reminder and broke eye contact with him. "Aliya said he would leave us alone once he had her. It seemed like a small sacrifice to make," he muttered.

"And you believed her? What was Aliya's plan for getting rid of the contagion once he left with my mate? Whether he would've forced another melding or not once he got hold of her, he wasn't going to save us from that threat. *Hel* did that. It was her power that shifted it from our world. He would've left us to die. And now Aliya's let it back in," Bast said.

"Aliya will be dealt with," Nerida said, her voice so low it was nothing more than a growl.

"This can wait. Show me to your injured, Earth Lord. I will heal them," Kairon said, cutting through the tension again. He was obviously used to navigating a political world.

It was nightfall before Ra finally got back in touch with him. Kairon had healed the two scouts Bast had brought with him of the wounds Aliya's kidnappers had inflicted and stabilised the worst of the injuries among Mica's people. No one touched by the contagion had survived, but the stronghold's violent throes of agony had caused rockfalls and a number of accidents that left behind an overflowing infirmary. Elementals healed quickly and Mica had his own healing mages, but they were fully engaged in trying to heal the injured stronghold so it wouldn't put anyone else at risk.

Kairon's blood-red power was the fastest way to get people back on their feet and to safety.

The vampyr had selflessly used his superior healing ability to help, or perhaps it would be more accurate to say he'd calculatingly used his healing ability. Bast was certain Kairon was keeping track of goodwill won and debts owed. Either way, he was grateful his own people were recovered enough to fly so they weren't stuck there and no one could fault the vampyr's dedication. Kairon was slumped asleep on a couch in the guest suite they'd been shown to when it had become clear he was fading, exhausted by his power expenditure.

"How are you holding up?" Ra asked when Bast answered the phone.

Bast sighed and ignored the question he was too broken to answer. "Did you find Tir?"

"That bad, huh?" Ra said, but he quickly got back to business. "Yeah. They're here with me now. I'll put you on speaker."

"I can't take you to your mate, Bastion," Tir's sibilant voice said a moment later.

Bast's hand clenched tight on the table he was sitting at and his wings trembled as he fought to keep from raising his voice. "Why not? You helped her before. He'll kill her!"

"Perhaps. But Sol was never one to throw away power and she proved she has that in abundance when the two of you shifted the contagion. I think he will reconsider his approach now he has her in his possession. Regardless, I can't portal somewhere the most powerful world-traveller in existence rules. He would sense the incursion before we even set foot there and his entire army would be waiting. That's if he didn't just collapse my portal and kill us en route. There's a reason he's an emperor. His magic is vast. Far greater than mine."

Bast slammed his fist down in frustration. "Fine. Can you at least bring Kaia back to us?"

"Watch your tone, Bastion. I am not your minion. You owe me a life debt already. Don't forget it," Tir said.

Bast opened his mouth and then swallowed back the harsh words. Tir was right. He needed their help and he wasn't going to get it by throwing his weight around.

"Please," he begged, voice cracking.

Tir sighed. "Children are precious. You know I would bring her back even if you hadn't asked, but I can't get a lock on her. Something is blocking me. If you can find her, and she's still on these Earths, I can get us there."

"I have someone who can track her once Ra gets us a location close enough—a vampyr from the new reality. I was hoping you might be able to help me portal us and some of his people back to the City."

"He's one of the vampyr? I've been trying to reach out to them but they're wary of me. I have a soft spot for the underdogs."

Bast smiled to himself. He was well aware of Tir's soft spot, what with all their links to the human separatists. He'd been counting on it. It was no surprise the vampyr were wary of Tir. If you weren't used to the writhing tentacles emerging from their scalp and the rows of razor sharp teeth on their jaw with too many hinges, they were fairly intimidating.

As if sensing he was the topic of discussion, Kairon stirred across the room and sat up to watch Bast talk. He didn't need to have the phone on speaker at his end for Kairon to keep track of the conversation and his translation spell was still attached to the vampyr. Although he'd noticed Kairon was already picking up their language.

"I'm letting him and some of his people live in the City of Souls on a trial basis. They'll help us track Kaia and then we'll see where we end up. I can't risk flying back if Hel..." Bast's words trailed off as his throat closed and the sharp ever-present ache in his chest grew even worse.

"Is six hours long enough for you to find his people? I'll portal to wherever you are then," Tir said.

Bast shot a querying look in the vampyr's direction and he nodded.

"My people move fast. Get us to a safe location and I will call them to me," Kairon said.

"See you in six hours," Bast confirmed, ending the call.

MICA LOOKED the closest to haggard Bast had ever seen him as they bid the Earth Lord farewell just outside the soaring entrance cave to his stronghold. His collared shirt was untucked on one side, there was dirt smudged down one cheek and a stain suspiciously like blood on the crumpled knee of his pants. Tension tightened his eyes, making his usually ageless face appear older, although his copper wings were still held perfectly tight to his back. He might be messy, but he'd regained some of the control he was so well known for.

"Travel safe," Mica said, his voice gravelly and distant and his eyes already searching the nearby rock formations for only he knew what.

Bast opened his mouth to respond but a noise from above had him throwing a shield of magic over the group as a shower of limestone rained down on them. He scowled at the reckless insult from the stronghold before noticing a fresh cut on Mica's face from the debris. That was concerning. He'd have to ask his scouts what they sensed from the traumatised stronghold once they were clear because, even damaged, it shouldn't have done anything to accidentally injure its lord. Not to mention the breach of guest-right without a direct order. Mica's gaze uncharacteristically dropped to his feet and he winced. The stronghold was clearly unstable. Empathy warred with Bast's lingering anger as he realised this damage to its psyche would not heal easily.

"Do you need anything?" he asked, finally.

Mica looked up in surprise and then ran a tired hand over his face. "Not unless you can portal away that contagion for me. Even if we could figure out how to heal the gaping hole in my home's core, the threat of the contagion's presence in such a vulnerable position is making it fearful. Unpredictable."

That looked like an understatement given Mica's condition. Bast wouldn't be surprised if the sentience in the caves was all but rabid with fear. Even contained behind shields, the contagion's threat of total annihilation was a constant dark discomfit in the back of his mind. It would be so much worse for the stronghold that had to deal with it nestled in the very heart of its body.

"I need Hel for that. When I get her back, we'll come and get rid of it," Bast said.

Mica winced. They both knew he had no way of getting to her and she may well die at any moment while he stood helpless worlds away.

Kairon had been standing so silently wrapped in shadow nearby that they both startled a little as his soft voice broke into their conversation. "I will talk to the other voices of my people and see if there is anything we can try for your stronghold, Lord Mica. Our healing comes from lifeblood though, and your caves have none."

Mica nodded. "I appreciate anything you can do. Go well."

Bast nodded and his scouts scooped up the ends of the sling they would use to carry Kairon as the vampyr settled himself into its seat. Bast couldn't risk carrying it himself in case he fell from the sky when something happened to Hel. The constant threat was like waiting for an axe to fall on his soul and he rubbed his aching heart as he struggled to control the burning helpless need to protect her.

Without another word, he powered up from the ground, launching himself into the sky faster than was necessary in the vain hope he could outfly the crushing despair for a moment. He was quickly forced to rein himself in. His scouts couldn't hope to keep pace with him even if they hadn't been weighed down with a passenger and he circled back to them in a wide arc over the trees of the forest city bordering Mica's home.

Kairon had told them he'd call his people to him on an outcrop of rock overlooking the grassland near where Bast had first spotted the vampyr. They flew there in silence, although he was all too conscious of the worried glances Tijmen and Blaine were shooting him.

The sun was setting in tones of burnt amber as they arrived at the outcrop and the three elementals quickly took up sentry positions while Kairon sunk to a crouch on the reddened earth and pulled a dagger from his belt. The vampyr was still an unknown quantity and Bast could feel the tension radiating from his scouts as they kept one eye on the potential threat behind them even as they scanned the horizon for predators. Kairon ignored them all, focused entirely on himself and the circle he'd drawn in the earth as he dragged a blade across his palm and let the viscous dark-red liquid drop to the dry ground. His soft voice echoed in the air around them as he chanted something in his native language the translation spell failed to decipher, rhythmic and thrumming with power. After long minutes, the words faded until all that remained was a barely audible low hum.

Bast glanced back down at the earth and saw the drops of Kairon's blood hadn't sunk into the ground but were suspended spheres of red vibrating softly in time to the ongoing bass of the vampyr's call.

Forcing himself to turn and face outward, Bast watched as full darkness fell on the landscape, stretching his awareness wide. The wyrms that had threatened them on the way to Mica's stronghold were unlikely to burrow through this rock to attack them, but there were plenty of other threats in the night and he couldn't afford to let himself be distracted.

Even so, he almost missed the first shadowy form slipping through the night as they approached their position. Kairon's people were hunters, predators, and they moved with an eerie silence and alarming speed, barely disturbing the long grass around them.

"Welcome," Bast said softly, his voice carrying into the night.

If these people would be living in his city, he needed to show them some courtesy. He also needed them to know he was in charge and he wasn't prey for them to stalk.

The figure froze in place, all but invisible, and the low hum paused for a moment as Kairon spoke.

"I'm safe, Ez. They're allies," he called down to her.

"Ezme is wary of strangers and constantly hungry. Don't sneak up on her or she'll bite," Kairon added for their benefit, letting amusement into his voice.

It was meant as a joke to cut the tension but Bast suspected there was truth in the statement. Kairon had vicious looking fangs and had shown no signs of eating the food brought to their suite earlier.

When the human and elemental realities had melded together it had become clear that there were areas of synergy and overlap between the two Earths—historical events that were similar, buildings that were almost identical, and folklore and stories that echoed each other. Kairon's vampyr people seemed very reminiscent of human vampire lore, although they clearly didn't disintegrate into dust in sunlight. When things settled down, philosophers and theoretical physicists would no doubt study the similarities between the two and try to figure out the relationship between them.

As he'd been pondering the nature of the meldings, Ezme had silently stalked up to their position, giving Bast and his men a wide berth as she settled into a crouch near Kairon.

"They can understand me?" she asked Kairon, voice so low Bast almost missed it.

"Lord Bastion has a magic that translates. So, mind your manners," Kairon replied before continuing his low thrumming call to his people.

Bast grinned for a moment, the prickly nature of the vampyr reminding him of his Hellcat. They would get on well. The thought brought the reality of Hel's situation crashing down on him again. Rubbing the mating mark she'd left on his chest with her power, his heart ached with her absence.

Three hours later, silence fell at last as Kairon ceased his call. He'd been joined by eight of his people—two men as stern and wary as Ezme, who walked like warriors, and, to Bast's surprise because it showed a level of trust he hadn't expected, a young family of two mothers and their three children. Two of them were young enough to be strapped to their parents' backs to travel faster and one jogged proudly at their side, though they couldn't be much older than nine or ten.

The children were curled up in the lee of a boulder sleeping as they waited for Tir while the adults talked quietly nearby. Ezme and the two men had shifted to the edges of the outcrop they stood on without needing to be asked, helping to keep watch.

Feeling Kairon approach his position, Bast turned to face him.

"This Tir you spoke to will create a magic gate to your home?" Kairon asked.

"Yes," Bast said, realising from Kairon's tone of voice that it was not a magic the vampyr were familiar with. Not that he could blame them. Not many of his people were aware of it either. The only people in their Earths who could portal were Tir and... Well, Hel wasn't even here anymore. So, it was just Tir. And neither they nor Hel came from this world.

"How far is your city from here?" Kairon asked.

Bast smiled wryly. "Maybe something you should've asked before deciding to come."

"The distance doesn't matter so long as my clan will be safe," Kairon said.

Bast could understand that. It was what had taken him to

the City of Souls decades earlier when he'd been hunted by his own brother, a pariah to his people. "It's at least a twelve hour flight for one of my kind, mostly over the ocean. My span of control is only over the city itself. There are a few other free settlements on the islands of Aotearoa and Lady Nerida claims control of the surrounding ocean once you clear the coast."

"Such a small territory and yet the other rulers respect your power," Kairon said.

Bast scoffed loudly and then lowered his voice as it startled the children. "My magic is unique. Combined with my mate's it is even more so. I can and do defend what's mine ruthlessly and they know that. But to say they respect me would be stretching it. They hate that my power comes from the dead."

Kairon seemed wary. "They are unlikely to be thrilled that our magic and sustenance comes from blood then, although in some respects our power is your inverse in that it stems from life."

"My city will welcome you. Before the first melding, the elemental free city there was always the home of those who didn't fit elsewhere and since then we've attracted the humans who aren't willing to be ruled by the courts as well. It's a city of independent thinkers. You will need to talk to the human tangata whenua about how you use blood, though, and respect whatever requests they make of you. The body, including blood, is tapu—sacred—for them."

"Blood is sacred to my people, also. How could it not be when it gives us life and power? We will make it work."

A tingle like the ghost of a phantom limb skittered across Bast's awareness, the dregs of Hel's power warning him of a portal forming nearby just as a soft glow filled the air.

"Stop," Bast cried at a blur of shadowy motion as two of Kairon's people launched an attack towards Tir emerging from the swirling portal while another positioned himself between the children and the perceived threat.

Tir didn't need his protection, though. They'd already looped several of the tentacles undulating from their scalp around the vampyrs' limbs to keep them away and the five petals of their jaw bared in a hissing rictus of sharp teeth.

"Is that the one we wait for?" Kairon asked, voice low and urgent as a child woke and whimpered into the still night.

"I am Tir. Tell your men to stand down or I will stand them down for you," Tir said, their voice calm and conversational despite the tense atmosphere.

"It's a little hard to stand down when you're holding us contained," one of the vampyr spoke up.

Tir's open jaws spread wider as their smile stretched and they released the sentries, letting their tentacles flow freely to the ground again.

"You didn't think to warn them?" Tir asked Bast as the vampyr warily stepped clear.

Bast winced. He'd been too distracted by his thoughts of Hel to remember how startling Tir could be for those who hadn't met them. "Sorry."

Tir inclined their head in acknowledgment of the apology. "Come. I don't want to hold this portal open longer than needed. We can make our introductions once we're back to safety."

"Are you sure that thing is safe?" one of the children's mothers asked as she watched the shifting play of shadows and light that made up the portal.

"I swear by the blood in my veins that you and your children will come to no harm from it," Tir replied, and Bast wondered how they knew such a phrasing would reassure the vampyr. Had they visited the vampyr's world before it melded with theirs or had they been meeting with others of their kind since the second melding? He'd have to remember to ask them later.

"If we're ready, let me go through first to show you," Bast said, stepping toward the portal and glancing in question at Kairon.

He didn't have time to stand around waiting. They needed to bring Kaia home. And then he needed to spend every remaining breath he had finding a way to save his mate.

CHAPTER 2
HEL

Hel woke to lungs burning for oxygen, the prick of claws clenched tight around her throat, and the heavy weight of a body kneeling on her outstretched wings and pinning her arms to the bed. They must've been going at it for a while because her lung capacity was far greater than a human's and her vision when she blinked her eyes open was blurring and covered in black splotches spreading wider by the second.

From what she could see, her attacker was slender but strong with skin as red as her face was probably turning as she tried and failed to gasp for breath. Reaching for her power, she tried to do something to free herself as she struggled to move. Anything.

Fuck.

There was a barrier between her and her magic.

It was a smooth impassable shield that felt like the all-too-familiar searing heat of her father's power. Her mind scrabbled in vain against the block while her body twitched beneath the figure attacking her. In desperation, she tried to draw on Bast's power instead of hers, only to find it was nothing more than ethereal dregs stretching tight and thin into the distance. He was so very far away. Even as she lay dying on this strange bed, the ache of his absence in her chest and through his marks on her wings momentarily distracted her from everything else.

Her mouth opened to scream, but it was strangled to silence. Literally. There was nothing she could do. No weapon she could grab. No power she could use. This was it. After a lifetime running from her father, he'd finally succeeded in capturing her and he wasn't even going to kill her himself.

"He killed all my family. Now I'll kill his," a disembodied voice hissed above her, fading in and out like a broken radio along with her consciousness.

She glared up at the figure, refusing to surrender. If she was going out, she'd do it raging against her fate. That was how she'd always lived. That was how she'd die.

Just as she felt like the tide of unconsciousness would drag her under into death, the pressure on her neck disappeared, but the fingers remained. She stared up in confusion as the weight pinning her to the bed lifted clear and an agonised scream not her own filled the air. The hands that had been strangling her were still resting on her collarbone, but they were now disconnected from the body of her attacker. Severed. The familiar metallic smell of blood filled the air and she tried again to do something. Take some action. It didn't work.

As her vision started to clear, a blade wreathed in starlight flame emerged from her attacker's chest. The red skin of the person smoked and blackened before her eyes, searing heat cracking through their body in lines like lightning radiating out from the puncture wound as the stomach-churning scent of cooking meat joined the smell of blood. The only skin that remained untouched was the person's face twisting in agony as their tortured noises went on and on. And still she lay there all but paralysed. Unable to move. Unable to do anything but watch.

Another silhouette came into view as she stared in horror at the person being tortured to death suspended in the air above her. This one was tall and male with horns curling up from his hair and sweeping wings of white stardust flared wide and crackling with the lightning of his power. His eyes swirled with vast galaxies and arrogance.

His voice was the last thing she heard as her eyes slipped closed against her will.

"Sleep, little star. And forget. I will deal with this traitor and we will try again."

HEL WOKE on silk sheets in a bed wide enough that her lax wings weren't hanging off either side where they sprawled across the infinitely soft fabric. As she blinked her eyes open, a room slowly came into focus, hazy with a glittering white sheen. It took her a moment to realise the effect was caused by the magicked gauzy curtains of light hanging from the ceiling obscuring what she could see. She took a deep breath, filling her lungs that ached with ... something. Something missing? Running her hands over her chest, she tried and failed to find what was causing her to feel like some essential part of her wasn't there.

Sitting up, she looked around again. Was she supposed to know this place? Her body told her it was familiar, but a distant part of her brain rebelled against that feeling. She could smell the power in the fabric around her, its molten heat comforting against the cold absence she couldn't quite shake and didn't want to. That absence was important. She held it close like a treasure, guarding it against the gentle light washing against her that tempted her to let everything go and float in the essence of a life-giving star.

Glancing down, she absently stroked the soft, loose-fitting gown of burnished sun-kissed gold. Why did that colour feel wrong? A lock of her silver hair slipped forward into her vision and she immediately felt comforted, though she couldn't say why. Something about the colour echoed in her soul. Silver was right. More right than the gold. Wasn't it?

When she finally swung her feet down to the floor to stand, her bare feet met a hard, warm stone glinting with sparks of light like hidden galaxies in its depths. The room that was revealed when she pushed away the enclosing fabric was huge, with a ceiling that soared into a domed shape spelled to look exactly like the night sky. Well, *a* night sky anyway. The constellations of the stars felt alien. Shaking her head in confusion, she pushed the thought away. She belonged here. Nothing was alien.

A shower and some clean clothes should've eased whatever dragging ache was pulling at her chest, but even as she turned the water off she still couldn't shake a grief she couldn't explain. There were no mirrors in the bathroom, but she caught a hint of her reflection in the glass as she turned away after showering—a pattern of black feathers etched across her silver wingspan.

For one brief moment, clarity hit and a name sounded in her mind like a clarion call—*Bast. Mate.* Then the brain fog she kept forgetting to notice descended again and it was gone.

When she emerged from the bathroom dressed in a floor-length dress of the same burnished gold she'd woken in, there was a meal waiting on the table for her. Unease ran through her veins at the thought of someone being in her space while she showered and she clutched for a weapon that no longer hung from her belt. Frowning, she scanned the room in vain for any hint of where her baton might be and for whoever had left the food until a forced calm washed over her once more in a wave of warmth. Sighing, she let herself slide down onto a dining chair.

When she scooped up the first mouthful of her meal, the fresh fruit and warm porridge-like cereal burst in heavy flavours across her tongue. It was more vibrant than she could remember anything she'd previously consumed being and had a hint of the magical kick of her kawakawa tea back home. Her thoughts caught on the word home and a montage of disconnected images flashed through her mind. Steaming cups of tea with her whānau, her family. Bast's black wings draped behind him as he sat on a barstool in the kitchen. Ra's laugh ringing out as he teased them over breakfast. Little Kaia bringing her a cup of tea in bed and snuggling close as her electric blue feathers tickled her skin. She held tight to those pictures, using them as an anchor to hold her mind steady against the tide of magic threatening to keep her submerged. Who the fuck was messing with her mind?

The gentle tide of power turned into a torrent as the door opened and a looming figure dressed from head to toe in black-accented burnished gold stepped into the room, his huge sparkling wings draping around him like a cloak. Hel swayed back in her seat under the weight of the power coming from him and held the seat of her wooden chair in a white-knuckled grip as she fought to stay present and aware. She could swear she'd never seen this man before but he seemed so familiar. A flash of screaming and burned flesh filled her memory and then dissipated like smoke. Gone before she could grasp onto it.

"Good. You're finally awake," the man said, smiling with a flash of perfect white teeth that matched his wings that were the colour of a white-hot star and held with military precision behind him. Wings that looked like hers rather than an elemental's—angled shards of overlapping condensed stardust—although he didn't have the benefit of a mating mark across their metallic-seeming surface to give the appearance of feathers.

He was danger.

Hel stood slowly as he approached and took the smallest step back despite the pressure of the magic around her whispering for her to relax. To let him close. To do anything he asked. She didn't need to breathe as often as a human and she'd paused her inhalation the instant the man entered the room, as if even breathing the same air as him might put her at risk. Her pulse stayed stubbornly, artificially, calm even as her body thrummed with the need to fight or flee.

The man paused within arm's reach and extended a hand to tilt her chin up so she was staring into his boundless eyes that seemed to contain entire galaxies. They were wearier than she expected. Tired. As if he carried a great weight. Jerking her chin away from him, she resisted the magical pressure to comply.

"Interesting. I suppose it's not surprising that you would be partially immune to my influence given we share the same DNA," he said.

Hel forced her strained memory to function. She'd never met this man before, but if she concentrated she could remember Tir describing him—towering over those around him with wings made of stardust and flowing locks of molten ebony. Her eyes flicked over the man's black hair, which was an exact match for her own before it turned the silver of Bast's power when she was transformed by Tir's efforts into something like her original form but also different.

"Are you my father?" she asked. Her body tensed in visceral hatred as she spoke the word, an instinctive reaction even his seductive power couldn't overcome.

His smile stretched a little wider. "After a fashion, I suppose. I am Sol, Emperor of Suns, Traveller of Worlds ... and any number of other titles my subjects bestow upon me."

Hel frowned as she tried to follow his explanation. What did *after a fashion* mean? She couldn't make herself care as a fresh wave of magic sparked through the point where he was touching her and washed away all her concerns.

"How did you portal the contagion here, little star? You caused a lot of trouble for me," he said.

Sol's voice was gently chiding, like a parent's, but there was a sinister edge hidden beneath it that left her shivering. She was struggling to form any thoughts at all now but survival instincts honed by decades of being hunted screamed at her not to answer.

"I want to go home," she said firmly, reaching for her own magic she'd forgotten about until that point and jerking in surprise as she smacked up against a smooth fiery barrier blocking her from using it. She couldn't portal across the room, let alone across worlds.

Sol looped his arm through hers and propelled her to a nearby sofa before sitting her down and gently stroking her hair. "This is your home, little star. I need you here by my side so we can save the people here from the contagion just like you saved the people of the Melded Earths."

She couldn't fault the logic, but there was something rotten at its core. Something she couldn't let herself forget even as her thoughts kept slipping away. Finally, it came to her.

"You killed so many of the Earths' people."

"Emperors must make hard decisions."

"I can't shift the contagion," Hel said.

It was the truth. She might've formed the portals, but it was Bast's soulweaving that had shifted the contagion and there was no power in the world that could force her to betray her mate to this man. Thinking of Bast cleared her head a little. She knew if Bast came here, Sol would never let him leave. She could see it in the desperation lingering beneath Sol's words. The thought of what someone like Sol would do with Bast's ability to harness the magic released by the so-called emperor's mass murder was enough to steel her against the lure of his influence.

Sol's smile slipped into a slight frown as he sensed her resistance but as he went to reply, the door opened again and a woman entered.

"There you are, darling," she said, smiling sweetly at Sol.

Hel blinked in surprise as her sluggish brain produced a name to go with the familiar white and gold image—Aliya, Lady of Air.

"What are *you* doing here?" she asked, but then another wave of Sol's power swept through her from his gentle touch on her hair and she relaxed back into the sofa, only half-caring to listen to the response.

"I told you to wait in the library, Aliya," Sol replied, clear dominance entering his voice.

"And miss the chance to chat with your lovely guest? We're old friends, aren't we, Helaine?" Aliya was speaking in a cajoling sweet tone entirely unlike how she usually addressed her.

Hel blinked as she listened to the click of Aliya's crystal heels coming closer and shook her head to try and clear the brain fog. The elemental must know Sol was keeping her mind sedated with his power.

"If that's how you define friendship, I feel sorry for you," Hel muttered and Aliya's eyes sharpened into a scowl.

"She is partially immune to my influence. There is too much of me in her," Sol explained over her head as if she wasn't right there sitting next to him. She wished she had the energy to push his arm away.

"Hmmm ... maybe I should take her for a ride then and compare," Aliya said, lips turning up into a smirking pout as she trailed her eyes down Sol's body.

"That's enough, Aliya. Leave us."

Hel couldn't help but smile as the Lady of Air hissed in frustration and glared at Sol in challenge before spinning on her heel and stalking from the room. "I won't come second place to anyone, Sol," Aliya snapped over her shoulder as she slammed the door.

Sol sighed and Hel once again noticed the sense of fatigue in him. "She is becoming a problem."

"She's a bitch," Hel replied.

"A bitch in heat is easy to manage, but she's getting ideas above her station."

Hel couldn't help a moment of sympathy for Aliya. The Lady of Air might thoroughly deserve one of Hel's blades to the chest, but no one deserved to be spoken of with such derision. And why was Sol talking to Hel as if she were a confidant?

"She's a ruler in her own right. Why is she here?"

Sol scoffed. "She controls a single territory of a single world. Her power is nothing compared to mine. She won't be here for long. Her presence is a momentary indulgence. A reward for finally delivering you when she failed for so long."

"She seems to think she's more permanent if she's worried about me taking her place," Hel said, her slow as molasses brain scrambling for a way to get her father to open up to her. If she could drive a bigger wedge between these two, maybe she could convince Aliya it was in her interests to take her home.

"She's not someone you need to worry about anymore," Sol said, voice firm as he shut down the topic.

Hel took the opportunity to shift further away from him on the couch as a million questions swirled in her head she was sure Sol wouldn't deign to answer. So, she went for something simple.

"Where are we?"

"Come see for yourself," Sol said, rising from his seat and holding an arm out for her to follow.

Dragging her still sluggish body out from the comfort of her perch, Hel followed him across the room to a floor-to-ceiling window. As they neared the wall, Sol absently waved a hand and the entire side of the room collapsed in on itself, cascading back from the window like folding origami until there was an opening to the outside that stretched as wide as their combined wingspans. The extra brightness threw Sol's ageless face into sharp relief and she could see even more clearly the signs of strain in the tension of his jaw and the muscles around his eyes. She was quickly distracted by the view, though.

The opening he'd created led out onto a balcony that shone like a mirror reflecting the world around it. There was no balustrade to obstruct her sightline out to a planet that was unlike anything Hel had ever seen. Swirls of purples, blues, and greens drifted in the sky, a playful aurora with drifting tendrils almost low enough to touch. But as she squinted up into the brightness above, she noticed the planes on which the colour shifted were a little too regular, like they were constructed rather than a natural phenomenon.

The sun loomed large in the sky—a pure searing white that matched the colour of Sol's wings and power.

Their outlook was high above the planet's surface in a building much taller than the rest of those in the city surrounding them. Each structure she could see was a twisting architectural marvel that seemed to defy physics—an overt display of power and resources.

"The planet is Travaris," Sol explained, his eyes trained on her as she looked out over the city. "It's a crossroads of sorts. A staging platform inset with portals that can take one anywhere in my empire."

"You built all this?" Hel asked.

"Yes."

"Who lives here?"

"Whoever I want. My military command is here, although only a fraction of my forces are. They're mostly scattered throughout the other worlds. A large portion of the current population are contagion refugees. Usually I would shift them on quickly, but the contagion spreads through any new portals I form so I can't find new worlds for them like I usually would. We're limited to using the portals I'm shielding that pre-dated the contagion until we find a solution, and even that is becoming dangerous. You are the solution to all that," Sol said.

Hel glanced over at him and shivered at the predatory gleam in his eye. "I told you I can't shift the contagion."

"The evidence is to the contrary."

"If you knew the contagion was spreading through any new portals, why did you keep opening them to the Melded Earths?" Hel asked.

"I had to find you. You have always been my only hope of staunching the contagion's darkness. It's your purpose for being. But I didn't expect you to be so powerful or so unique. That power gives you a choice you didn't have before."

"What choice?" Hel asked.

"The choice to save myriad worlds and *live*."

"And if I can't shift the contagion like you want?"

Sol shook his head like she was a disappointing child. "I won't let the worlds succumb. Either you choose to help me, or I use you to end this like I always intended. And if that happens, little star, you're choosing to die. Sleep on it."

Hel couldn't even take a single step away from him before her body followed the command against her will and she slipped into unconsciousness.

CHAPTER 3
BAST

Tir's portal took them to the rooftop of Soul Tower where Ra and Isabelle were waiting to meet them despite it being ridiculous o'clock in the early hours of the morning. Bast had barely processed the familiar winds of the city pushing at his wings as he stepped clear before Ra was pulling him into a tight embrace.

"We'll bring them both home," Ra promised.

Bast swallowed hard and pushed down the pain of Hel's absence for the thousandth time. He didn't trust his voice just then so all he could do was nod before pulling back to face their guests coming through the portal after him, stretching his translation spell to Ra and Isabelle as he did so. It wouldn't have stuck with most humans but it did with these two who were his chosen family courtesy of his mark on their skin that gave them a permanent connection to his power.

"Nau mai, haere mai. Welcome. I'm Isabelle, the tower manager here. We'll have you all settled in no time," Isabelle said as they emerged, her face splitting into a broad smile as she spied the children.

Kairon inclined his head in a shallow bow. "Thank you."

"And I'm Ra. Nice to meet you," Ra added, making a point of clasping each vampyr's hand in greeting as they exchanged names.

"It's late and you're all exhausted. We can talk more in the morning," Bast forced himself to say when the introductions were complete, even though what he really wanted to do was leave right now and not stop hunting until he found Kaia and Hel.

Ra followed him back to his penthouse as Isabelle led the vampyr down the elevators to the guest quarters two floors below and Tir disappeared off to their quarters.

"Is there any update?" Bast asked his friend.

"Not yet. As you suspected, they screened their flight with magic so they didn't show up in any satellite imagery once they cleared the Earth Stronghold. We've centred our search on Aliya's territory, of course. I've got all our networks searching for any whisper of her presence. Someone will let something slip."

"If Hel dies and I go with her, ask Ivy for help when you locate Kaia. You'll need someone with enough elemental magic to protect you from whoever's guarding her."

"No one is dying," Ra almost growled. "Go and get some sleep and stop talking that way."

Bast sighed and looked out at the shining lights of the city through the curving windows of his home. The space felt empty without Hel's fractious intoxicating presence filling it. Ra squeezed his shoulder in comfort before propelling him toward the hallway to his bedroom.

Hel's absence had been a constant itch in the back of his

mind in the living room, but in the bedroom it became a whirlpool of need that threatened to suck him under. Drawing in a shaky breath, he didn't even bother getting undressed before falling down on the bed on top of the covers. What was the point when every move was weighed down by the knowledge his mate could be taken from him at any second?

HEL'S WINGS slid across the sensitive inner surface of his own as she clung to him with a desperation she'd never show in the real world. They were in their bedroom at the tower, but it was decorated how it had been that first time they'd been together. The night their mating bond had formed. There was no sign of the twisted metal sculpture of salvaged weapons Hel had quietly put up on the wall a couple of weeks after she'd just as quietly stopped ever sleeping in her own bed.

"I miss you," Bast whispered in her ear, pulling her even tighter to his body as if he could pull her back to the Melded Earths if he just got close enough to her. It was instinct to grip the delicate skin of her ear in his teeth the way he knew drove her crazy as he drew in a deep breath of her familiar scent. Her breathless moan in response sent shivers through him.

He'd never attempted to connect with someone through dreams before, but there was no mistaking how real this felt as the mating bond allowed them this stolen moment together. Hel's essence still felt impossibly far away, but the sensation of their powers constantly twining and wending their way around each other that had faded to only a shadow was now a pulsing sliver of light in the darkness of their separation.

He knew he needed to take the opportunity to find out

what was happening to her, but he couldn't help but let himself sink into her embrace for a few more breaths as she tilted her head up to him and kissed him with a need that was every bit as frantic as that first time. It was his turn to groan as their tongues battled and her body pressed against his at every possible point of connection, grinding against his hard length.

Reluctantly, he pulled away far enough to look down into her eyes. They needed to take advantage of this opportunity before they woke. It might not be enough to give him access to his powers, but at least they could communicate.

"This is a lucid dream. We don't have much time. Where are you?" he asked.

Hel blinked in confusion for a moment and then understanding dawned in her eyes and she switched gears from revelling in their connection to the seriousness of her predicament. "On his planet. Travaris."

"Are you in danger?" he asked, expecting Hel to roll her eyes at the question with such an obvious answer but needing to hear her response from her own lips. To his surprise, she paused, thoughtful.

"Not immediately. Sol wants me to shift the contagion here like we did at home. He's being more accommodating while he thinks there's a chance I might agree. He's using his power to try and manipulate me, to make me forget you and home, but I have some sort of immunity to it. It's a constant battle, though. This dream is the first time I've had a genuinely clear thought since I got here. Oh, and Aliya is here."

Bast's eyebrows shot up in surprise. "What's she up to?"

"She seems to think she can sleep her way to power with him. At least he doesn't seem as susceptible to her charms as you elementals are."

Bast snorted. "Not all of us," he said firmly, pulling Hel closer again so he could feel the reassuring beat of her heartbeat against him. Her proximity distracted him for a breath. The mating bond between them overwhelming his senses as it responded to the juxtaposition of being side by side but also separated by a distance more vast than he could comprehend.

"If this is a dream, why the fuck are we wearing clothes?" he murmured.

As soon as the words passed his lips he was rewarded with the familiar soft warmth of Hel's naked skin against his own and he started tracing kisses down her neck. The need to touch and claim was overwhelming after their forced separation.

"Focus, necromancer," Hel teased, the old insult now more of an endearment.

Sighing, Bast paused his movements and leaned his forehead against his mate's. "Are you able to portal home?" Bast asked.

"Sol's blocked my power, but there are multiple permanent portals here. At least one of them must go to our Melded Earths. Don't worry about me. I'll figure something out."

Hel spoke with confidence, but Bast could feel that her emotions didn't match. His hellcat had little hope of making it home.

"Don't give up. I'll search from this side. The portal must be somewhere in the Air Court and we'll be over there fetching Kaia soon. We'll find it and then we'll find you. I won't ever give up on you."

Hel's face filled with concern. "Kaia's still gone?" she asked.

Bast winced as guilt reared up and slapped him. "I had to turn back when you were taken and I lost her. Ra and Kairon will find her, though. And when we save her, I will burn wherever she was taken to the ground. No one messes with my family."

Hel must've sensed his conflicting emotions because she reached out and cradled his face before tracing gentle fingers across his lips. "I'd expect nothing less. Even though it is NOT your fault she was taken."

Her faith in him was all he needed to shore up his failing hope. Letting his hands roam as she continued her gentle exploration, he revelled in the feel of her wings trembling at his touch and the familiar curves of her skin drawing his hands south.

The physical world seemed far distant in the softness of the dream. There were no noises or people to disrupt them. The city outside the windows was a hazy blur. Such details were not important here. All that mattered was connecting with his mate.

Overtaken by a sense of urgency, he gripped her neck, pulling her mouth to his as desire flooded him like she might be ripped away at any moment. Hel responded by jumping into his arms as he backed her against the nearest wall, wrapping her legs tight around his waist where she was already levering herself higher to guide him inside her.

They both gasped as he entered her, their throbbing need for each other seeming to fill the very air around them. As desperate as he was, he was still careful to use his arm snaked up her back to keep her wings from being crushed against the wall. His need to protect her carrying through even to the dream realm. Would she wake with bruises if he let go?

Time was both endless and fleeting in the dream and he knew this could be taken from them at any moment. As their mouths devoured each other and his free hand sought out *every place he knew would make her gasp, the world began to dim and so too did their sense of each other. The harder he clung, the deeper he tried to bury himself inside of her, the less substantial she became.*

Hel's whisper echoed in his mind as he bolted upright in bed, a cry of frustration leaving him as he returned to the real world.

"Kia kaha. Stay strong, my love. Bring Kaia home. I can take care of myself," she whispered.

"I'll bring BOTH of you home," he responded to his mate, but he had no idea if she heard his thoughts or not.

Waking after the dream was like reliving that moment when Hel was stolen from him all over again. There was no getting back to sleep after that and judging by the light coming through the windows he'd slept until mid-morning anyway. Isabelle confirmed over breakfast that the vampyr hadn't emerged from their suite yet. He'd have to check in with Kairon soon but the memory of Hel's body against his was driving him to seek out Ra on the comms floor and see if he'd found anything yet. It would've been easier to text, but he wanted the reassurance of his friend by his side while he stared at the screens himself.

He knew as soon as he saw the tension in Ra's body as he paced between his staff searching satellite feeds that he hadn't made any progress.

"We'll figure it out. I know we don't have much time," Ra said before Bast could even ask.

His friend was afraid. For Hel, but also for him.

"Hel's situation is stable right now. We have a little

time," he said, reminding himself as much as he was reassuring Ra. He had to trust her assessment of her father was correct.

Ra raised an eyebrow in question but didn't follow up with more questions while they were surrounded by people.

"Shall we go chat to your latest adoptees, then? Maybe give them a tour before things get crazy with the hunt?" Ra offered.

Bast tipped his chin up in assent and let the man he called brother wrap an arm in comfort around him as they headed to the elevators.

It was the stern vampyr Ezme who answered the door to their suite when Bast and Ra knocked a few minutes later. She looked like she was about to pat them down for weapons, but Kairon called out from behind her before she had the chance.

"Let them in, Ez. We're in their home. If they wanted us dead, we already would be," Kairon chided.

Bast blinked in surprise when they entered the main living area to find the incongruous picture of Kairon, who looked an awful lot like a goth punk with his bone piercings and black leather, down on the floor colouring with beeswax crayons with the youngest children. But on reflection, it fit with the protective vibe Kairon had going. He was sure the decision not to stand was a conscious one. The vampyr was silently restating his intentions to make a home here. Or perhaps shamelessly appealing to their emotions through the children to endear Bast to let them stay. Bast's mouth twitched in a smile at the manipulative move he could totally relate to as he gave Kairon an up-nod in greeting and settled on the couch the vampyr gestured to.

The youngest of the vampyr looked up at him as they sat, a little boy with dark red hair. "Hi. I'm hungry," he said.

"Hush, Dryn. Your breakfast is waiting for you in the kitchen," Kairon said, a gentle warning in his tone.

"It's yuck!" Dryn cried.

Bast was so used to Isabelle taking care of everything without needing any guidance or assistance that he hadn't even thought to check what she'd organised for food. "Do you have everything you need?" he asked Kairon.

"We do. Your clan-mother brought us packages of blood donations. She said she'll arrange a regular supply as soon as she can. Dryn just isn't used to not drinking fresh from the vein."

Ra cocked his head in question from beside him. "Are any of you?"

Kairon smiled. "No. But it is a sensible way to reduce any awkwardness as we settle." It was clear from his tone that he was both grateful and not keen to continue drinking that way for long.

"How do you usually feed?" Ra asked.

"A bite on the wrist is simplest. Our healing power means we can numb the area and ensure there is no wound or scar left behind. It is the power it contains as much as the blood that sustains us, so we only need a little. It doesn't always have to be from a person, although we need that power regularly as part of our diet. Any magical creature will do. Your predators are a rich meal when we can find one that isn't too dangerous to hunt."

"I'm guessing the power fades in blood that's been stored?" Bast said.

Kairon nodded. "We have to consume more that way."

Ra was already rolling up his perfectly tailored shirt

sleeve beside him, revealing his muscled forearm. "Would you like a snack, Dryn?" he offered, holding out his arm.

"Dryn needs to learn manners. You don't have to..." Kairon started saying, but Bast could see the gratitude on his face.

"It's my honour. I can't very well ask anyone to do something I'm not willing to do myself and I'll need to help Ana set up a schedule of some sort for you to feed," Ra said.

Dryn was staring at Kairon with pleading eyes like any other three year old who'd been offered a treat they weren't sure they were allowed.

"Go on then," Kairon said.

Bast watched in fascination as the boy trotted right up to Ra and held his wrist in a tiny gentle hand.

"Thank you," Dryn said solemnly, making eye contact with his friend in a way that was clearly a rote-learned show of respect. Then his face screwed up in concentration as he brought Ra's wrist to his lips and sunk in his fangs.

"He's only just learned how to anaesthetise with his bite," Kairon explained. "Our children learn by feeding from their parents. I'll heal you when he's done."

Dryn only swallowed a few times before he pulled away. Kairon was there within a split-second, his uncannily fast movement on display as he wrapped long fingers around Ra's wrist. Bast felt the vampyr's power surge for a moment and when he stepped away, there was no sign that Ra had ever been bitten.

"Easy as," his friend said, winking at Dryn and smiling.

Dryn held out a crayon to Ra and gestured to the paper nearby. "Ra draw?"

"Sure thing, bud," Ra said, sliding down onto the floor next to the kid.

Ra had always been that way. Quick to make friends. Unafraid of the unknown. That's how they'd ended up meeting each other mere hours after the first melding. He'd been the one jumping in to help the elementals whose buildings were collapsing when everyone around them was in shock or running scared, and he'd adopted Bast immediately even when everyone else was terrified of him.

"We thought we could take your family on a tour while we wait for any intel to come through on Kaia's location," Bast said.

Kairon inclined his head. "We'd be honoured, and I will be ready to accompany you when you find her."

Conscious that the children might tire, Bast and Ra kept their tour on the shorter side, taking the time to explain the various concourses and the mixture of elemental and human architecture. There was a trick to understanding how to navigate their city but Zee, their magical engineer, had made it as simple as they could when they were reinforcing the foundations and integrating the buildings together after the first melding. The kids were delighted to learn there was a secret code they could learn to tell them which buildings had public roof terrace and concourse access, which were private and what functions they undertook courtesy of the subtle colour markings on their façades.

Kairon quizzed him about the souls in the city as they walked, fascinated by the soulweaving magic he'd described as the other side of the coin from his own. Perhaps if Kairon proved trustworthy, Bast would have Ra show the vampyr the database they used to help manage the souls that thronged the city in sectors protecting it and reporting any unusual activity. For now, Bast glossed over the fact that he had eyes everywhere and would know any move the vampyr made.

They wound up at the Spiderhive, staring up at the brutalist beehive-shaped building from its dilapidated forecourt.

"We get the occasional griffin and dragon venturing close to the city from Matiu Somes Island in the harbour, but they mostly know to avoid us. The Spiderhive is one of the biggest safety risks in the city. It's heavily warded, but the arachdryn nesting inside are extremely dangerous. They're huge winged spiders with hairs on their limbs that leave a nasty sting and large fangs with venom. There's no direct route for them to access the city but they use the wyrm tunnels to hunt in the old botanical gardens that border us to the southwest," Bast explained.

"Probably not the best prey for us then," Tayn, one of the children's mothers said.

Bast winced at the thought. "It would be like biting a mouthful of stinging nettles."

"What's that?" Dryn's big sister Lana asked, pointing to a tree overgrown with vegetation nearby where a glint of metal was reflecting in the sunshine.

"That's a slide," Ra said, carrying on as he noted the confusion on her face. "It's for play. You sit at the top and slide to the bottom."

"Can I use it?" Lana asked Kairon.

After getting a nod from Ra, Kairon told her "If you stay in sight."

The three children all ran over and Bast couldn't help his small smile. They carried on talking nearby as their soft laughs carried on the breeze. Kairon had picked up on the fact they'd been attacked recently when he'd sat in on the council meeting before Hel was taken and he was particularly interested in the way they'd used the Spiderhive as a trap for the attacking force.

They were mid-conversation when a stray branch snapping sent every vampyr with them moving so fast towards the slide it was like the hunters disappeared from their side and reappeared in the distance.

"Oh fuck," Ra said, following on Bast's heels as he launched into a run himself.

By the time they reached the spot where the children had been playing, Ezme and one of their mums had pinned two humans to the ground with their fangs bared right in their faces.

"What happened?" Bast asked, keeping his voice calm.

It was one of the humans who replied, his voice whining. "All we did was tell them to go back where they came from. You need to protect us from them, Lord Bastion."

Bast shook his head in disgust and looked over at Kairon. "What did you see happen?" he asked, and the vampyr looked surprised for a moment as if he'd not expected the courtesy of being asked for his take.

"They were looming over the children and pointing their fingers in their faces. Perhaps my people overreacted. But they know from experience that you don't get a second chance to save your children's lives," Kairon said.

Ezme hissed in annoyance and the human beneath her flinched at the lethal sounding noise.

"Please let them up," Bast said, waiting patiently for them to look to Kairon for direction before complying.

The humans stepped closer to him as if for protection once they were back on their feet. He wondered what made them think he would ever take their side in something like this. Staring at the two of them, he held eye contact and let his soulweaving power show through until they looked down at the ground in submission.

"You bring shame to the city when you threaten our guests. Even more so when they are children. Report to Niko when you go back to the city. I'm sure he can find you something to do that will remind you how we welcome people who need a home here," Bast said, making a mental note to message the spokesperson for the local humans on their ruling partnership to give him a heads up. Ra was already subtly taking a photo so they could find the two again.

"Thank you for looking out for our children," Tayn said to him, as the humans slunk away. "Do you have any of your own?" she asked.

Bast shook his head by habit, but it was the first time he'd really processed the idea that, thanks to their work designing the shielding for Hel, children were actually a possibility for him now. His whole life he'd thought the soul taint of his magic meant he would remain childless. The thought threw him into a bittersweet memory of making love to Hel and suggesting she remove her contraceptive implant one day in the heat of the moment. She'd told him it wasn't happening, but he could pretend if he wanted. He honestly hadn't thought any more about it. It was a path he'd always assumed his life could never take. Would his mate ever want to have children? Would he? He wasn't sure how either of them would feel about it, given their histories. It would have to wait because his mate was worlds away and they were still no closer to bringing her home. Fuck, he missed her so much. He'd give anything just to be able to plan any kind of future with her, children or not.

THEY FINALLY CAUGHT a break on Kaia's location that evening from the unlikeliest of sources—the half-brother who despised him.

The voice message Ty left him didn't tell them much—*I have someone you'll want to speak to. Best hurry or I can't guarantee he'll be in one piece.*

After a quick deliberation with Ra, or argument more like, Bast recruited Tir to take him alone to the Fire Court. Ra needed to keep on top of things back at the Tower and Bast wasn't prepared to trust his brother's good intentions, given how many times Ty had tried to kill him. He already had two loved ones being held captive. He didn't need to put anyone else in harm's way.

The Fire Court stronghold was lodged in the side of a volcano on an island near Italy. Tir portalled them back to the beach where Bast had fended off Ty's attack months earlier when they'd been hunting the Archivist. Neither of them wanted to risk appearing on the volcano itself and invoking a defensive response from the stronghold before it realised who they were.

"I will wait here for you," Tir said, as the liquid shadow of their portal slipped closed.

"Thank you."

"No need. I'm not doing this for you. I'm doing it for her."

Bast wasn't sure if they meant Hel or Kaia, possibly both. It didn't matter. He was just grateful Tir had saved him the day or more the return trip would've taken him to fly there.

Launching himself into the air, he headed straight up to

the formal entrance of the stronghold and the familiar and still threatening lava falls that created its walls before cascading down to the black rock below.

He was expecting Ty, or at least one of his scouts, to intercept him before he got there, but the guards stayed hovering in the distance and there was no sign of his brother until he stepped into the orange-lit cavernous entry chamber.

"*Brother*," Ty's voice was slurred as he emerged from the uncharacteristically gloomy interior.

Bast frowned. It wasn't like Ty to acknowledge they were family given he was just as likely to greet him with poison, an assassin's blade, or a predator's attack. As his half-brother moved closer, he noticed Ty's fiery-coloured wings were haphazardly folded behind him and his suit was askew.

"Greetings Ty," Bast said, warily making his way further into the volcano that had tried to trap him and his mate the last time they were here.

As he finally stepped into arm's reach of his half-brother, he caught a waft of whisky and realised what was behind Ty's uncharacteristic behaviour and appearance.

"You're drunk," he pointed out.

Ty reached out and stabbed a finger into his chest. Hard. Bast raised an eyebrow and held his ground.

"And you're always there. Why won't you stop being there?"

Bast stayed silent, wondering where this was going.

"Do you know how hard it was to be orphaned at thirteen and take over as Fire Lord? Everyone thought I was too young. And they were right. I *was* too young. Elemental rulers are centuries old and I was barely a decade. I was a fucking liability. Even my own people were asking if the title should've gone to you because you were a whole two years older. And you were a damn *necromancer*. And then you wouldn't fucking die and every time I failed those voices got a little louder. Do you know how many people I've had to kill for that?"

If Bast wasn't so desperate to get to Kaia, he might've actually felt sorry for Ty. Sometimes he forgot they'd both been children all those years ago. They hadn't grown up together despite sharing a father. Bast had been farmed out to foster parents the second his mother died in childbirth and he hadn't been allowed near the stronghold for fear he'd taint his family with his necromancy. The Fire Stronghold and its court had been a distant thing he observed across an impassable sea.

As it was, he didn't have time for this trip down memory lane. Kaia was scared and alone. His mate was in mortal danger. He needed whatever intel Ty had, assuming there was some and this wasn't just a drunken prank.

"I was never a threat to your rule. I have no interest in returning to the Fire Court. Why did you call me here?" Bast said.

Ty tilted his head, considering. "You really don't, do you? I thought you killed our father to take over," he said. As if it was some revelation that Bast wasn't gunning to replace him as Fire Lord despite the fact Ty had known for months it was Aliya who'd killed their father and not Bast like everyone believed.

"I'm Lord Soul. I have my own home, and a family who chose me just like I chose them. I neither need nor want your position. We aren't rivals. I just want to keep my people safe and find my mate," Bast said.

"Aliya said you would come for me."

Bast snorted. "Aliya's a fucking traitor and she used you

just like she used our father. I don't give a shit about revenge. I give a shit about our world being torn to pieces."

Ty nodded, straightening where he stood as he donned the control of an elemental lord once more. "You're right. Follow me."

Bast sighed in exasperation as his brother stalked off into the stronghold without another word of explanation. Luckily their destination wasn't far, just a short winding staircase to some holding cells. Ty shoved the door open ahead of them and Bast was assailed with the scent of piss, burning flesh, and blood as he entered behind him. A white-winged scout hung naked from two butcher's hooks through his wings over a pool of lava, his bare feet a blackened mess of burns. His chest was criss-crossed with lash marks that must've come from a flaming whip.

"Speak," Ty snapped at the tortured captive, all signs of his drunkenness now gone.

The elemental didn't wait a second before words poured out from him, his will thoroughly broken. "She's been taken to Caelus's territory."

"You're welcome," Ty added to Bast, before waving a hand that sent the man crashing down into the pool of lava in the floor, his screams quickly silenced as he succumbed.

Bast winced at the callous ruthlessness, but he understood it. Elemental politics had always been brutal. If it saved Kaia, he could live with it. It's not like he could've stopped Ty in his own stronghold anyway. If the elemental had been senior enough in Aliya's court to know this information, there was no way he was an innocent. Reaching out, Bast caught his brother's shoulder as he tried to push past him.

"Thank you, Ty. You didn't have to do this."

Ty met his gaze. "She is a child. She should never have been taken. We are even now, yes?"

Bast bit back the retort that nothing could make up for the years he'd been hunted by Ty's assassins as a child, nor for Ty helping Aliya to kill him on Matiu when his souls had had to resurrect him. This was an olive branch, and it was up to him to be the bigger person here.

"Not even. But perhaps we can start the tally afresh."

Ty nodded. "Good enough. Go well, Lord Soul. Bring your girl home."

CHAPTER 4
HEL

Waking from her dream with Bast was like sinking back beneath the waves after a single gasp of life-giving oxygen. At least her mind was the clearest it had been since she'd first awoken on Travaris, but that wasn't saying much. The constant pressure of Sol's magic luring her to submit was exhausting in its temptation. She was so very tired. And it would be so easy just to tell him what he needed to know.

Shaking her head, she refocused.

No.

She could never betray Bast to him, both for Bast's sake and the worlds'. So many worlds. She could feel them all around her—all those points of connection that usually fed her magic on the tips of her awareness. It would've been a treasure trove of power for her if only her father's barrier in her mind wasn't insurmountable. Ugh. She didn't even want to think of him as her father.

All of that was a distraction. She'd told Bast she'd find a way out of there, even if she was ninety percent certain she would fail. She wasn't going to just roll over and die for the bastard who'd been hunting her for her entire life. He could fuck right off.

Taking advantage of the anger burning through her to push back Sol's drugging influence, she rolled out of bed where someone had creepily carried her and undressed her *again*. Rifling through the clothing she'd been provided, she found something slightly more substantial than the pyjamas and lightweight gauzy gown she'd been wearing earlier. Pants and a fitted singlet made her feel a bit more normal. Even if they were still nothing like the robust black leather and thick linen she wore at home. Where the fuck had they put her things? She'd kill for a weapon. Literally. She'd never felt so murderous, and that was saying something.

Standing indecisively for a moment, she looked toward the wall that had opened onto the balcony Sol had taken her to and then toward the door to the rest of the building that Aliya had entered and left by. She had no idea where to even start searching for a way to open the wall because it had seemed to respond to Sol's mere presence. The door was a much smaller space to search for an opening mechanism and she knew for sure that people who weren't Sol could open it because Aliya had come and gone without assistance. She was also reluctant to venture outside onto a strange planet without some kind of weapon and there was a reasonable chance she would find someone through that door she could take one from. Plus, there was the slightest pull inside her toward the balcony that she didn't trust. Almost like Sol's influence was daring her to go out there. That pull alone would have been enough to send her running in the other direction.

Her stomach growled as she headed across the room and

she grabbed a slice of toast from the table to eat on the way ... somewhere. Wherever she could get to before someone stopped her. She wouldn't know if she didn't try. And, who knew? Maybe Sol's magical influence that kept sucking her under would fade once she was outside the bedroom.

The first barrier to her plan, unsurprisingly, was the door. It had no obvious handle on this side. In fact, it was so closely fitted it was almost invisible in the wall. If she hadn't seen Aliya coming in earlier she might've missed it was there at all. As she ran her fingers along the near invisible joins, seeking anything that might open it, she wondered how long ago Aliya's visit had been. She was getting really fucking sick of unconsciousness and the blank space of lost time in her memories. The gnawing hunger in her belly suggested it could've been the day before. Although, who even knew how long a day was on this planet? For all she knew, it could be tidally locked and night would never come at all. She doubted it, though. Even without access to her magic, she could feel the essence of the world she'd found herself in and nothing about it felt static.

On her fourth increasingly desperate search of the door, her fingertips picked up the slightest of depressions. She tried everything she could think of to activate what she hoped was the opening mechanism—pushing, stroking, tapping, scraping at the edges with her fingernails. None of it worked.

Claustrophobia threatened to set in despite the sedative effect of the magic surrounding her. She wasn't made to be caged. Freedom was everything to her and always had been. Her breaths came faster as her movements became more frantic. Maybe it was operated by magic? Aliya got through on her own, though, so it obviously didn't require the kind of power she and Sol had. She might not be able to access her own power, but she could access the tiniest distant mist of Bast's soulweaving. Not enough to do anything at all, really. Except maybe nudge a magical door handle.

Focusing deep inside herself, she concentrated on the memory of his presence in her dream—his warm lips against hers, his skin sliding against her own—and then she pooled the dregs of his magic, aching with effort, into the tip of her index finger before pressing it one last time to the depression in the wall. Her mouth stretched in a silent grin as the door finally swung open. Yes! One step closer to freedom.

There were two ways she could play this. One was to creep through whatever this building was, silent and deadly, and hope no one noticed her. The other was to fake a confidence she'd left behind on the Melded Earths and pretend she had every right to be there. Sol was her father, after all, even if she wished she could disown him. Did his people know she was a captive here? Would they dare challenge her even if they did? She was going to go for it. If it looked like she was going to be attacked for wandering free, she could always claim ignorance and say she'd been confused by his compulsion.

Decision made, she stepped through the door with her head held high and looked each way up and down the sharply curving passageway she'd emerged into. Oh great. It looked like this place was going to be a fucking maze. Because of course it was. Popping back into the room briefly, she tugged the sheet from the bed and slipped it under the bottom of the door so just the corner of one golden silk edge was poking out into the hallway. The last thing she needed was to walk in circles and not realise she'd ended up right back where she started. The door was almost as invisible on this side as it was on the other except for a thin glowing gold band surrounding it she suspected would be replicated in every other door she came across.

Marker in place, she turned decisively to her right and set off around the gently curving corridor. She was quickly out of sight of her bedroom's door, but she'd been correct about the interior design. Every twelve steps or so she passed another golden outline on one side or the other. Did they lead to more bedrooms? Or was this a prison level and they really were cells? She didn't particularly want to open one and find herself in someone else's space without a blade or her power to defend herself, especially if they were dangerous captives. Someone had already tried to kill her. If she was going to take someone on without weapons, she needed the element of surprise.

As she strode forward, she wondered what kinds of people she'd come across here. A crossroads of worlds would have species she'd never seen before, which meant she'd have no idea what they were capable of. Stepping as silently and quickly as she could, she slowed her breath to a rate far below what a human could've comfortably sustained. The last thing she needed was someone with sensitive hearing realising she was coming up on them before she clocked their presence, and the hallway was deathly quiet.

The bright white floor her silent footsteps crossed was only broken up by a single curving line of glowing red light running just off its centre. It must've had some meaning to the occupants of the building, but if it was a navigation aid it was of no use to her. The starkness of the floor colour was softened by the annoyingly comforting golden glow emanating from the walls and ceiling. The air was fresh but carried a hint of the scent of her father's power—a subliminal reminder of his dominance for anyone occupying the space.

It was impossible to tell how far the circular corridor extended, but it wasn't too long before she came across another corridor that ran perpendicular to the one she was traversing. The red line of light on the floor was intersected by a blue one leading down the new path to her left. Presumably, it would take her further into the building, which might be a bad move but seemed to be her only choice if she wasn't going to open one of the other doors. The blue glow reminded her once more of how helpless she was without access to her power. As she pivoted to follow it, she reached again for her magic and let out a silent breath of frustration as she once again smacked up against the barrier in her mind.

It didn't take long to reach the end of the new passageway. The building was obviously much taller than it was wide, unlike the Spiderhive back home that had a similar warren of circular passageways but was more squat than soaring. Hel's steps slowed as she approached an open space ahead that looked like a central circulating area. With her sharp vision, she could see a large hole in the middle of both floor and ceiling that was letting sunlight into the chamber and would make it possible for winged people to traverse up or down floors without bothering with stairs or whatever passed for an elevator in this world. She'd be very exposed if she entered that atrium—vulnerable to attack from every level of the building.

As she neared the opening into the chamber, a familiar tentacled figure came into view and she paused in surprise before she noticed the subtle differences between whoever this was and the Archivist Tir back home. For one, their garment was nothing like the clothes she'd seen Tir in. It was more similar to the soft gold robes she'd worn the first time she'd awoken here, whereas Tir's fashion sense was more akin to her black leather. As she silently stepped closer, she noticed the person ahead was a little shorter than Tir as well, and their tentacles undulating down to the floor were a dusky blue—a shade lighter than Tir's midnight colouring.

She catalogued the differences between this person and her friend in a single glance, but what really held her attention was the curved short sword hanging from their waist. A grim smile stretched across her face as she crept closer. Finally. A chance to arm herself.

She had no idea if this person shared Tir's portalling ability, but it was fairly likely they shared their rows of razor-sharp teeth and were local to her father. They would be dangerous and she couldn't afford for them to raise an alarm. It was just as well she healed faster and didn't need to breathe as much as most other beings. Those tentacles weren't going to be fun. There were too many to restrain them all. A fast and silent ambush was the only way to approach this one, even if she felt like she'd need to apologise to Tir later for it. Hopefully they weren't actually related.

Drawing in a deep fortifying breath to fill her lungs, she stalked closer to the oblivious person who was staring down at something in front of them. She wasn't going to kill them. Not if she could help it. She didn't think she'd be able to look Tir in the eye again if she did. Instead, she wrapped one muscled forearm around their tentacles and neck alike, bracing herself to tighten her hold until she was certain she was either choking them or stopping vital blood flow regardless of what their internal anatomy looked like. Everyone's brains were in their head weren't they? And their hearts were somewhere else? Fuck. She didn't even know.

A soundless exhaled scream left her victim as she held tight. Tentacles that had gently swayed down to the floor now thrashed wildly, whipping at her face and body. Their nails clawed at her arms leaving long welts. As panic set in for them, they managed to coil a tentacle around her face and she tucked her chin down as far as she could into their back to reduce the pressure as they tried to choke her in turn. A sharp ache in her neck on existing bruising she'd forgotten was there had her freezing for a moment as residual memory crashed into her. Her grip slackened and she flinched as images of the brutality Sol had shown as he'd tortured whoever it was to death filled her mind. She couldn't even blame whoever it was for attacking her after those words they'd uttered. They'd been taking their revenge the only way they could think to and she understood that mentality all too well. Now wasn't the time to think about it. Steeling herself to do what was needed, she tightened her grip once more.

After long minutes of silent struggle, the body in her arms finally went lax. They became a dead weight dragging on her straining arms, but the tentacle around her throat still held tight. Fucking great. How long would their tentacles keep moving while the rest of their body was unconscious? She had no choice but to hold tight and hope she didn't accidentally kill the hapless being. Or lose consciousness herself. If they were human, she would have let go long since.

Her vision was turning spotty from lack of air by the time the tentacle around her neck finally cooled and loosened, sliding down her skin like a dying snake. Finally, she let the body slide to her feet, taking a moment to press a finger to their skin and check for a heartbeat. It was still there. Shallow and slow. She had no idea how long they would be out for.

Pushing their slack tentacles to the side, she unclipped the belt holding their short sword and awkwardly extracted it from underneath them. Smiling, she saw three throwing daggers she hadn't noticed sheathed on the opposite side of the belt from the sword. Perfect. Working quickly, she slung the belt around her own waist, her sense of control increasing as the weight settled on her hips. It was only now she had a weapon that she didn't feel naked.

A quick search of the person's pockets revealed nothing else except something that was probably a comms device. She wished she could take it and use it to keep an ear on the guards, but she couldn't risk being tracked by it so that was out. Instead, she took the device and jogged to one of the nearby potted trees encircling the area, burying it out of sight in a substance like a bioluminescent sphagnum moss at its base. It probably wouldn't take long to find, but every second might make the difference in getting clear.

Once she was confident the comms device was hidden as well as it was going to be, Hel bit her lip and glanced around the space as she considered which way to go. She could look for a stairwell, but would it be any better coming across someone in an enclosed space like that as opposed to the opening in the centre of the building where at least she could flee in all directions? Of course, she could also be attacked from all directions. Slipping closer to the hole, she balanced near the edge of the drop to crane her neck up and see how much higher the building loomed. Surprisingly, there were only another couple of levels before it opened out to the sky, but there was a slight sheen to the view that made her think there was a magical barrier at the entrance. That made sense.

Sol wouldn't leave his building open to such an easy line of attack. But the question was, would it let someone like her out?

When she peered down, she quickly decided it was worth checking even if it set off an alarm because the levels beneath stretched far further than even Soul Tower at home. The holes through each floor got increasingly wider the further down she looked so the drop appeared to yawn beneath her feet. It was lucky she didn't get vertigo. There were no balustrades, but the edges of each ring of suspended floor and ceiling glowed with the same golden light as the walls in the corridor. When she looked up, it created a view of concentric circles of light. She could only imagine what that would look like from the ground floor so far below. It must seem to stretch into infinity.

Movement caught her eye as she watched, winged people flitting from floor to floor far below. She needed to get a move on before someone noticed her. Decision made, she launched herself out into the open space, snapping her wings out and catching the still air in a way that was still a novelty to her after a lifetime of being wingless. She'd never attempted flying in such a small area and it took her a moment to find her balance as she executed the corkscrew turns needed to rise up through the building.

Unwilling to barrel headfirst through what was likely Sol's magic above, she awkwardly drew the short sword from the sheath at her waist as she powered up with short sharp wingbeats. Holding it straight up above her, she let the tip of the sword be the first thing to breech the subtle sheen of white-hot magic above. It didn't spark or rebound, so that was promising. Instead, it sunk slowly into the sky above like it was passing through molasses. She had about two seconds to decide if she should let her body follow suit. Fuck it. She needed out. Surely Sol wouldn't put his own people at risk with whatever this shielding was.

With aching control of her beating wings, she surged up as slowly as she was able, letting the sword sink through the barrier until her hand and wrist met the magic as well. The familiar searing heat of Sol's power washed over her skin, but it wasn't burning her. Either this shield was designed to let people exit, or it was somehow attuned to her as a relative of Sol's. Either way, she took full advantage and put on a flurry of wingbeats to shoot up into the freedom of the alien sky above.

The unfamiliar sun's light was fading as she propelled herself clear of the towering building she'd been stuck inside, but the auroral lights of the sphere of power surrounding the city remained constant—the flashing purples and blues reflecting off the silver of her wings.

Instinctively, she reached for her power to try and sense the location of the portals she knew were nearby, but she immediately hit up against that infuriating smooth barrier in her mind. There weren't as many people flying as she'd expected, suggesting most of the city's inhabitants weren't winged. Keeping her ascending spiral going another two rotations, she considered which direction to head. Westward had the least number of shadowy forms flitting in the sky and something about the auroral lights in that direction captured her eye. The domelike quality to the lights there connected with the ground in a series of thick glowing columns. Straining to send her awareness that way, the barely-there presence of Bast's power in her veins that was all that was available to her twinged in response—death.

That sounded like her kind of place.

Setting a course for the far distant play of light, she focused her attention on flying as fast as she was able without any power to bolster her wingbeats. Her muscles tensed waiting for a blow that never came as she constantly scanned the airspace around her, but no one was approaching. The lack of any guards or pursuit made her more nervous rather than less, and she thought back to the subconscious lure she'd felt toward the balcony. Her exit had been too easy. Had Sol allowed her to leave? Encouraged her even? Had she set her direction based on her own instincts or his insidious influence? Her flight stuttered for a moment and she dropped a little closer to the ground.

Catching herself with a surging wingbeat, she glanced down to see she was passing over a large park of some kind—alien plants arranged in sweeping curves of beauty. But in among that beauty were patches of despair.

People were gathered along the flowing paths of the garden, clustering around small fires as night descended. People with the familiar flowing tentacles of Tir's kind. She really should find out what they called themselves. Tir was the only one of their people on the Melded Earths so most people never thought to even ask. They were just Tir, the Archivist. Hel had tried to ask where they were from, but they'd always deflected. Was this their home world? If so, they weren't being well done by, because as she passed over their people she could see ragged clothing and children who seemed to be settling down under blankets outdoors for the night when not so far away there was a whole city of buildings that presumably contained places they could've slept. She wished she could risk investigating further for Tir's sake, but she couldn't trust them not to return her to her father. And they probably wouldn't be friendly once they learned she'd attacked one of them only minutes earlier.

Powering higher, she turned her gaze away from whatever it was she'd been passing over. She didn't have time to figure out if it was a slum, refugee camp, or simple preference. She doubted the latter, given Tir had always seemed to appreciate the bedroom they'd been provided in Soul Tower.

The sun had set by the time she reached the columns of auroral light she'd been aiming for. As they loomed large ahead, her dulled senses finally processed what they were— containment for the spheres of contagion she and Bast had sent to this world in retaliation when the second melding hit. For the last few minutes she'd been flying over abandoned buildings, a mini-settlement outside the city, and guilt hit hard. Was this the explanation for the homeless people she'd passed over on the way there?

She was about to drop down to the ground to investigate when she felt it. An absence, a darkness, far greater than she'd ever felt before. The worst outbreak of the contagion she'd ever come across. So vast that, even with her magic inaccessible, she could still pick up on the sickening power signature.

Drawn on by morbid curiosity and a deep need to sight the immense danger, she wove through the columns of magic holding back the smaller patches of devoured reality until she came to a large circle of scorched earth where nothing remained. The arid ground wasn't caused by the contagion, because there would have been nothing left if it was, but a huge destructive force had cleared the area around a seething black mass of contagion-ridden portal up ahead. She instinctively knew what it was even without access to her power. This was the source of the contagion, or at least a portal to where it resided. It was the origin point from which it had spread to this world, and from here on to hers. The place where it all started.

Nearby, the other portals Sol had mentioned, the twelve that pre-dated the contagion, encircled the area. It had probably made sense to group them together before the contagion hit so it was easier to defend the planet against any potential threats that came through, but now it meant the raging absence was a constant threat to them.

As she drew closer, she dropped lower and lower until she landed on the barren earth well clear of the seething absence. All she could do was stare in horror at the looming darkness. It was so hungry. So destructive. A mindless devouring presence.

"Do you see now why you need to help me?" Sol said from behind her.

Hel's heart skipped a beat as she spun to face him, and she launched all three throwing daggers at her belt at him before she could think better of it. How long had he been following her? Or had he portalled there only a moment earlier? Sol didn't even blink as she sensed his power surge and the metal flashing through the air evaporated in bursts of searing heat like the core of a star.

Hel swallowed hard. He was so much more powerful than her. So effortlessly in control. What hope did she have of standing against him? "I already told you I can't move it," she said, voice quiet.

Sol took a threatening step toward her and she realised she couldn't move, her feet fused to the dry blackened ground beneath her feet. "Then shall I use you how I intended right from the start? Throw you through that portal and force our power into a pincer to explode it out of existence and bar the contagion's core from reaching through this world forever?"

Hel stared at him in horror. The gateway ahead was a mass of writhing darkness containing the vastness of dead stars and worlds the contagion had already consumed. Imagining a death like that seemed worse than any other. Through Bast's power and the souls she could now hear when it was flowing through her, she knew there was a place beyond this plane where the living went in death. A place she could be with her mate even if they both died. But not if the contagion took her. The devouring energy was a black hole that consumed everything, leaving nothing behind, not even a soul. It was worse than death. Worse than destruction.

Firm hands closed around her arms as Sol lifted her rigid paralysed body. She couldn't move, couldn't cry out. Even her tear ducts refused to let her grief run free. What had she done by coming here? It couldn't end like this.

CHAPTER 5

BAST

"She's near La Paz!" Ra yelled, bursting into Bast's penthouse the evening after he returned from the Fire Court.

Ra had been scouring the satellite feeds of the Air Court's territory for any trace of Kaia since the second Bast got back from the Fire Court and passed on that she was somewhere in Caelus's territory. Caelus was Aliya's delegate ruler for the South American continent—powerful in his own right and many centuries old. Bast was almost flattered that Aliya had ensured her righthand man was the one to oversee Kaia's capture. It meant she knew how much of a threat he was. It also meant it would be really fucking tricky to rescue Kaia.

Bast surged to his feet, abandoning the meal he'd been eating. "You've got her location?"

"Not exact. But there have been two sightings of Caelus around the city and one of our local couriers confirmed there was an unexplained surge of elemental power through the ley lines in the area exactly like the kind an untrained teenager might cause."

Bast blanched at the news, his excitement tempered in an instant. What had happened to make Kaia's power surge that way and had she survived the experience? He could only hope having one of Aliya's most powerful mages on hand would keep her safe. Her untrained power could be more deadly to her than her kidnappers. Surely they wouldn't go to the trouble of capturing her only to let her die. Unless she'd been using her magic to try and escape. Then who knew what force they might've used to stop her.

"We need to get over there. Now," Bast snapped, reaching for his travel gear.

"I called Tir and Kairon on the way up. They'll be here as soon as they're ready and we can head straight out. I have our people finding a safe place outside La Paz to portal into. They'll send the details through so Tir can get a lock," Ra said.

Bast's brain hitched on the 'we' in Ra's sentence. The thought of losing him when Hel and Kaia were already missing was more than he could bear.

"You aren't coming with me. I need you here," Bast snapped.

Ra just raised an eyebrow and pulled him into a one-armed embrace. "Sorry, bro. I'm not letting you go without back-up and I *need* to be there for Kaia."

Bast opened his mouth to keep arguing, but one look at his friend's face told him he wasn't going to get anywhere. Ra had always been stubborn like that and he was too loyal not to do what he thought was necessary to protect his family. Ra had always made his own choices.

"Mica's blaming me for the damage to his stronghold," Bast said, changing the subject instead of voicing the order he wished he could give for his friend to stay safe here in the Tower.

He'd messaged an update to the Earth Lord earlier in the day given Ty would've already updated the council members and they were still hoping Mica would let Kaia train in his court. They needed to keep the communication lines open. Mica's reply had been terse: *I am too busy dealing with the damage you caused.* It wasn't clear whether he'd meant too busy to communicate or too busy to train Kaia once she was found, and Bast hadn't wanted to push his luck. He could deal with whatever was going on with the Earth Lord once Kaia was home safe.

He regretted raising the subject as soon as he brought it up because Ra's face twisted into an uncharacteristic sneer. It took a lot to turn Ra against someone, but it seemed Mica had offended his sense of loyalty enough that whatever spark had been growing between them had turned into something much more toxic.

"The fucking nerve of that man," Ra said, so mad he almost spat. "First he held Kaia's need for training over you like blackmail for your good behaviour as if he'd even be willing to leave her to self-destruct from her power. Then he treats Hel like she's a worse threat than that fucking emperor and backs the council in trying to hand her over to her father even though he *knew* you were mates. And now he's blaming you for the damage done when Aliya took Hel when he should have been fucking protecting her as his guest? Why isn't he waging war on the Air Court instead of getting stuck into you?"

"To be fair, no one has seen any sign of Aliya and I doubt any of his people are in a state to wage a war. You should've seen them. They were totally incapacitated by the damage to the Stronghold. I think one or more of the ley lines in the nexus there have been severely affected as well. They're dealing with the psychological impacts of the stronghold's pain and amputating part of its essence, but they're also dealing with whatever it's doing to the source of their power."

"Don't you dare defend him," Ra said, still fuming.

Bast sighed and returned the hug his friend had given him just before. Mica's actions had hurt Ra deeply, even though they'd made no commitments to each other. He knew Ra would be feeling like his earlier interest in Mica was a betrayal of Bast and the city now they might be at odds.

"We need to give him time and see if he comes round. He's still our best bet for training Kaia. Even if Nerida is more sympathetic, she's too wary of outsiders. She'd never let someone stay for as long as Kaia needs and she definitely wouldn't let anyone accompany her even if she did. And the other courts would be more likely to kill her than train her. We need him."

"Speak for yourself," Ra muttered, and Bast couldn't help the small smile at his friend's petulant tone.

Their conversation was interrupted by a knock at the door, quickly followed by the familiar buzz against his senses as Tir opened a portal near the floor-to-ceiling windows and stepped through. He'd always wondered how the Archivist avoided opening a portal inside someone's body, but they'd yet to come even close so he guessed there must be a way. A soft knock on the door moments later had Ra letting an armed-to-the-teeth Kairon into the penthouse as Bast turned to greet Tir.

"Just let me grab a weapon or six," Ra called from the door as he headed towards one of their locked storage cupboards. "Don't you dare fucking leave without me."

Bast rolled his eyes. "Wouldn't dream of it," he muttered.

"So, what's the plan?" Ra asked once he'd returned.

There was no sign of whatever weapons he'd secreted around his person but knowing his friend, there was at least one gun, probably several blades, and a garotte. He didn't wait for an answer as he strode right over to the touchscreen on the wall and pulled up a map of La Paz and its surrounds. It was marked with several flags of interest he pointed to as he explained. Two shaded areas covered most of the city and extended to the north and west.

"Rumour is Caelus operates from a base somewhere near La Paz when he's in that part of the continent, a crystal mountain constructed of air magic, but no one has the exact location. That's the most likely place he's holding Kaia as it would be the least likely to be found and the most defensible. The shaded areas relate to the power surge we think came from Kaia. Our courier gave us the rough location based on his memory of it, although a lot of it is guesswork as it depends on how the surge travelled along the ley lines. It's not necessarily a straight line and, as you know, the ley lines themselves shift position enough to make the search area wider than I'd like."

"If we cover enough ground in those areas, I should get close enough to be able to track her. Ana kindly gave me some of her blood to use. It will take a little longer than if we had some of Kaia's blood, but they are close enough relations that it should still work," Kairon said.

"Excellent. I can cast a glamour on us to keep us from the notice of any but the most powerful magic users. Then we just have the problem of finding the safest place to portal into that won't disturb the ley lines in a way that might be noticed by the Air Court's scouts," Bast said, looking over at Tir in question.

Ra selected another icon on the map and it became criss-crossed with swathes of bright lines that showed the potential locations of ley lines in the area.

"Here," Tir said, pointing to the Valley of the Moon south of the city. "The mess of ley lines there is similar to your Matiu Island. It will hide our entrance."

"And the rock ghasts there will mean there won't be anyone around to launch an ambush," Kairon added, receiving surprised looks from the rest of them.

"What the fuck is a rock ghast? Do I even want to know?" Ra asked.

"You didn't have those in your reality?" Kairon asked and everyone shook their heads in response.

"They're blood-suckers like most of the predators from my Earth, but unlike most animals, they take their nutrition from the magic it contains rather than its physical properties. Ghasts are a bit like vampyr in that respect and it means they have some ... unique ... abilities. They're a little smaller than a human with leathery wings, but only to glide not to fly. They hide in the rock pinnacles in places like the valley where they can launch down onto their prey. Although no one from my world goes in there, so mostly they hunt from the outer edges into the surrounding countryside," Kairon explained.

"What kind of abilities are we talking?" Ra asked.

"They change the colour of their skin to blend with their surroundings and become basically invisible. They can exhale a colourless gas that will leave their victims dizzy and confused for ten minutes or so. And they can puncture your skin with just the barest touch of the digits on their hands or feet. They often bleed out livestock by making a hundred or more draining holes that way and then feed from the trail of blood left behind on the ground. It means they don't have to risk injury the way a normal fight would."

"Delightful," Ra said in a dry voice.

"They sound delicious," Tir added, the petals of their jaw stretching into a wide, toothy grin.

"Ra will be too slow to escape them," Kairon said, eyeing up his human friend.

Ra rolled his eyes. "No worries. I'll hitch a ride with my guy over there with the wings."

Bast shook his head with a wry smile, still worried for Ra but reassured that he'd at least let go of some of his anger at Mica to return to his usual irreverent ways.

"I can fly low with Ra and keep a lookout for you. I assume the two of you can keep yourselves safe?" Bast said.

"Like I said, they sound delicious. They will have more to worry about from me, than me from them," Tir said, still smiling.

"I'm much more powerful than most of my people and they will sense that. They're likely to hold back unless they're really starving," Kairon said, but the tone of his voice said they may well be hungry.

"What are we waiting for then? Let's go," Ra said.

THE LIQUID SHADOW of Tir's portals was familiar to Bast now, but the adrenaline of wondering what would face him once he stepped through never faded. When they emerged into the sandstone and clay stalagmites of the Valley of the Moon, the swirl of local souls that whispered their greetings to him did nothing to reassure him. He would have ready access to his power at least, but there was a reason for that. It was because so many people had died there. The ghasts had capitalised on the unknowing humans and elementals after the second melding.

It was night in Bolivia, a little past midnight, and the crescent moon gave only the barest glow to the chimneys of white sandstone stretching above them like giants crowding close. He couldn't feel the ley lines himself, but he wondered if the tangled nexus here would one day form another sentient stronghold and, if it did, whether that would require the courts to split their territory five ways instead of four.

First Ra, then Kairon and Tir followed behind him on silent footsteps as Tir let the portal snap closed. The portal had led them just far enough into the rough paths to escape notice from outside, but close enough that it shouldn't take them too long to clear the danger of the ghasts and leave the death trap of the sandstone maze behind.

For this trip, he and Ra had opted for the magicked leather harness he could use to carry his friend clipped to his front with minimal strain like a tandem skydive, rather than one that would have him hanging below. It was a little awkward but would allow him to fly close enough to the ground to keep an eye on Kairon without risking sending Ra crashing face-first into a pinnacle of stone.

It only took a few seconds to get airborne and wrap a shield of illusion around himself and Ra to hide them from sight. All of them moved as swiftly as possible, although Tir was glancing around them with a look of avid interest that suggested they might not have been kidding about hunting down one of the ghasts to get a taste.

If Bast thought he'd seen Kairon move fast before, it was nothing compared to the speed with which the vampyr traversed the stairs and paths cut into the clay. Bast had thought he would have to hover and fly slowly to keep pace, but they were travelling at a reasonable speed. The problem was that visibility was getting progressively worse as clouds drifted in front of the moon. Dropping a little lower, Bast flew closer to the spiny natural crenelations where he could keep better track of Kairon's shadowy form. Tir had dropped behind, but he wasn't so concerned for the Archivist, given they could portal away if things got too bad.

Ra's sudden shout was the only warning that he'd become too focused on tracking the people below him and not enough on their surroundings. He'd thought his glamour would keep them hidden from the ghasts, given it masked all sight, sound, and scent of their presence from the world, but he should've remembered Kairon's comment about how they consumed the power within their victim's blood. The ghasts clearly had other senses he hadn't managed to screen them from and as the weight of two leathery bodies landed one on each of his wings, he realised the ghasts' camouflage had made them every bit as invisible as he'd hoped to be. He'd imagined them like a chameleon, thinking they'd be noticeable to the trained eye. That wasn't the case. He still couldn't see the fucking things and they were literally riding him.

Hampered by Ra hanging from his front, he sent a blast of pure death magic out through his wings. Blood-curdling screeches filled the air as the creatures fell free. He winced as chilled air moved through his wings, now riddled with holes like they'd been pellet-shot where the ghasts had gripped tight. His magic had protected him from the worst of it and he knew he'd be healed in no time, but his wings were sensitive and it fucking *hurt*.

Cursing to himself, he looked down to see Kairon somehow sensing the location of the ghasts despite their invisibility and diving into a series of acrobatic moves to avoid the same fate Bast had suffered. He sent another swathe of magic to surround the vampyr in a dome as he ran. Shadows flickered and screams cut off as the ghasts quickly realised these people were not prey.

If only they'd realised a little sooner, he thought, irritated he'd been taken by surprise.

Once Kairon was clear of the rock formations, he circled back to check on Tir. The Archivist had a new hole in their cheek but otherwise seemed in no particular hurry. Tir glanced up as they passed and licked their lips. Clearly, they'd managed to find a snack and the creatures were now, wisely, steering clear of them.

Flying back to Kairon, Bast stumbled as he landed and Ra stepped clear so he could stretch his legs while they waited for Tir to join them. Without a word, the vampyr stepped close and hovered his hands over the already healing holes in Bast's wings, letting his blood-red power flow bathe them. For a moment, Kairon's power failed to penetrate through the network of Bast's magic running through his wings. Their magics of life and death were like oil and water, unable to mix and co-exist until Bast carefully adjusted his own power to let Kairon's healing take effect.

Sweet relief spread through the holes tunnelled in his wings as soon as the vampyr's magic made it through, accelerating his naturally advanced healing ability. Bast twitched at the tickle of his skin and feathers as he felt the damage knitting closed. He nodded his thanks when Kairon finally removed his hands and the vampyr flashed him a fang-baring smile before reaching into his pocket for the vial of Ana's blood.

As Kairon began chanting softly under his breath, his hair drifted in a breeze that seemed to only affect him. The vampyr spun in place, turning and turning as he searched for the pull of Kaia's blood. The vial in his hand glowed progressively brighter with his power until he came to rest facing north. It wasn't much to go on at this stage. North encompassed the entire of La Paz and most of the shaded search areas. Still, it was a start.

Kairon looked up as Tir finally joined them and smirked. "Cute," he said, pointing to the new perfectly circular hole in one of Tir's cheeks. "Want me to make you a piece of jewellery for that or heal it up?"

Tir's eyes lit up. "Like your bone jewellery? Is that how you got your piercings? That would be so kind of you."

Kairon let out a nearly silent chuckle. "No. We pierce with sharp implements much as anyone else would. Even my people aren't crazy enough for that. I'll hook you up with something when we get home."

Bast was impatient to move on, but the realisation each of these uniquely powerful creatures now called his city home was both reassuring and nerve-wracking. He hoped his people would grow used to them before anyone caused another incident. Tir had mostly stuck to the Tower since they arrived, or wherever they went when they portalled away, but Kairon and his people were highly unlikely to confine themselves that way. He had faith the city would accept them. It was foundational to who they were. There would always be individuals who needed a reminder that everyone deserved a home, though.

"Could I fly you ahead to figure out our destination and swing back for Ra and Tir once we know where Kaia's being held?" Bast asked Kairon.

The vampyr shook his head. "Flying won't work. Without a sample of Kaia's blood, I just get a vague sensation of direction and I need to keep my feet connected to the earth to ground it."

Bast sighed. Nothing was ever easy.

"I will leave and come back when you need me. That way you won't need to travel to my speed," Tir said.

Ra had issued everyone with a sat phone before they left in case they got separated so at least they didn't have to worry about how long it would take to find Tir this time.

"Thank you, Tir," Bast said.

"Good hunting," Ra added with a smile as Tir slipped back toward ghast territory with an eager step.

Ra mapped their location on his GPS once they were back underway and confirmed their current route would take them either skirting the eastern edge of the city to head north or straight through its heart. Only time would tell which.

Kairon moved in fits and starts beneath them as they flew. At times, he ran almost as fast as he'd moved through the Valley of Moons. Often, he slipped more uncertainly through the shadows as he held the vial before him in a clenched fist, the red glow of his magic sneaking out between his fingers to cast a sinister air to his face. They couldn't take a straight path—partly because of the vagaries of the tracking spell that seemed like one of the most temperamental Bast had come across, and partly because they needed to avoid populated areas and any airspace where scouts were patrolling. They were in the depths of Air Court territory and they couldn't risk anyone noticing them beneath Bast's cloaking spell.

As they drew nearer to the city, Bast dropped to the ground so that he could extend his glamour to encompass Kairon and so both he and Ra would be free to defend themselves if needed. It was tricky to wield a weapon with a human strapped to your front even if magic did make them all but weightless.

The tracking spell took them through the eastern parts of La Paz, down low-rise residential streets of human buildings that had long since been abandoned for the safety of the magically reinforced elemental structures closer to the city centre. It was still the dark early hours of the morning as they moved through the city and few people were out and about. Sunrise would be a few hours away at the earliest. Hopefully, they'd be well clear of the city by then.

Scattered along the old human footpaths were the remains of rusted metal tree sculptures clawing at the night sky with their branches of spiked talons pointing upward. They must've been made from some sort of welded old pipework, the empty circles of shorn-off downpipe dripping dark liquid down onto the broken concrete they were crossing. Perhaps the metal pipes had once drained water. Now, they drained the crumpled body of some poor man who'd clearly been dropped from a height onto the sharp sculpture. The only mercy in his death was that he wouldn't have survived a single breath past the impact. The body must've only been there a day or two because the flesh was still mostly on his bones, the ripe scent of decomposition washing over them as they passed.

Bast glanced away, all too aware he had enacted the same death on traitors in his territory in an attempt to speak the only language the Air Court understood. He didn't leave them there to rot and scare his own people afterwards, though. A glimpse on the edge of his awareness had Bast turning his head to the roof of a half-collapsed building to see a jaguar staring down, eyeing up the body. He'd be surprised if it was still there come morning.

Three blocks later they passed one of this area's smaller cousins of the arachdryn, the winged spider monsters from home, being feasted on by a juvenile nocturnal mountain dragon that hissed in warning as they passed, somehow able to sense their presence just like the rock ghasts had. The early hours of the morning belonged to predators and the citizens of La Paz knew to stay clear.

The souls in the area watched him warily as they passed, unsure whether his intrusion in their city was one they should help or hinder. Not that they could stand against him if he really flexed his power.

Reaching out to them, he broadcast a call for help. *I'm searching for a missing child. Have you seen her? As soon as we find her, I promise we'll be gone.* He sent them a collection of images and feelings that made up his understanding of Kaia along with the message—her playfulness, determination, and willingness to befriend almost anyone, including his grumpy reluctant mate. A stab of pain shot through him as he sent the souls his memories of Kaia and Hel together.

Bast could feel the dead swirling around him as they considered his request before finally a single soul replied. This lingering dead man felt almost ancient, like he'd been waiting on this side of the veil a long, long time. *She is not in the city, soulweaver. Look elsewhere.*

Bast passed the message on to Kairon and Ra in a whisper, the vampyr merely nodding in response before returning his focus to the vial in his hand. Sweat was beading on his pale skin now and though he hadn't slowed his pace, the search was obviously sapping his energy reserves.

"Save your strength. The souls are confident she isn't here. Let's run to the northern edge of the city and then pick the trail back up from there," Bast suggested, and Kairon gratefully nodded in agreement, letting the red of his power fade from view.

They were passing through an area of red-brick housing marching up a weathered hillside when raw power rushed through him and a female soul wrapped itself around his essence sending chills to the tips of his feathers.

Soulweaver. Wait.

Why? Bast asked the soul.

There is a woman here. A mother. Hiding because she carries a soulweaver in her womb. She is dying, the soul replied.

Through the filter of his magical protections, he could feel the pain of the soul's death in childbirth. He wondered what had happened that an elemental would pass like that. Unless she'd also conceived a soulweaver. It was unlikely, though. Luckily, his kind was rare.

Ra looked at him in question as he launched back into

the air and circled in place above the dilapidated residential area where they'd been forced to jog along a cobblestone road riven with cracks and wyrm holes.

Casting his power out in a soft net of silver only he could see, he let the soul direct it where she wanted his attention. The sparking mist settled on a hovel nestled in the hillside nearby. He dropped back down to where Kairon and Ra were waiting, speaking in a soft whisper even though his shielding was still in place. There was no point taking chances.

"I need to stop at a house nearby and see if I can help someone," he said.

Ra shook his head in mock disapproval. "Honestly. I don't know how you've maintained a rep for being ruthless this long. You're a total softy."

Bast rolled his eyes and shoved his shoulder. "Shut it. So are you. And you'll still sneak up on someone from behind and use that garotte hidden at your wrist when the situation warrants."

"Will you need my assistance?" Kairon asked.

"I may do. She's this way," Bast said, launching himself back up into the air and flying low to keep his protections stretched around the other two men.

It didn't take long to make their way along a path that was more like an urban bush trail than a road to the isolated property. The door was barely held in place by its rusted hinges, sitting at an awkward angle. He knocked anyway. There was no point risking getting shot at by whoever was inside. His knocks fell into silence, no sign of any movement in response breaking through the sounds of the night. It wasn't a good sign.

"Can you hear anything?" he asked Kairon.

"A fading heartbeat and struggling breath on the other side of the door," the vampyr replied, urgency in his tone.

"No one else is in there?" Bast checked.

Kairon shook his head.

The door took two attempts to open. He had no idea how a delirious, dying pregnant elemental had managed to close it in the first place. When they entered, Kairon hissed in concern from behind him, darting around his wings to reach the woman draped over an old musty mattress lying on the bare floor. The red of the vampyr's power had filled the space before Bast even had a chance to explain what was going on.

Ra clasped his shoulder in reassurance and murmured in his ear. "I can see what this is. I'll keep watch at the door." He must've felt the soulweaving power of the baby growing inside the woman through his bond with Bast.

"She's like you?" Kairon asked, his voice showing his frustration as his power ran off her body just like it had run off Bast's earlier. Unlike Bast, the baby growing inside the woman couldn't control the mass of the power of the dead coalescing around her to let Kairon's healing work.

Souls swirled in the tiny space, drawn by the baby's danger and pain just like they'd been drawn to Hel before Bast had constructed the shielding that kept her safe. The dead were unable to stay away even though they knew they were causing the mother and unborn child's death.

"Her baby is like me. I need to construct a shield for her to protect them from the child's power. Once it's in place, you should be able to heal her," Bast said.

Kairon looked like he had a million questions, but he knew better than to waste time asking them. Bast went to work constructing the protections from the soul taint that would've consumed the mother within days without his shielding. For the hundredth time, he said a silent thank you to Ra and Zee's technology that had let him apply science to his power and design this shielding that had saved his mate and would now save this woman as well. Anchored in her wing structure and with the help of the soul who'd contacted him for help, he was fairly certain the shielding would last long enough even without his presence to keep it refreshed. This woman wasn't like Hel, who had his power permanently running through her veins, twining with her own, to keep the shielding in place. Luckily, it only needed to function until the baby was born.

Judging by the swell of her belly, that would only be a matter of days or weeks. She'd toughed it out this far and he'd found her just in time. This would be enough to save her. The baby might be more tricky. Their wings were not yet fully formed to hold the shielding. Their mother's protection would extend to them for now, but he'd have to revisit the pair soon after the birth to see what he could do for the child.

Stepping clear as the last structure of the spell snapped into place, the souls that had been swarming the room around him were finally released from the compulsion that drew them to the unborn child.

Thank you, a dozen voices whispered in his mind.

The woman's breathing steadied a little. Even with only the renewed red glow of Kairon's power lighting her face, Bast could see her body had wasted away to skin and bone while she lay there for however long she had been. It was long minutes before a strangled moan sounded from her and she tried to sit up, the strength in her arms failing her as her heavy wings hung limp and exhausted on the mattress.

"Here," Bast said, reaching around her shoulders to help

and digging an energy bar and bottle of water out of his pack to give her.

Holding the food to her lips, he silently willed her the strength to chew and swallow as even that seemed too much effort. His heart hurt as he watched. They couldn't stay here with her, nor could they risk giving their position away by calling for help.

"Do you have family here? Someone you can call?"

Her eyes flicked to a bag nearby and he pulled it over to her, taking her slight nod as permission to rifle through it until he found a sat-phone powered down in one of the pockets. It also contained more food and a lantern he set on the floor and turned on.

The bright LED light revealed Kairon was sitting slumped against a wall nearby with his eyes closed. The vampyr was obviously running low on energy himself after running all night while wielding the tracking spell and healing both Bast and the woman.

"You okay?" he asked, touching the vampyr gently to check he was still conscious.

"I need to feed. It can wait, though. Take care of her," he said.

Bast turned his attention back to the woman who was chewing a little faster now as some colour came back into her face.

"Does anyone know your child is a soulweaver?" he asked.

She looked up at him with fear in her eyes as she shook her head and eyed up the distinctive black of his wings that made him instantly recognisable to his kind.

"Good. You and the child are safe for now. I can return and help once they're born. Just don't do anything drastic before I get back here," he said, all too aware of how history had shown soulweaving babies were dealt with—left in the woods to join the dead.

Powering the elemental's phone on, he programmed her number into his own. He couldn't risk giving her his in case she gave it to someone who could track him.

"You'll be okay here until help can come?" he asked.

"Yes," she croaked. "My family aren't far. They think I'm travelling. They will come when I call."

Bast ignored the flash of irritation he felt at that. Of course they'd come when she called. Because she wasn't a soulweaver. His own family had abandoned him as soon as he left the womb. Although he guessed he should be grateful they didn't try and kill him before he was capable of defending himself. They'd assumed he'd die way before that.

Pulling his power to himself, he wrapped it around the woman, holding her gaze and forcing his will into his command. He hated doing this, but there was no way he could risk letting her talk when they were deep in Aliya's territory.

"We were never here," he said, making her believe the statement as truth. She didn't have enough magic to fight the compulsion.

Her eyes lost focus a little as she repeated his words back to him. "You were never here."

Reaching a hand down, Bast pulled Kairon to his feet and propelled him out the door to where Ra was waiting. He made sure to push the door back into place to keep the woman safe until she called for help.

"How long will your magic confuse her?" Kairon asked.

"Not long. We need to be gone before she makes that call. Can you feed from me?" Bast asked.

Kairon looked surprised and tilted his head as he considered the question. "I am honoured you would offer. But I don't think so, no. Our powers don't play nicely together. I suspect your blood would be like a kind of poison to my kind."

Ra was already rolling up a sleeve. "See. I told you you'd need me along. Portable snack bar at your service," he said, smiling his familiar cheeky grin at Kairon as he held his wrist out to the vampyr.

Kairon smiled. "You are a very unique individual," he said. "Thank you."

Bast snorted. "You have no idea."

Kairon paused as he gripped Ra's forearm in gentle fingers and looked concerned. "Bast's magic has touched you."

"Is that a problem? Holy shit, did I poison little Dryn when I fed him?" Ra asked.

Kairon looked relieved at the reminder. "We would've known right away if you had. He's too young to handle that kind of stress without anyone noticing. It must be little enough not to matter."

"The bond I have with Ra is the closest thing to normal elemental magic I'm capable of. My power may come from death, but my bond with Ra gifts him life. I guess it's the closest I get to your power as well. If my power is dangerous to you, I wouldn't try feeding from Hel, though."

Ra guffawed as Kairon bit down on his wrist. "Can you imagine? She'd stab him before he even bared a fang."

Bast smirked at the reminder of his mate's prickly exterior. "Well, yes. That too. But I meant that given she can wield my soulweaving power herself, she's probably dangerous in blood as well as attitude."

His smile faded as his words made the constant knowledge of her absence slam into him again and it was all he could do to stay on his feet.

"We'll bring her home," Ra promised, correctly reading his expression.

"Or die trying," Bast replied, voice flat with renewed despair.

CHAPTER 6
HEL

"Wait!" Hel cried, annoyed her voice was more of a croak.

She *wasn't* scared of him, dammit. Even if she couldn't move. Sol's steps slowed as he carried her toward the writhing contagion, but he didn't stop.

"I can't shift the contagion right now but I can figure out how to do it again," she said, desperate to buy herself some time while she figured out a way through this shitshow that didn't involve Bast falling into the hands of her father.

"Is it because you need the power surge from a melding? I can always make another," Sol offered.

"No!" Hel lied, horrified by the thought of any more death.

So many people had died already and she couldn't help but feel responsible. If she had never been stolen away as a baby, if she'd just handed herself over to him as an adult, neither of the meldings would ever have happened.

She shuddered in revulsion as Sol bundled her up into his arms and powered up into the air.

"You're lying. Is that how you did it? I've tried moving the contagion myself with a power boost but it never worked. Maybe it's something about being on the planet being melded," he mused, sounding too fucking smug at having 'cracked' it. "It won't take long to set up the structures here. A few days, maybe a week, given I don't have to hide them or defend them here. The shards are made by a fascinating people who can weave dimensions. Would you like to meet them, little star?" he asked.

Hel opened her mouth but no words came out. Swallowing, she tried again. "So many people will die. *Your* people," she whispered.

It was Bast's power that actually shifted the contagion. If Sol caused a melding here and Bast wasn't around, she would fail at his task and all those people would die for *nothing*.

"They will die eventually regardless. Either of old age or when the contagion wins through. The worlds I'm shielding the portals to are full to capacity and it's taking all my power to keep the taint away from them. I can't leave Travaris or the contagion will run out of control, which means I can't go create portals on a planet clear of contagion to find new worlds to move to. Even if I could, it takes vast amounts of time to hunt for a world that can sustain life. This is the *only* solution."

Well, that explained why he'd never come for her himself on the Melded Earths. He was essentially trapped here. "You can't play God like that. You killed millions."

"Yes, I did. Are you any better? How many people do you think died when you shifted the contagion here? You saw the remains of the settlement. Did you see the refugees, too?"

A rushing sound filled Hel's ears and she thought she might vomit. "The spheres we sent were contained. They can't spread."

"And yet if you drop one on top of somebody, they will still die."

A sob wracked her body and she shook with the effort of holding back a silent scream. It might not be the level of destruction Sol had wrought, but how could she claim to be any different to him? She hadn't thought twice before lobbing those spheres of contagion back at him. In her head, she'd been saving their people. Clearing the contagion away from those she loved. She hadn't even thought about where it was going. She should've known better. It was never those in power who paid the price.

Like father, like daughter, she thought, bitterly.

"You can save the rest of them now, though," Sol said, voice cajoling as he landed them back on the balcony by her chambers.

"By killing them?" Hel asked, both her voice and spirit broken.

"By whatever means necessary," Sol said.

Probably sensing she was at her limit, Sol left her alone to recover from his revelations. It was all she could do to stagger to the too-soft bed and curl up in a ball wrapped tight in her wings. How many people had died when she sent the contagion here? Ten? Fifty? One hundred? Were there children? And how many more would die when Sol forced a melding on Travaris thinking it would give her the power to shift the contagion?

She'd spent too long unconscious to want to ever sleep again, but she couldn't make herself get out of bed. Tears flowed down her cheeks until her pillow was sodden.

Turning her face down into the wet fabric, she screamed as loud as she could, giving voice to all the guilt and pain that took up so much space inside her she thought she might explode and yet still did nothing to fill the aching absence of her mate.

She needed Bast here. Needed to lean on his broad shoulders just a little until she could bear to keep moving again. She'd never needed anyone like that before, but a few months with him and she was a different person and the world was a different place. She hated that weakness as much as she craved it. She was so tired. Had been alone so long. She couldn't go back to that.

There were no good options.

Sol had said she had a few days at least. Surely, she could come up with something in that time. Escaping alone wasn't enough because not only would Sol send his people to chase her down, she'd be dooming this world to succumb to the contagion. It wasn't an abstract location devoid of people in her mind anymore. It was filled with people just like Tir, and children who were probably much like Kaia.

Fuck.

How could she save them all?

HER DREAMS that night were filled with scenes from home she could sense were true but without the ability to touch or talk like when she'd shared her dream with Bast. It was like a movie reel of what was happening to those she loved who were too far away to comfort. An agonising peek that only made her feel more helpless.

Ana sat crying in her bedroom, her usually tidy silken

hair of white straggling around her face in tangled knots. A mourning wail broke from her mouth as she rocked in place all alone—"Auē!"

Hel reached out disembodied hands to her friend, but they passed through her body like air. No matter how many times she tried, she couldn't touch her, couldn't pull her into her arms to offer even that small inadequate comfort.

Had the worst happened to Kaia? Why had she been left alone? Where were Bast and Ra?

The thought had a hook pulling in her chest and the image blurred as the world spun.

BAST AND RA huddled in the darkness watching a hunched form holding a vial of blood—Kairon, the vampyr she'd met so briefly. The men were deep in conversation, pointing over unfamiliar terrain, their eyes searching the darkness around them for any sign of ambush.

She watched as a current of air glowing faintly gold drifted ever closer to their position. It tasted of nefarious air magic, and they were oblivious. Why couldn't they sense it?

Throwing herself between her mate and the invisible danger, she opened her mouth to scream a warning. Bast's head jerked up as his eyes searched for a presence that wasn't there, confused.

The scenes playing through her mind changed again before she could do more than curse the divide between the waking world and the one of dreams that meant any warning would go unheard.

KAIA'S BODY slumped in a cell of crystalline walls like Aliya's Air Court stronghold. Desperate to find her location, Hel tried and failed to peer through the seemingly transparent walls to the space outside that remained a vague blur no matter how hard she tried.

Kaia's eyes in her young face looked almost as old as her grieving mother's and her quiet sobs rent the air with anguish. The bright electric blue of her wings had faded to a wan grey in a way that should not have been possible—her body drained of energy and power. Brittle feathers trembled as she let out a cough that wracked her slight body. The movement created a strange clinking noise and Hel glanced down to notice a collar of thick black metal ringed Kaia's neck, connected by a cable of magic to the nearest wall. It was sucking the power from her very bones and feeding it some-where else.

Hel tried to follow the trail. To see who she needed to kill. But once again, control escaped her and the scene moved on.

Whoever they were. They were dead. NO ONE treated her family that way and lived.

FAMILIAR ARMS WRAPPED around her body, pulling her in close, and she sighed in relief. Soft lips brushed her hair. Resting her hand on her star-blue mark on Bast's chest over his heart, relief flooded through her at the renewed connection.

"My love," Bast whispered.

His voice was enough to remind her of her fear for him and dread filled her as she realised he must've fallen asleep.

"You need to wake. Now. Something's stalking you. A cloud of Air Court power," she gasped into his neck, clinging to him even as she told him to leave. "And find Kaia quickly. They're draining her dry. Her cell is constructed like Aliya's stronghold and reeks of air magic," Hel said.

Bast was gone as suddenly as he'd appeared, leaving her floating in darkness, their connection stretching thin once more. She let out a mourning call of her own that echoed Ana's—Auē!

The voices of the dead surrounded her, audible briefly while Bast's power still flowed through her more strongly but fading in volume the longer she stayed in the place between waking and sleep, living and dead.

A voice from her past called from the darkness. Her mother's voice—Amira.

She couldn't quite make out the words as her connection to Bast grew thin and distant once more.

WHEN SHE WOKE, she screamed her frustration into the light-filled gauze surrounding her bed. Everyone she loved needed her and she wasn't there. Why had the universe finally given her a family only to taunt her with their pain?

Stalking from bed, she dropped to the ground and trained in a way she hadn't since she'd arrived on this forsaken planet, forcing her body through push-ups and hand-to-hand combat drills until she was breathless and aching. At last, all she could do was lie panting on her back on the bare floor.

She didn't clock her mistake until it was too late. Lying prone, too much of her skin was exposed to the magic infusing the bounds of the room. She barely had time to process she was drowning in her father's influence before calm descended and her pain was pushed into a tiny screaming voice buried deep inside.

Her personality was still a tenuous thing when Sol returned for her that afternoon, Aliya hanging off his arm as he sauntered into Hel's room, both of them dressed in inverse pictures of white and gold silk. Their white-gold wings were close enough in colour at a casual glance that the two could've been related. Gross. But closer inspection revealed that Sol's wings seemed made of pure starlight while Aliya's were almost tacky in comparison, threaded through with feathers of gold like gaudy jewellery.

"Little star. Come, get dressed. We're dining with the Anvanthar tonight in honour of their new contract," Sol said.

She'd noticed the fine clothing hanging in her room when she awoke, but she'd ignored it. She wasn't a doll to be dressed. The mental haze that constantly tried to suck her down into compliance had been easier to regain while Sol wasn't around, but she could feel the fight leaving her tense muscles as his power flooded the room and she was moving to pick up the clothes before she could even process the change.

"Good girl," Aliya said, with a smug smile.

That was enough to break through the compulsion for a moment and she glared at the Lady of Air. There wasn't enough magic in the world to convince her to take that kind of shit from the woman who'd killed her mate and pinned him to her wall like a bug.

"Fuck off," Hel shot back at her.

"Aliya, we spoke about this. Behave," Sol said, a sharp edge sneaking into his tone.

Aliya pouted and swept over to one of the low-backed love seats, draping her white-gold wings around her like a skirt as she let the thigh-high split in her dress reveal the length of her bare legs.

"She's going to make us late," Aliya pouted.

"That is not your concern," Sol said. "Besides, you love making an entrance."

Hel rolled her eyes in disgust and found her feet still moving to take her behind an intricate dressing screen despite her reluctance. Sol must've decided to try endearing himself to her again instead of his threats because he'd allowed her a floor-length dress of black, rather than dressing her in his colours of gold and white. Although she would still be thoroughly branded by the pieces of jewellery awaiting her on the dressing table which all shone with the bright white light of his wings and incorporated what she assumed was his sigil—a scattered pattern of stars. By the time she'd donned them all, she felt like a walking advertisement for his empire. The earrings, draping pendant, arm cuffs, bracelets, and rings on almost every finger would've been enough on their own to make her feel like a jewellery store model, but the delicate diadem draping over her horns and hair was total fucking overkill.

Still, her hands never faltered as she donned everything in a forcefully relaxed haze. As each piece of metal touched her skin, she felt his influence tightening around her. This was how he was ensuring she didn't embarrass him tonight.

The final pieces of the outfit were black three-inch stilettos that she noticed with satisfaction would make her just a touch taller than Aliya. They also seemed solid enough to stab someone in the throat in a pinch, which was reassuring given the sword she'd stolen the previous day was nowhere to be found.

"I need a weapon. I'm defenceless without access to my power," she said as she stepped back into the main living space.

Sol's eyes tracked up and down her body, checking each of his drugging ornaments were secured. "That won't be necessary. No one would dare attack you in front of me."

Hel frowned as her brain scrambled to remember something important sparked by those words and she rubbed at her throat that twinged with a phantom pain. Was that true? Hadn't someone tried to harm her? The harder she chased the memory, the more ethereal it became.

Sol stood and approached her, tucking a loose strand of hair behind her ear. "Your mind is so strong, little star. You will be such an asset by my side. Perhaps I will give you your own worlds to rule one day."

Hel stumbled back as unfamiliar and unwelcome want rushed through her. She didn't need power like that, did she? Shaking her head, she tried to banish the uncomfortable sensations, but they didn't dissipate until Aliya slipped under Sol's arm and knocked his hand free from her as she stepped into his body.

"And me, my light? When will you give me the world you promised me?" Aliya asked.

It might be the first time Hel had been grateful for one of Aliya's obnoxious interjections because it gave her the time to gather the threads of herself back together. Sol deftly extricated himself from Aliya's embrace and looped his arm through Hel's, heading toward the balcony rather than the interior door and leaving Aliya to trail along behind them.

"I upheld my end of our bargain, Lady Air. If you can't wrest control from the chaos on your world without my help then you don't deserve to hold it," he said.

Aliya's silence in response spoke volumes. Her seething behind them was a visceral thing Hel felt in her bones as she walked outside. She wasn't sure who was the more immediate threat. The murderous elemental at her back or the insidious influence of her father by her side. As Sol stayed too close for comfort, Hel strained her muscles to keep her wings furled tight to her back in an effort to avoid brushing against the stardust of his, keeping as much distance as he'd allow between them.

"We're circling the building to the right and dropping down three floors to one of the ballrooms. Stay close behind me," Sol said, ignoring Aliya's quiet tantrum behind them as they stepped out into the night.

Hel paused for a moment as she watched her father launch himself over the edge, turning her head to stare into the distance where the columns of auroral light hiding the contagion weren't quite visible. She'd barely processed the urge to flee when an intangible tug at her body sent her swooping down behind Sol's impossibly broad wingspan.

Flight was still a novelty to her, but at least she was adept enough at landing now that she didn't embarrass herself when she touched down on the stretch of golden carpet that stretched like a landing strip on the balcony. Tiles of white stone lit the air around them making the entryway appear almost as if it was daytime. However, she did stumble when Aliya's wings clipped her on the way past as she was still finding her balance on the narrow heels of her shoes. Who the fuck thought stilettos were a sensible choice for flight? Or anything else for that matter. Jabbing an elbow into the Lady of Air's ribs before the elemental could get clear, Hel smirked in satisfaction as Aliya let out a pained gasp and stumbled even worse than she had.

Sol grabbed Aliya's elbow as if to catch her, but her pleased smile quickly turned frigid as he hissed in her ear. "I warned you, Aliya. If you're going to behave like a child, you will be treated like one."

Aliya froze in shock as Sol turned away from her to place Hel's hand in the crook of his arm before heading toward the soaring entranceway to the ballroom. A steward slipped in behind them to direct Aliya to wherever she'd been banished for the night. Hel didn't look. She already knew the Lady of Air would be fuming. Just one more reason to watch her back.

The doorway ahead of them towered with majesty and, on either side of it, sitting statue-still but for their venomous tongues lolling to the side, were two of the biggest starhounds she'd ever seen. They easily came up to her shoulders even with her heels on. A lifetime of running from them like prey made her breath catch in fear and she hated herself a little as she clung tighter to Sol's arm. He patted her hand reassuringly.

"You have nothing to fear from them so long as you don't run," he murmured, the threat in that statement all too clear.

As they entered a glittering room of floating platforms holding tables laden with sparkling place settings, a sharp crack like thunder was followed by total silence falling in the space that had been filled with alien voices and the clink of glassware only moments earlier.

A disembodied voice echoed through the space announcing their presence—"His imperial highness, Sol— Emperor of Suns, Light of the Avanthian Multiverse, wielder of Starkiller, Traveller of Worlds. And his little star —Saviour of the Freed Galaxies and his most exquisite creation."

Hel hid her frown at the introduction that was just slightly off in a way she couldn't quite put her finger on. They made her sound like an object, not a daughter. Did she not even warrant her real name? Did her mother not have any input into her 'creation'? Sol's titles reminded her of Tir's description of him—*his sword is called Starkiller and his power is so great the name could well be fact.* The contagion destroyed whole stars and planets, but that was different. It destroyed everything. Was Sol really powerful enough to kill a star? Were stars even alive? She faltered as she glanced over at the well-worn hilt of his blade hanging from his back, realising his nickname for her might be more sinister than she'd thought.

"Smile, little star," Sol murmured in her ear as his power wrapped around them and took them into the air with no effort from either of their wings.

He was taking them up to the highest of the floating platforms, one that drifted just below the twinkling draping lights of the chandeliers hanging from the ceiling that cast an electric white and blue glow like the heart of the hottest of suns to match Sol's power signature.

Hel tilted her head to the side as she thought about that. Her own power had only the plasma blue plus Bast's silver entwined through it. What parts of Sol's power had she missed out on inheriting? Definitely whatever he was using to hold her enthralled, but she suspected it was more than that. He was several orders of magnitude more powerful than she would ever be.

Free to glance around the room as they ascended

through no effort of her own, Hel noticed species she'd never seen before sitting side by side at elaborate tables on the floating platforms she suspected had some hierarchical significance. Her eyes caught on a group of Tir's people and Sol noticed her attention.

"Ah, yes. You have met one of them before, have you not? The ceptae are a fascinating species, but Tir is particularly so. The power to portal is not common. I intend to track them down once I can leave Travaris again."

Hel kept quiet despite the fear his words sparked, not wanting to risk betraying anything about her friend to Sol. Far below, her eyes caught a flash of familiar white wings being led to one of the few tables on the floor of the vast chamber. The steward had carried through on Sol's threat to sit Aliya at the equivalent of a kiddy table. If she hadn't been so overwhelmed she might've smirked. She couldn't think of someone more deserving.

The platform they landed on held a table already fully occupied but for a thronelike chair at the head and one immediately to its right. There were ten people seated and Hel froze for a moment as she noticed the one to the left of the throne was the spitting image of the man who'd chased her across the skies until she and Bast had killed him on a deserted beach months earlier. They had exactly the same red skin, leathery bat-like wings, double-hinged jaw, and eyes that glowed like the starhounds that had hunted her. Another wave of Sol's calm washed over her before she could tense up and a distant voice in the back of her mind fumed at the artificial feeling of trust towards whoever it was in that seat.

She didn't have time to pull herself free from Sol's influence, though, because the second her heels touched the silver of the platform, everyone was standing and Sol was introducing her to a blur of peoples she was thoroughly unfamiliar with—these were the Avanthians who had built the shards that enabled the meldings and the mass-murder of three worlds of people along with it.

The Avanthians were the least human-appearing of the species she'd come across. Not because they didn't appear bipedal with arms and fingers to wield the cutlery set out for them, but because their bodies seemed to constantly shift from second to second. Each change on its own was subtle, but the overall effect was that they looked completely different from one minute to the next. What had Sol said they could do? Weave dimensions? They looked like their anatomy was constantly weaving every version of themselves that existed into itself in a never-ending cycle.

Names passed in a blur of artificial calm and smiles as they made their way around the table. Strangely, the most incongruous person at the table wasn't the species who were alien to her, but someone who looked an awful lot like her—a young woman at the foot of the table who couldn't have been more than eighteen with twisting horns emerging from her blond hair and feathered wings the colour of auroral lights draping down her back. Hel might've paused to speak to her, but Sol was propelling her on toward their places. She supposed the entire rest of the room was probably waiting for them to sit before being served. That was a lot of people.

Pulling her focus back, she did her best to pay more attention as she was introduced to the person who'd be sitting to her right.

"Little star, may I present Laylarth. She's the most powerful of my Avanthian mages and the original architect of the shards of stasis," Sol said.

It took another nudge of Sol's power for Hel to extend her hand. Had Laylarth willingly given her father the tools of her Melded Earths' apocalypse? Or was she subject to the same overwhelming urge to please him as Hel was, but without the immunity to fight it?

Either way, she couldn't forget what this mage had wrought. Dragging her personality from where it had been crushed somewhere deep inside by her father's power, she managed to say something that passed for her true feelings. At least, as much as Sol's enforced politeness would allow.

"I wish I could say it was a pleasure."

Sol tutted and squeezed her hand that was still looped over his arm hard enough to make it ache.

"Play nicely, little star," he chided. "I apologise, Laylarth. She appears to be holding a grudge."

"I understand," the woman replied, her soft voice becoming sibilant partway through the word as something in the biology of her mouth shifted.

"And this is General Tarn," Sol said, gesturing to the bat-winged man on his other side as he took his place at the head of the table. "I believe you met one of his cousins already."

Hel bared her teeth in something she knew looked nothing like a smile. "Should I apologise? He died well—telling my mate exactly what we needed to know," she taunted.

Sol placed a hand on the nape of her neck and every piece of jewellery she was wearing flared briefly until her face relaxed and she sunk into the chair in a haze of almost drunken stupor.

"Her resistance is almost refreshing," he said, addressing his words to the General.

"Respectfully, we don't have time for the refreshment.

Send me to her world with a battalion or three and let's see how long she keeps resisting," Tarn said.

Hel knew that threat should spark something in her, but the warm glow from the metal on her skin kept her pliant, not allowing her to feel the panic she should have at his words.

"If she's still holding out when the shards are ready, you may launch an incursion into the Melded Earths. I'm sure the combination of your soldiers and the contagion that large a portal would let through to her world will have her complying soon enough," Sol replied, before turning back to her where she sat wishing her wings would fit in a chair with a back so she could've had something solid to lean on. She needed something, anything, to anchor her in this surreal floating space.

"General Tarn has a nickname in the colonies—the Ravager," Sol told her, reaching out to tuck a napkin on her lap as if she were still a child. "You must try the dumplings. I bet you've never tasted anything like them."

CHAPTER 7
BAST

Bast blinked awake, groggy and disoriented, to the knowledge that something was very wrong. The last thing he remembered was Kairon feeding from Ra. Well, the last thing that wasn't the sweet agony of visiting his mate in his dreams again. Now, both Kairon and Ra were slumped nearby asleep and a bright light like a flare hung over their heads. Fuck. Some sort of sentry air magic had caught them and called for scouts and he had no idea how long they'd been out.

There was no time to wake his friends and they likely wouldn't stir until they left the area tainted with sedative power. Straining with effort and fighting the urge to just lie down and rest his eyes, Bast managed to haul the two men upright, one under each arm, and use his power to launch them into the sky as he renewed his glamour and shielding. Wincing, he noticed tiny golden sparks where the edges of his shield that should've been invisible met the grey light of dawn around them. Was that because they were still within the spell's bounds or had it attached itself to them somehow?

Calling deep on the magic that lingered in the dead town they were flying above, he burned whatever it was away from him. The move probably keyed in their searchers to how powerful he was, if they weren't already aware, but there was nothing else he could do.

Kairon finally showed some signs of waking as the spell dissipated, jerking in Bast's arms and making his biceps bulge with effort to avoid dropping him.

"We're airborne. Stay still," Bast whispered.

"Fuck. What happened?" Kairon asked. Apparently, all it took for him to pick up on human swearing was a day in their company.

"We triggered a sentry spell that knocked us out and sent a signal to every Air Scout in the area."

As if saying the words aloud had been the catalyst, five figures appeared ahead of them, flying in a search pattern. A glance over his shoulder showed more elementals narrowing in on their position from behind. He couldn't face them like this, weighed down with no hands free, but looking down he saw there was almost no cover for them on the ground.

"There," Kairon said, pointing at a dark circular shadow nestled in the earth.

"No way. That's a fucking wyrm hole. Or worse," Ra slurred, finally awake as well.

A burst of energy radiated from somewhere behind him and the glints of flashing light on his shielding returned. They wouldn't usually have sensed him. Someone had obviously been training in defending against soulweaving power. Although how they'd managed it when he was the only living soulweaver was a mystery. The thought reminded him of the baby they'd saved and he wondered if his kind weren't as rare as everyone thought. Did the Air Court have one hidden away?

Bast cursed as another burst of energy, this time from whoever was flying above, sunk down around them and the air they were breathing lost its oxygen. Fuck, he hated air mages. Give him a rage-filled fire mage lobbing fireballs and dragons at him over their insidious suffocating murder any day.

"Pick a direction and fly. I'll take care of anyone in your way," Kairon said, seemingly unaffected by the fact that each breath they took lacked what their lungs needed to keep them conscious.

Bast couldn't afford to delay. Trusting in Kairon's abilities, he shot east as fast as his magic would propel him, which was still an order of magnitude faster than these soldiers even with his incapacitation growing with each unsatisfying inhalation. Ra's face was turning a disturbing shade of red. Dropping lower, Bast skimmed close to the ground so that if he fell from the sky he, hopefully, wouldn't kill his chosen brother before the magical attack did.

A red flash of Kairon's magic went off like a bomb around them and the welcome sight of elementals tumbling from the air flashed in his peripheral vision. Their wings crumpled behind them as they lost consciousness instantly instead of this slow strangulation they'd inflicted on them. Spying a lake ahead, he crossed his fingers that the elemental magic smothering them would respond to the most basic of changes in surrounding and that the lake wasn't filled with anything too nasty. He would've warned Kairon and Ra they were about to get very wet, but the exertion plus the lack of oxygen was stealing his words.

Without much finesse at all, he dropped them into the

water, using his power to smooth out the inevitable ripples as he pushed them into its depths. Elemental magic was a strange thing. It all came from the same source—the ley lines that crisscrossed the earth—but through training and the influence of the strongholds, they fashioned it around the focus of their element in such a way that they often created a weakness in their constructs that didn't need to be there. This one was no different, the air magic sloughing off them as they sunk into the cool water. At least they hadn't learned how to fix that problem along with their new trick of getting past his shields. He'd need to investigate that later. When Ra wasn't about to drown on him.

Kairon had twisted free of his hold just before they hit the water but Ra was struggling in his arms. Letting his friend go, he gave him a sharp push toward the surface, following close behind him. His oxygen-starved muscles burned with effort as he kicked upward against the drag of sodden wings. They breached the surface almost simultaneously, gasping in life-giving air as they treaded water and scanned the air for anyone following. He caught a flash of wings in the distance back the way they'd come as Caelus's people searched the ground for their bodies. For now, they'd thankfully miscalculated Bast's speed and his ability to function without air. The scouts would spread their search wider as soon as they realised there were no dying bodies hidden on the earth, though. They needed to get moving.

As he wrapped an arm each around Kairon and Ra to lift them clear, something hidden beneath the surface of the lake wrapped around his leg, twining up until he felt something suction onto his stomach.

"What the fuck is that?" Ra yelped, drawing a dagger and stabbing it down into the murky water.

Bast pushed free of his companions to shoot a swathe of death magic into the depths, but more neon-coloured tentacles were clearing the water around him every second.

Kairon swore from nearby "Kranthum. The suckers on the tentacles are like leeches."

"A fucking kraken leach? Why does everything from your version of Earth have to feed on blood?" Ra gasped.

The kranthum must've had a few rich meals lately dining on the unsuspecting elementals and humans because the lake around them was swimming with souls. Grasping for more power from the dead, Bast dragged the three of them clear of the water by slicing raw power through an ever-multiplying number of tentacles.

With a grim smile, he left a simulacrum of their appearance flailing in the water once they were out of reach. With any luck, it might lure some of their pursuers into the kranthum's arms. Then he focused all his energy on speeding over the bare beige landscape looking for anywhere they could lie low and get back on track to finding Kaia.

Hel had told him in their dream that the girl was somewhere that reeked of air magic. Given Caelus was the most powerful mage in the area, he'd be surprised if she wasn't in his hidden base. They needed Kairon to get them directions with the tracing spell again. But first, they needed to fly clear of anything trying to kill them or eat them.

Frustration threatened to overtake him as he spent long minutes scanning the exposed plains below them for any hint of cover. He didn't risk landing until the earth finally shifted to gently rolling hills with enough valleys and folds to screen them from view.

"You need to rest," Ra said, as he stumbled a little setting him down.

"We need to confirm where Kaia is," he corrected, glancing over at Kairon who looked as exhausted as he felt.

The vampyr nodded. "I'll get a new lock and then I can see if the vampyr clan near here will answer my call. We need all the help we can get."

Pulling out the vial of Ana's blood, Kairon began to chant the refrain of the tracing spell, but this time he stopped almost immediately and stared in confusion to the north.

"She's nearby," he said, pointing up into what looked like vacant airspace.

Bast nodded. "Caelus's mountain base must be there. It's covered by a powerful glamour. I'll figure out how to reveal it while you call the clan."

"And I'll check in with our people and let Tir know to be ready," Ra added.

"Can you stay safe here if I go scout ahead?" Bast asked.

"I will take care of your human," Kairon said, his mouth twitching into a grin as Ra raised his middle finger at him for the teasing comment.

Bast hesitated a moment and then launched back into the air. Ra could take care of himself against most threats other than magic. And if he didn't trust Kairon at this point they had bigger problems. Kaia had been gone too long. They needed to get her free before anything as bad as he was imagining happened.

Caelus's base, like all Air Court complexes, leaned in hard to the higher-than-thou god complex air-branding. It wasn't quite at the level of Aliya's flying stronghold, but only because that kind of vast waste of power only worked with the sentience of the strongholds to keep it functioning in the absence of its Lady. If Aliya compared her stronghold to a heaven in the sky, Caelus compared his to Mount Olympus

—nestled in magically artificed clouds and snow flurries that hid it from the view of the casual observer somewhere at the peak of the mountain Bast couldn't see as he ascended in flight. It was only by virtue of the strength of his magic that he could even hold course toward what appeared to him to just be vacant airspace and he knew any satellite imagery would only show an illusion of rolling brown hillsides below.

Like all senior court members, Caelus was ruthless about protecting his space, privacy, and power. The only photos of the base that were available online were carefully orchestrated to not reveal any defensive secrets and to enhance their ridiculous posturing. Which all meant Bast had no clue what he was looking for.

Conscious that his magical shielding may trigger a warning system of some kind, Bast kept his awareness stretched wide for any sign of an alarm, giving a wide berth to the scouts who'd been looking for them and were now arriving back empty-handed.

Remembering the air magic traps they'd faced earlier, he focused his magical senses on searching for more. Now that he knew what he was looking for, he could sense the sinister clouds like the one they'd been caught in. They thronged the air around him like aerial mines, forcing him to duck and weave because the only direct routes were the ones Caelus's people were taking. Despite the annoyance, they also gave him his first indication of where this mountain was, though. It must be in the large area of space the magical protections encircled.

Finally, he gave up his attempt to see with his own eyes and simply hovered in place, communing with the souls surrounding the area and hoping they would be amenable to helping a stranger. Lucky for him, it wasn't just the Air

Court faithful who'd died here. The souls of those tortured to death in the basement of the structure hidden ahead were all too happy to respond to his call, giving him a virtual tour of the mountain and base in a whirlwind of images he caught and held in his mind's eye.

A low growl escaped him as an image of Kaia flashed across his awareness—sunken-eyed, hollow-cheeked, grey-skinned, and fucking *chained to a wall*. It was all he could do not to charge upward to her right then, but they needed a plan and they needed Tir on hand to get them free after.

Lost in his focus on the souls, he drifted slowly forward in his hover. As he passed a boundary of some kind, a full-body shiver trembled through him and a moment later he could finally make out the crystal mountain and base ahead. He breathed a silent sigh of relief that proximity alone was enough to reveal it. He'd been worried he was going to have to rely on the dead to lead them blind the whole way there.

A series of tumbling almost free-falling barrel-rolls had him dodging the aerial traps much faster on the return trip to where Kairon and Ra were waiting for him. The vampyr had a thin bone dagger to his throat the instant he adjusted his shields so the two could see and touch him. Bast froze where he stood, a reckless grin stretching across his face as the adrenaline of his acrobatics finally caught up with him and he waited for the vampyr to realise who he was. Kairon dropped his arm and re-sheathed the weapon just as fast as he'd drawn it.

"You need to be more careful or I might not stop in time," Kairon said.

Bast shrugged and looked over to Ra. "Did you find anything useful, brother?"

"Tir can track us once we call them on the sat-phone. So,

all we need to do is get the phone to Kaia and they'll portal straight there to get us home. Caelus and any high-level magic users will sense the disturbance in the ley lines, but if we get out fast enough that shouldn't matter. Tir also scanned the area somehow when we talked. They said there's something that smells of Sol's magic nearby."

"A portal?" Bast asked, heart racing with excitement at the thought of being able to reach his mate.

"They said it definitely isn't an active open portal. Beyond that, they can't tell from this distance. It could be something that needs triggering like whatever Aliya used to get Hel out of the Earth Stronghold, it could be a defensive magic, or it could be something Caelus isn't even aware of that was put there to monitor him."

Bast growled in frustration. With Kaia so close, he couldn't help the way his thoughts kept turning to what would happen after they found her. He pushed back desperation for the thousandth time as his need for Hel threatened to overwhelm him.

"Whatever it is, you probably wouldn't be able to find it without Tir and it may well be heavily guarded. Eyes on the prize, bro. We're bringing Kaia home. Then we can figure out how to save Hel. Don't go flying off to chase who the fuck knows what," Ra said.

Bast made a non-committal sound. Ra was right. But this was also the closest thing to a lead they had to reaching Hel and he wasn't likely to be able to return easily once they'd breached the base and put the Air Court on alert.

"How will we climb a mountain we can't see?" Kairon asked.

"Once we get through the outer boundary, we'll be able to see it. The dead will lead us that far," Bast replied.

"I have put out a call to my people. Whoever they can spare from the local clan will be here by nightfall. Children are precious to us and I can sense their anger through the call. They dislike your Caelus and his mountain. They will help," Kairon said. "I suggest we all rest while we can. I'll take first watch."

Bast might've insisted on taking the watch himself, but he was exhausted after the magic he'd expended getting them here and staying hidden. The chance that he might get to hold his mate in his arms in his dreams again was enough to have him settling into a shaded hollow in the earth and stretching one of his wings over his face to sink into blessed darkness.

B ast blinked on *the soft black sheets of his bedroom at home and smiled as Hel nestled deeper into his embrace, running her nose up his neck before pressing a kiss just below his ear.*

"I don't know what to do," she whispered, sounding defeated as she leaned her forehead against him.

Bast brushed the silver hair from her face, stroking a finger down one of her twisting horns as he did so in a move that made her shiver. Tipping up her chin, he lost himself in her eyes and the feel of her body against him. These dreams were the only time the agony of her absence abated and he needed her naked skin pressed to his like he needed the breath in his lungs.

"We'll figure it out. Just hold on a little longer," he said.

"Sol's threatening to send an army to the Melded Earths

to get me to comply. And he's going to cause another melding here."

Hel's guilt throbbed like a mortal wound through their connection and a tear rolled down her cheek. Bast pressed kisses down the path it took, heartbroken by the taste of the salt on his lips.

"I'll come for you. We'll figure out another way to shift the contagion when I get there," he said.

Hel disappeared from his arms in a split second, now standing clothed and shaking with emotion next to the bed. The sudden change was a stark reminder this was only a dream and they'd never really been touching.

"No! You can't come here. He's too powerful. You'll become just another weapon to him. He'll use you and use you and we will never be free," she said, voice low and urgent.

"I won't leave you there. I can't," Bast said, letting Hel feel every ounce of his need for her, pushing it down their connection so she wouldn't be able to keep hiding from what they were both feeling.

"Don't do that. Don't make me weak. You have no idea what he could do with your power, with our powers together. I need to get out on my own. Don't you dare try and come here, Bastion."

Bast stood as well, his anger rising to match hers but his desire rising just as fast. This was familiar territory, this antagonism between them. They had always burned hardest for each other when they burned at each other.

They stood frozen in the dreamscape for a second as a raft of complex emotions flowed between them, amplifying their bond, and then they lunged for each other. Hel's clothing ripped free with barely more than a touch as he grabbed at the *offending shirt that had appeared on her body and tore it in half.*

There was no more talking. They both knew they'd only end at loggerheads. Words wouldn't stop the stubborn refusal to be saved that he could feel from his mate, but their rising passion might help ease the debilitating ache of her absence, at least for as long as it lasted.

Dropping his head, he sucked hard on her nipple, drawing it into his mouth and closing his teeth over it just tightly enough to make her cry out before moaning in pleasure. Her wings had curved around him instinctually. The feel of his mark on their soft surface rubbing against his own sensitive feathers was almost too much to bear.

Before he drowned in the sensation, a delicious sharp pain cut through the overwhelm—Hel's nails dragging down his skin as she clawed at every part of him she could reach before gripping his hair in a tight fist and pulling his head up so she could claim his mouth in another kiss.

Spinning her away from him, he pushed her forward so she was bent over the edge of the bed before him. His hands sunk down to the soft swell of her hips as he knelt behind her and pulled her toward his mouth. The scent of her arousal was driving him crazy. He was desperate to get his lips on her and banish the taste of her despairing tears from his tongue...

It was all Bast could do not to punch Kairon in the face when the vampyr's urgent grip on his shoulder sent him winging back to the waking world. Fucking cock-blocked by consciousness. Again.

Swallowing the pained noise he couldn't risk letting loose, he clung tight to the fading sensation of his mate's power slipping through his soul like the most fleeting and delicious fantasy.

Distantly, he was aware he'd reassured Kairon he was conscious enough to take over keeping watch. In reality, he was barely present in this world as his essence clung to Hel's through their bond, enwrapping it like the precious gift she was. It wasn't enough to hold her to him. It couldn't be when they were literal worlds apart. All it did was prolong the agony of their separation.

A stray noise in the wild brought him back to himself and he turned to keep watch over Ra's sleeping form beside him. He had other people depending on him, too. Other family. He couldn't go to Hel. Yet. But once Kaia was safe, all bets were off.

CHAPTER 8
HEL

Hel screamed in frustration as the bedroom disappeared from her dream and the temperature seemed to drop several degrees. Bast was gone. Again. And she hadn't extracted a promise from him about not coming to find her before he left. The knowledge she might see him in her dreams was all that had kept her going through the rest of the dinner with her father, but now she worried all it had done was make her infuriating mate even more determined to save her.

The darkness now surrounding her was familiar. A threshold she'd visited several times before that no longer held any fear. The place between the living and the dead was just another world to travel, another point of connection between realities and worlds that could feed her power just like the souls here siphoned the power of the numerous dead through to Bast—One place. Two power sources—It was another demonstration of how she and her mate just fit. When he wasn't being a stubborn ass about saving her. Despair filled her again at the thought. She knew Bast had a protector *complex. There was no way he would wait for her to get free. He was coming.*

Hel gave voice to his name with a frustrated sigh despite the fact he could no longer hear her. "Oh, Bast."

"Your relationship with him is a weakness," an achingly familiar woman's voice sounded from the darkness.

Her words echoed Hel's own from earlier, but her heart still violently rejected the statement even as she blinked back tears she couldn't shed because she didn't have a body in this place.

"Mother?" she asked.

"I am no more your mother than Sol is your father, girl," Amira said, her voice harsh in the echoing void.

"What are you talking about?"

"Your weakness will let Sol win. I won't let that happen. Not after everything he did," Amira said.

"What do you mean Sol's not my father?" Hel snapped again.

Her frustration at Amira's bullshit outweighed any joy she might've felt at their reunion. Not that they'd ever been all that close. Her mother, or guardian—whatever—had died protecting her when she was twelve, taking Hel's only friend with her as she was dragged away by Sol's starhounds. Amira had never been affectionate but Hel's memory of her abrasive edges must have softened over time because she couldn't help the stab of hurt she felt at the woman's cruel tone.

"You need to know exactly what you are so you don't give in to what he wants. You're not his spawn. He made you from his power. You're nothing more than a construct—an experiment. You're just a clone of the part of himself he needed to send through the gate as a bomb to destroy it from the other side. It might be the one time he's ever shown self-sacrifice.

Killing you would be like removing one of his organs—a non-essential one."

Hel's mind spun in confusion at Amira's words. "What the fuck are you talking about? That doesn't make any sense. I'm not even male. I'm not his fucking clone."

"Only because I twisted his creation at conception when he forced me to bear you inside my body," Amira said, bitterness in every word. "I see you found your winged form again —the one you had at birth—but even Tir couldn't undo that earliest of changes when you were nothing more than a collection of cells. Sol never truly understood my people's shapeshifting power, especially on something as small as an embryo. He never realised what we're capable of. That's his weakness. He doesn't understand your so-called mate's power, either. He believes the stories he's spun about his own supremacy and he can't even see that it was only your combined magic that shifted the contagion to Travaris. And now you have the chance to finally win the battle and stop him from succeeding."

"How?" Hel asked, only half paying attention to the conversation as her mind struggled to process Amira's revelations.

Was she even really a person? It sounded like she was nothing more than a complicated spell cobbled together by Sol and then corrupted by Amira. A collection of DNA and forced shapeshifting that had formed whatever weird mix of body parts and magic she now possessed.

"By dying before he gets the chance to use you," Amira said, and as the words fell into the surrounding darkness, the chill of the place between grew infinitely colder, wrapping around Hel's soul in a chokehold.

Voices in the dark whispered to her—

You were never meant to be.

Let go of your false existence.

Deny him his tool.

Stop living.

Stop breathing.

Just. Stop.

Hel's awareness grew vague. Dizziness took hold, threatening to unravel her as she lacked any way to find her bearings. The heartbeat in her body, far distant, stuttered and paused. Somewhere, worlds away, Bast's did too.

No.

She wouldn't let that happen. Couldn't. If she died, Bast died. Maybe she wasn't really a person, but he sure was. She would protect him. Always. Just like he protected her.

Forcing the deadly despair away, she steeled herself against Amira's conniving influence. Her renewed determination made the cold recede and the voices fall silent. The dead didn't hold power of their own. They could only channel it to the soulweavers. It was the self-destructive thought process Amira had sparked that had been the real threat to her. Magic was a matter of willpower and her own mind had been unmaking her through Amira's cunning manipulation. The place between the living and dead wasn't somewhere you could afford to lose your way.

A sob left her as she mourned her lack of family and this one last crushing betrayal by the only mother she'd ever known. She was all alone. Even her murderous father wasn't really her parent.

The thought was strangely freeing. Whatever stray sense of familial obligation she had felt was gone. Maybe she hadn't started as a real person, but she was more than a fucking magical implement.

"Fuck you, Amira. You're as bad as he is," she said.

And then she ripped her mind free from the place between and followed the twisting line of blue and silver magic anchoring her back to her body.

Hel didn't know how long she sat staring vacantly at the gauzy curtains surrounding the unfamiliar bed after she woke. She felt untethered and she hated that she felt that way. Sol and Amira shouldn't have that kind of power over her mental state. They didn't deserve it.

With a shaking hand, she reached up and touched the horns twisting up from her head. Were they courtesy of Sol's cloning or Amira's meddling? Turning on her side, she stretched her wing out and stared at its silvery breadth marked with the black feathered pattern of Bast's mating mark. It was another way someone else's magic had shaped her, Bast's and Tir's, but she had a new perspective on it now. Some of the warmth seeped back into her chilled body as she traced a finger down her wing that was the colour of Bast's power. They had shifted her to this form to *save* her when every other part of her had been created for either sacrifice or revenge.

This part of her—the silver of her wings and hair, Bast's mark, the black of her horns—they were all created from love. Her *real* family's love. Her whānau back home in the City of Souls. The only family that mattered.

Something that had been broken inside her set itself at the thought. The mating bond she thought she'd already fully accepted nestled in just a touch deeper as she owned it with everything she was. She didn't need its validation. She would've worked things through on her own given a little space from the whirlwind of attacks, ambush, and kidnapping that had been her life for the past few months. But in that dark place where she was right then—alone with so little hope of escape, ridden with guilt at the deaths carried out to secure her and the deaths that had been promised were still to come—it was a shortcut to the stability she needed.

She *must* be a person because Bast couldn't have formed a bond with her otherwise. Bast wouldn't love her otherwise. It was okay to lean on him a little to get through this. He would protect her even when he wasn't there. Just like she did him.

Drawing in a deep breath, she shoved to her feet. Sitting on the bed waiting for Sol to come and pressure her into doing something she wasn't even capable of would achieve nothing. She needed a plan. And until she had one, staying in motion was the best she could do. A solution wasn't going to just fall into her lap.

The scent of baked goods wafted over her as she crossed the room. Someone had left clothes and food while she was sleeping again and she hadn't even stirred despite the fact she'd never slept through that kind of intrusion in her life before she came there. Fucking Sol and his drugging power. It leached into her all night from the floor and walls of her room. That was probably half of why she'd almost been caught by Amira's trap—she hadn't been able to wake. Shaking her head, she rejected the constant barrage of foreign emotions Sol was pushing at her through the bespelled room. Movement would help that, too.

She half expected the door to be locked now that Sol had realised she could get through it, but the opening mechanism still responded to the drop of Bast's magic she could access.

That wasn't a good sign. It meant Sol was fine with what she was doing. *Just keep moving,* she reminded herself. She wasn't going to find a solution lying in bed. There was nothing else she could do. Mind made up, she was striding around the curving corridor and back toward the central atrium of the building mere seconds after she'd shoved her feet into the closest thing to sturdy boots she could find.

If she thought Sol might let her fly outside again, she was mistaken. The second she set foot into the circular chamber surrounding the building's hollow core, wings of white-hot power flashed before her. Sol dropped onto the landing from above so quickly he was only the blur of a shooting star until he came to rest. Aliya followed closely behind, slower but still with the graceful ease of long practice that Hel envied. She still had to concentrate not to fall on her face when she landed.

"Ah. There you are. Sometime, you must tell me how you're opening the doors without access to your power," Sol said, taking her elbow and directing her toward one of several passageways she hadn't had the chance to explore yet that radiated like spokes from where they stood.

"Sure. Right after you tell me how I was made," Hel shot back, voice heavy with sarcasm. If he didn't know how she was opening the doors, she wouldn't be stupid enough to tell him.

Sol's steps faltered for a moment and he hummed in what could have been surprise. "How did you come by that phrasing, little star?"

Hel tugged her arm free and would've stopped walking but Aliya was following so closely behind she had no choice but to carry on wherever Sol was leading her.

"Why do you keep calling me that?" Hel asked, her

annoyance at the manipulative endearment finally getting the best of her as they stepped into a richly appointed study.

An imposing desk that looked to be made of something like amber dominated the space. The same substance made up a series of picture frames as tall as she was that ringed the curving walls of the room. She couldn't help but step closer to the nearest one in fascination as it held her gaze. The middle section of the gold-hued resin seemed to conduct magic, glowing with Sol's power as a series of alien land-scapes flashed across its surface. She could tell the images weren't from Travaris or the Melded Earths. The sun was too red, the plants were thoroughly unfamiliar, and the people going about their day were like nothing she'd ever seen even at Sol's extravagant dinner.

She could feel Sol watching as if he could read her thoughts if he peered close enough. "Because you are a little piece of me. And I am the closest thing to a living star you will find."

Hel spun to face him, her head cocked in question. Were his words literal or was he talking about his imperial persona? The soft swish of fabric nearby reminded her they weren't alone as Aliya walked to a drinks tray against the wall and poured herself a glass of alcohol glowing with some sort of soft bioluminescence.

"Why is she here?" Hel asked, desperate for answers, but not so desperate she wanted Aliya to listen in.

"Your *maker* thought I might have some insight into how to get you to do as you're told," Aliya said with a smirk.

Hel watched the Air Lady warily. Why hadn't Aliya already given away the secrets that would make her comply? Even if her heart was cold and dead, Aliya still understood mating bonds and the compulsion that could be achieved by threatening the other half of one's soul.

"Aliya, watch your tone," Sol warned, before turning his gaze back to Hel. "Forgive her rudeness. She doesn't understand your status here."

Aliya almost hissed in response. "She is nothing more than a stray creation and you value her more than your own child!"

Sol pivoted to face Aliya head-on and his vast power gathered in the air. The sudden smell of ozone drifted in the elegant space and sent static charges trembling through Hel's sensitive wings.

"Because she is *me*, a carefully curated part that I cut free. She might be unexpectedly tainted by the magic of others, but she is still entirely another piece of me walking the world. Whereas our child is diluted by also being a part of you. Hel will always outrank Stella because she is as much a father to the girl as I am. I have told you this before. When you have control of your world, I will allow you to take our daughter there and you can let her rule whatever you like. It will be good training for her. But she is not my heir and, given I have no intention of ever dying, there is no way she would inherit even if she was."

Hel's mind spun as she tried to process all the new information. Aliya and Sol had a child together? That explained so much. She'd never understood why the Lady of Air was so willing to betray her world for him, but this she could make sense of. And Hel was what? A father or a sister to this Stella? Another mother? This was too fucking weird. The memory of the young woman sitting at the foot of the table at the banquet dinner flashed through her mind. Feathered wings like Aliya's, horns like hers and Sol's. She'd been standing right next to their daughter, this Stella, without even realising it.

A raft of emotions flashed across Aliya's face before she regained control of herself and turned to Hel with a calculating look in her eyes. "If you want her to do as you ask, just torture her mate in front of her. Kill him, even. She won't be able to resist."

Hel's heart raced and panic set in as she scrambled to counteract Aliya's words and keep her mate safe. Damn her for being such a murderous conniving bitch.

"If you kill Bast, I'll die!" she snapped, and then immediately winced in regret.

Telling Sol that was a mistake. She should *not* have given away how important Bast was to her if he didn't already know. Why had Aliya kept that information to herself for so long anyway? She must've worried it would undermine Stella's position here.

Sol sighed like a disappointed parent. "Why would you weaken yourself that way, little star? We will have to disentangle you from each other."

Aliya smirked in response and Hel wished she could risk smacking the look right off the bitch's face.

"He makes me *stronger*," she shot back, and then mentally kicked herself again.

Why was she still talking? The shocking revelations of the previous hours had distracted her and Sol had toned his influence right down so that she almost hadn't noticed the subtle compulsion hanging in the air that was making her reveal the truths he needed. Biting her lip hard enough to draw blood, she used the pain and the coppery taste on her tongue to halt the betraying words being gently pulled from her.

"Is that so? Interesting. Aliya, darling. If I find you've been withholding information from me about this man and their bond, you will not be seeing Stella anytime this century. Do you understand?"

"Yes, my light," Aliya said, voice strained with fear.

"You will fetch Bastion for me. He has almost reached the child you stole. You can use the nascent portal there," Sol said, already turning away from Aliya in dismissal.

"That will let the contagion into the base there," Aliya said, genuine concern showing for once.

"Sacrifices must be made if you want to rule," he said, his gaze still assessing Hel like she was a new puzzle rather than watching Aliya. "I'll tell Stella to expect a visit from you on your return."

The implication was clear—only if Aliya did as she was told would she get to see her child. Aliya's breath was shaky as she inhaled deeply and sketched a shallow bow Sol didn't even notice before sweeping from the room. Hel took a deep shuddering breath of her own as she fought down the crushing fear that had filled her at Sol's order. Bast was too powerful to be captured by Aliya, wasn't he? Her heart sank as she realised he might well let himself be taken if he knew it would get him to her. And then, not only would Sol be able to use Bast's power, but he was going to break their bond as well. She curled in on herself as her body tensed in pain at the thought. Sol missed none of it.

"How does he make you stronger, little star?" Sol asked, his voice and his power cajoling. "Is that why you can open my doors without your magic? I could feel the foreign magic there inside you, tainting mine, but I thought it was a residue from the various shape changes that were forced on you."

Hel clenched her jaw tight against the need to tell him all her secrets. It was all she could do to stay silent.

"The differences between us are fascinating. When I heard the whispers from the Melded Earths, it didn't even occur to me you would really have tied yourself to someone in that way because you are a piece of me and I would never have done so. I guess it wasn't just your physical shape that Amira and your 'mate' changed," Sol continued. He sounded equal parts disgruntled and fascinated.

"I'm *nothing* like you," Hel said.

Sol's laugh filled the curving room, rich and poisonous in the way it further sapped her willpower. "They may have changed your sex and the colours of your body, but at your core, you are literally the same as me. I carved a part of my essence out to make you, sacrificed just enough of my power for you that you could fulfil your role. And you returned to me so much more complex. When you get over this childish aversion to us, you will make the perfect righthand person because I'll be delegating to myself." He seemed delighted by the idea. Smug.

Hel knew she should play up to his misunderstanding, gain his trust so she could stab him in the back. But she just wasn't capable of pretending what he said held any truth. She was *herself*. She might have started as a piece of him, but some combination of her life experience, her transformation, and however he had changed with the loss of her had left them galaxies apart in identity. Judging by the way he was using his own daughter to control Aliya, he couldn't seem to even comprehend the idea of whānau/family, whereas she could barely live with the guilt that she might've put the people she loved at risk.

So, fuck him. They were *not* the same. At all.

"If I'm so perfect why do you need Bast here to control me? Leave him where he is," Hel said when she finally got her stuttering thoughts under control.

Sol smirked. "Nice try. I've always been stubborn about my desires and you're the same. You need retraining before you can be what I need and I can't tolerate the risk to us he presents. No one has the power of life or death over any part of me. Aliya will bring him here and then I will fix the mess you've made with him."

Hel's eyes felt like she was blinking through molasses as she tried to rekindle her rage in defence against the constant pressure of his attempts at mental control. He was knocking her out again. Why the fuck couldn't he end a conversation like a normal person? She couldn't defend Bast from him if she was unconscious.

Sol patted her arm reassuringly.

"Don't worry. I won't be cruel to you. That would be like hurting myself. You won't even remember him once I'm done."

CHAPTER 9
BAST

Kairon's people emerged from the darkness in total silence. Twelve of them. If he squinted, Bast could just make out the faint glow of red from their eyes —a half-hidden manifestation of their power.

Kairon had disappeared an hour earlier to greet them and explain whatever needed explaining of their relationship. Each of the new vampyr greeted them with a handclasp as Kairon whispered introductions to Bast and Ra. They seemed hesitant. Wary. But at least they didn't show the kind of disgust elementals who didn't know him often displayed when they met him.

"They sense your power. It's not something we've come across before and it feels both deeply familiar and totally unrecognisable. They'll get used to it," Kairon explained in a low voice.

Bast just nodded. There was no time for niceties. They needed to get to Kaia before any more harm came to her and then he needed to save his mate.

"What's the plan here? You're best placed to know how

to deploy your people. I can overpower some of their defences, but they've improved their ability to counteract my power since we last fought and there are so many that we can't risk a full frontal assault. What do you suggest?" Bast said.

One of the vampyr hummed in approval. "Thank the lifeforce for men who can acknowledge other's expertise. Maybe we have a shot at this after all," she said.

Kairon glared at her as Bast fought to hide a smile. They weren't so different from his people back home.

"You know he can understand every word you say, right Laya?" he addressed the woman.

She just smirked and waved a lazy salute at Kairon. "I don't care as long as he understands how to get into that base as well."

Bast's brow furrowed as he watched the exchange. He should've guessed they would have their own reasons for being here. "Why did you come?" he asked.

Laya glanced at him and seemed to consider whether to answer. Whatever she saw in his face must've reassured her. "We have people missing, too. Five of them. But we didn't have the resources to get in and out. Kairon says you can get us close enough to see the damn place and you've got the exit covered."

Bast looked over at Ra. "Will Tir be able to handle this many people?"

Ra frowned and pulled out his sat-phone. "I'm sure they can, but I'll let them know. The question is more how much longer it will take all of us to get clear, especially if we're under attack."

"To answer your initial question about how to deploy us, we have several magic users in this group. Between us, we can lull the guards to sleep as we pass. It's a passive magic they shouldn't pick up on, but it will be short-lived. They'll be out maybe five minutes max once we pass by and it won't work once they realise what's happening and they're on alert. They've been learning to counteract our magic as well. That's why we think they're holding our people—to study them," Laya said.

Bast brought the images the souls had sent him to the forefront of his mind, grateful the dead were so willing to assist. They were just as keen to help him find Kaia as the missing vampyr and they'd plotted a route to where they were being held that glowed silver in his mind. The only problem was that it involved entering through a second-storey balcony that backed onto a steep crystal mountain face.

"How well can you climb on a smooth surface?" he asked the gathered vampyr.

"Far better than you or the human," Laya said, her people straightening in pride at her words.

"Lucky we can fly then. I'd race you, but it hardly seems fair," Bast said, grinning at the competitive light in her eyes. With the speed the vampyr travelled when they really went for it and the indirect route he'd need to take to avoid the guard spells it may have been a fairer competition than it seemed.

Bending down, he started sketching a rough map of the area on the bare earth with one of his blades as he explained how they needed to scale the artificial mountain and where they'd be entering the base from. Ra pulled up the topographical information that was available outside of the black spot that surrounded Caelus's base on his sat-phone, supplementing Bast's rough sketch with aerial imagery as much as they could.

"Will you be able to avoid any magical traps they've set? There shouldn't be as many once you pass the barrier that holds the glamour hiding the base," Bast said.

It was Kairon who replied. "I can sense most of your elemental magic. Healing your scouts and the Earth Lord's people tuned me into it."

Laya flicked him an interested look that said they'd be discussing that revelation later. "I can't say the same, but we should split up so we can divert attention away from what you're doing," she said.

"If you draw the guards elsewhere, I can hunt your people down if they're holding them near Kaia," Bast said, hoping that was true.

Laya was shaking her head before he finished speaking. "No. They won't trust you. At least one of us needs to be there."

"And we'll all need to meet up to portal everyone out anyway. I think we need to sacrifice tactics for speed," Ra added.

Bast frowned. Ra was right. Their greatest advantage was being able to leave instantly through Tir's portal. He'd need to make sure the gathered vampyr got there safely.

Sensing something was afoot, eager souls had flocked close in the hopes they could get some vengeance on the people who had tortured them to death. They were quick to agree to his plan to help guide their party and an image of three vampyr in another cell flashed in his mind as the dead continued scouting.

There are only three? Not five? he checked.

Two of the hovering souls coalesced in his awareness

more clearly. They thrummed with the same essence as Kairon and his people.

They are the only ones left, the two dead vampyr said.

A silent mourning keen that made his blood vibrate was the response when he passed on the news to Laya and her people. It was followed by growls of anger and bared fangs flashing in the darkness as the red glow of vampyr power throbbed like a heartbeat in the night.

"We hunt. Now," Laya snapped.

Bast and Ra shared a look and Ra jerked up his chin, gesturing toward the invisible threat ahead. His friend was right behind him like always, no matter the danger. He just hoped the link to his power would be enough to keep Ra safe when the chaos of battle descended.

Using one of the ropes Laya's people had brought with them, Bast had Ra and each of the vampyr take hold of it before infusing it with his power. He was surprised at how well it took his magic until he realised the rope was made of twined long hairs from some kind of predator they must've killed. His power flowed through the remains of the dead creature like it was made for just that purpose and the souls that had guided him to Caelus's base pressed close as they sensed the link to their power.

"The dead will lead us through the protections and glamour here until you can see for yourselves. They'll keep watch for attackers while you climb as well. I'll give you a communication spell so we can keep in touch while I fly ahead with Ra. The cells are on either side of the window we're entering through. We can split off to grab them all and have Tir form the portal in the window."

"I'll let Tir know," Ra murmured.

It barely qualified as a plan, but it was the best he could

do when they needed to get there before anyone else died. The grim expressions of the vampyr said they were well aware of the danger they would face, and they didn't care anymore than he did. None of them were prepared to let their people stay in that base a single night longer. Bast hadn't said anything earlier, but given the state the captives were in, he wasn't certain they would all survive another day. Waiting for better intel wasn't an option if they wanted to get them all home safe.

THE WORST PART of their approach by far was the first fifty paces. The souls might be able to lead them through, but something about the magical protections that hid the mountain meant everyone had to close their eyes to make the approach. Otherwise, they all ended up just walking in circles. Bast held tight to the front of the rope as he submerged himself in the senses of the surrounding dead to lead the way, pulling the train of ambushers along behind him. At least he could use the soul's vision to see where he was going. The vampyr were limited to only their superior hearing, and Ra didn't even have that to fall back on.

They were forced to move at a snail's pace so that no one tripped and gave away their position. The closer they got to the hidden mountain, the more noise travelled strangely, as if it was echoing off the crystal of its structure. The shuffle of a boot on loose scree tinkled like falling glass and everyone froze, holding their breath as they waited to see if the sound had given them away.

When they finally passed the barrier of the shielding, the group stared in silence at the imposing mountainous terrain ahead of them. It wasn't the size that was off-putting. It was the smooth crystal that would defy every hold and the precarious glass stones scattered through the path that they already knew would draw attention like a clarion alarm if they disturbed them. At least with only the dull moonlight to light their way they didn't have to worry about reflective glare. In daylight it would have been like walking through a prism. High above and ahead, stray flickers of white flashed in the sky where elemental scouts patrolled and a slight deepening of shadow was the only sign of the base they were aiming for.

Bast raised an eyebrow in silent question to Kairon: *Can you make it?*

Kairon jerked his head in assent and slipped past him to take the lead, pausing only long enough to let Bast press the communication spell to the hollow beneath his ear.

"Travel safe," Bast whispered.

"Watch your back," Kairon replied.

The vampyr flashed into the distance so fast and quiet it was like they'd never been there and Bast collected Ra and launched into the air a moment later. They didn't have any time to lose.

The flight up to the base was faster than Bast expected despite the extra weight of Ra in his arms. His friend sported a reckless grin the entire way at the aerial acrobatics involved in avoiding the traps of air magic designed to keep elemental attackers at bay. Ra had always been that way—finding the joy even in the darkest, most dangerous situations.

From time to time, the souls whispered to him when Kairon and his people were about to step somewhere they shouldn't far below, but the ground defences were proving to be as elemental-focused as they'd hoped. This close, they were designed for aerial attack, either from other courts or from predators like the dragons that belonged to the tongues of blue flame he could see flaring in the darkness on a distant snow-covered ridge. The Air Court didn't see humans as a threat and they hadn't yet got a grip on what was needed to keep the vampyr at bay. Between them, Kairon and Laya were perfectly capable of using their power to avoid any traps once Bast told them where they were.

Hovering in place by the window nearest the cells while they waited, Bast wrapped them in even more shadow and silence. Using just a touch of his magic to avoid notice, he started the process of delicately untangling the shielding on the building.

When the vampyr emerged within sight of the walls, Bast sensed their blood magic rolling forward to wash up against the crystal blockwork of the base. Soft susurrations nearby told him their power had found its mark, sending the two ground-based sentries hidden by a trick of the architecture into a deep sleep.

Their five minute grace period had started.

The window Bast was targeting had a conveniently broad crystal ledge for him to balance on. They were lucky it wasn't a sentient stronghold like Aliya's or just the touch of his feet on the surface would've alerted everyone to their presence. Bast disconnected Ra from the harness that held him close and his friend quickly turned to jimmy open the mechanics of the window as Bast deftly finished weaving his magic through the tiny alert spell running along its edges. Caelus had grown careless. He was too confident in his reputation and the other protections surrounding the base to worry about reinforcing windows despite their proximity to the prisoner holding cells. None of the Air Court expected an attacking force to get past the over-the-top glamour hiding the mountain.

Bast was stepping inside within half a dozen breaths, the vampyr swarming in silently behind as he furled his wings tight in the increasingly crowded space. He wished he could've watched them climb. They weren't even using ropes on the glass-like ice-cold surface of the base. Impressive. It wasn't until he turned back as the last person stepped through that he recognised the shielding on the window as a similar but unfamiliar variant to what he'd placed on the Spiderhive back home. It was one-way protection focused on keeping the people inside in, not any invaders out. No wonder it had been so easy to breach. It was just as well they had no intention of leaving the way they'd come.

Ra was already messaging Tir to get them to open the portal they needed in three minutes. They couldn't risk staying past the point at which the guards awoke from Kairon and Laya's sleep spells. They didn't have the numbers to defend against a rush of attackers when Caelus realised they were here.

Dull thumps from either end of the hallway heralded the vampyr putting the rest of the guards to sleep with their power. Bast didn't waste time as he strode in the direction the souls were beckoning him to reach Kaia, Ra close on his heels. He ignored the metallic smell of blood from the nearest dropped guard ahead. Who was he to tell the vampyr not to kill when their people had been taken from them and tortured to death? They'd just have to hope no one came across the bodies before they were done. A sleeping guard spied from afar would attract notice, but not necessarily alarm. But if someone noticed a guard lying in a pool of their own blood, it would immediately set off the defensive response they were trying to avoid.

Kaia was too young to create the kind of bond Bast had with her mother and Ra, but even without a connection, he could swear he felt her through the thick door they stopped at. He was probably sensing her ever growing elemental magic seeping out. In keeping with Air Court trickery, the door looked like a transparent crystal pane that should've revealed a view of the cell it barred, but instead showed a view of the icy night-time visage outside the base as if there wasn't even a room behind it.

Conscious they only had a minute or two before Tir appeared to take them home, Bast studied the magic on the door. It was keyed to respond only to Air Court power and for a moment he was stumped on how to break it without drawing attention. He was about to risk launching a brute force attack of power when one of the souls surrounding him, a local, channelled him a strand of soul magic that tasted of remembered air magic.

Thank you, he sent to the soul, surprised they had volunteered to help him in that way when they must've sworn allegiance to the Air Court when they lived.

She is just a child. Caelus is a parasite. This is wrong, the soul replied.

Bast sent the soul's offering of power towards both the door to Kaia's cell and the one the vampyr had gathered around further down the hallway and was rewarded with both swinging open to a sound much like a wet finger tracing the top of a crystal glass. The melodic vibration rang too loud in the quiet surrounding them. There was no way anyone nearby hadn't heard it. The game was up.

"Fuck. We need to hurry," Ra whispered.

A low groan greeted them as they charged into the room but the bundle of washed-out feathers and limbs on the floor where it had come from barely twitched.

"I'll fucking kill them," Ra growled through gritted teeth behind him as Bast stepped forward and knelt by the girl, scooping her too-light form up into his arms.

"Uncle Basti?" Kaia said, her voice barely more than a whisper and cracking with dehydration and lack of use.

"I'm here, baby girl."

"I knew you'd come," she said.

Bast swallowed back tears. He hadn't found her fast enough. Even a single hour like this was too long. With a surge of raging power matched by the surrounding souls, he disintegrated the collar defiling her neck and with it the sickly syphoning of her magic. He almost hoped the guards would arrive before Tir got here so he could show them exactly what it felt like to be drained to near death like his sweet little Kaia had been.

Kaia sobbed in relief as the weight of the collar and its leeching magic disappeared, wrapping her arms around Bast's neck in a weak hug. Bast stood still to avoid jostling her injured body, cradling the girl close to him like he had when she was just a baby and he'd paced her nursery, walking her back to sleep. He wished he could let her rest like she had then, but they needed to move.

The sound of metal on bone rang out from the hallway as they made their way back to the door and Bast gently handed Kaia over to Ra so he could draw his weapons. A white-winged elemental lunged at him as soon as he cleared the doorway, the magic of his attacker's sword turning the air around them even icier than it already was. The strike was clumsy in the too crowded space and Bast parried it easily, but the cold spread to his short sword making his hand stiffen and the bones of his fingers ache.

Liquid shadow spun nearby as Tir finally made their entrance. The swirling portal forming in the window they'd entered through was exactly where it should be. Bast glanced around and winced. The same couldn't be said for their people. There were vampyr and elementals everywhere he looked. He'd been so distracted by Kaia he hadn't noticed the battle had been joined and he couldn't risk letting loose a blast of power that might take out a friend.

The guards must have figured out how to block the vampyr magic that had cast sleep on them because the red glow of power filled the space but no one was dropping unconscious. They were, however, dropping the occasional limb amputated with surgical precision by what looked like Laya's blood magic if her proximity to the severed arm lying on the floor was any indication. Her fighters without battle magic were just as effective, using their fangs and weapons to tear through elemental flesh and feathers. They might be outnumbered, but they were powerful and out for revenge.

"Our ride's here," Bast said, not bothering to raise his voice as he blocked another strike from his attacker, shoving the weaker elemental back. He knew the vampyrs' sensitive hearing would pick up everything he said.

"Get Kaia out of here," he told Ra, waving his friend toward where Tir was guarding the portal as he kept his eyes on the elemental before him.

A flicker of motion revealed an opening and Bast stabbed his sword deep into the muscle and tendon of the man's shoulder. Twisting the blade as he yanked it back out for maximum damage, he followed up with a hard kick to the sternum that sent the elemental crumpling to the ground.

Kairon appeared from behind the fallen attacker, stepping on the elemental's wings as he climbed over him to approach Bast.

"We have our people," he said.

"Go. I'll cover you," Bast replied, scanning the hall again and smiling grimly as he realised there were no more allies to worry about ahead of him. He could finally send out a swathe of soulwoven power without worrying about who he'd hit.

The raw death magic blasted half a dozen Air Court soldiers to the ground. He held off the rest as Ra and the vampyr left. Most of them were through the portal when Ra came *back* through, minus Kaia.

"Come on, bro. Get your ass over here and let's go home," Ra said as Bast sent another blast of magic the other way down the corridor to buy them a moment of peace.

"I need to close the portal before someone strong enough to disable me gets here," Tir said, adding their voice of reason.

They'd both sensed his reluctance to leave now that Kaia was safe. He couldn't stop thinking about Sol's power that Tir had sensed somewhere in Caelus's base. It might be his only chance to reach Hel. As if responding to his thought, Aliya's voice rang out from shadows just past where he'd sent her people scrambling in retreat.

"Bastion. We need to talk," she said.

"Fuck off, Aliya," Ra shouted back, grabbing Bast's arm to pull him to safety.

Bast hesitated, resisting his friend's efforts.

"Can you take me to her?" Bast called to the Air Lady.

"Bast, no. She already killed you once," Ra hissed at him.

"I can. In exchange for a little help with a contagion issue I'm about to have downstairs," Aliya said.

"And will you bring them back, too?" Ra growled at Aliya as she picked her way through her dead and unconscious courtiers littering the hall.

Aliya's laughter tinkled through the space, enhanced by the trickery of the crystal walls surrounding them. "I can only promise a one-way trip. Can't his mate portal? I'm sure she can get him home."

"Except her power's blocked," Bast said.

The only sign of Aliya's surprise at the information he had was the slightest inquisitive cock of her head. "Well. I guess you'll have to unblock it," she said.

Bast turned to Ra. "I have to go. I can't leave her there. This is my best chance to reach her."

Ra looked like he couldn't decide whether to punch him or hug him. Finally, his shoulders slumped in defeat. "I know. You'd better both fucking come back to us. Kaia needs you. We all need you."

"I will. But you know what to do if I don't. I'm counting on you to protect her," Bast said.

"Of course. We've got you, bro." Ra clasped his hand and pulled him into a tight embrace. "Don't you dare die."

"Not planning on it," Bast said, but they both knew his odds were fifty-fifty at best. They weren't any better if he stayed put and Hel died on a far distant world, though.

"Come, then," Aliya said sweetly, sweeping her hand toward the way she'd come. She wasn't fooling anyone. She was a viper.

Ra gripped his arm one more time, hugging him tight, and then disappeared into the portal with Tir close behind him.

Tir paused at the threshold, holding Bast's eyes with their own. "Look after yourself, soulweaver. And hold tight to your bond with Helaine. Sol's power is greater than you think," Tir said.

Bast nodded in thanks, even though he didn't need the warning. He knew how powerful Sol must be to cause the meldings. But nothing on the Earths could make him let go of his bond to Hel. It wasn't even possible.

Once the portal closed, Aliya silently led him down a series of stairways and passages deep into the base. The view through the crystal walls still reflected the outside panorama, sometimes the distant lights of La Paz and sometimes the crevasses and façades of the mountain they were perched on, but he was pretty sure they were well inside its depths at this point.

"Why are you betraying your world for him?" Bast asked when he grew tired of walking in silence behind Aliya's swaying hips and the sweep of her white-gold wingspan.

Aliya glanced over her shoulder at him. "You'll understand once you're there," she said.

Bast frowned in annoyance at the cryptic response, but what else would he expect of the Air Lady?

Aliya finally halted by double doors of stone instead of crystal. They opened with a wave of her hand to reveal a star-blue portal that burned in his awareness where he could still use the thin connection to his mate's power. It tasted of burning ozone and an empire of suns—Sol.

"The contagion will find a way through shortly like a disease," Aliya said, her body blocking him from striding toward the gateway to join his mate. "I need you to do whatever it is you do to contain it so it doesn't destroy the base here."

Bast glanced around the room, searching for any sign of the reality taint that he'd missed, but there was nothing yet. He knew she was speaking the truth, though. He'd seen the spots of contagion that sprung up in the aftermath of Sol's portals before. Everything in him screamed to let the base succumb to the contagion after what they'd done to Kaia. If anyone deserved that death, it was Caelus. It wouldn't end there, though. Fuelled by all these people and without his presence to rein it in, the contagion would spread to the nearby city and from there he shuddered to think how fast it might travel.

"I can create a barrier around the portal that should hold it," he said.

"Will I be able to pass through?" Aliya asked.

"No," Bast said as he wondered what the fuck he was getting himself into.

Was she going to follow him? Would she stab him in the back the second he'd finished the containment? He would've challenged her right now but they were evenly matched and he couldn't afford to drain and injure himself with a fight when he was so close to reaching Hel.

"Fine. Do it," Aliya said.

He rolled his eyes at the order. "Don't confuse me for one of your underlings, Aliya. I am helping you only because it serves my purpose."

She shrugged. "I'd get on with it if you want your mate to still be there when you arrive."

They both stepped closer to the portal and Bast braced himself as he reached for his power to form the now-familiar spherical containment that he'd built so many times before. It was far easier with the contagion not actually here yet, but he was exhausted and running dry after expending so much magic to get them here. "You need to anchor this in the crystal of the walls and make sure there's a deterrent to keep people clear," he said.

Aliya frowned in concentration for a moment and he felt the breeze of her magic against his own as she did as he asked. For all her manipulation, she was still a master of the elemental magic craft and he couldn't help but admire the deft way she wove her magic with his.

"You've been studying soulweaving?" he asked, suspicious of the ease with which she was working.

"We found a necromancer child who's survived long enough to be useful," she said.

Bast growled in anger, clenching his fists in fury as he reminded himself once again that he couldn't afford to start a fight with her. "We will discuss that child's future when I return," he said through gritted teeth.

Aliya just shrugged. "If you return," she said, before brushing past him and stepping through the portal.

Bast took a deep breath, forcing himself to focus before stepping through after her.

Searing heat ripped through him as he crossed the threshold and his brain clouded with confusion the second he emerged. Swaying where he stood, he twisted in place as he tried to make sense of the unfamiliar surroundings. Unnoticed, the portal blinked out of existence behind him.

He was on a barren plain, surrounded by columns of plasma-blue light that reminded him of someone dear to him. Someone whose name hovered just out of reach in his mind. His brow furrowed as he reached for the information and fell short. Power surged nearby and a male voice sounded from his right. A hand reached out to grasp his shoulder, turning him toward the magic he'd felt.

"Hush, Bastion. Be calm. I'm here now," the man said.

He was tall. Taller than Bastion. With wings of starlight and hair of ebony that filled him with nostalgia for ... someone. Was it this man? It felt like him.

Strong rough fingers gripped his jaw and the man's thumb stroked Bast's cheek, making him frown in confusion as he leaned into the touch despite himself.

Why did this stranger feel so familiar?

CHAPTER 10
HEL

Hel paced the bedroom she'd been left in, stalking back and forth with wings still trembling in rage. No fucking way would she let Sol tear her and Bast apart. He was *hers*. And who the fuck did Sol think he was to send her to her room like a child? The lock on the door no longer responded to Bast's power and the walls felt like they were closing in as they infuriatingly lured her to be calm. She held tight to the anger that was her best defence mechanism against his insidious mind-control, needing every advantage she could get.

"Sol! Let me out of here! Don't you dare fucking touch him!" she yelled, not for the first time.

Her voice rasped on the words from her earlier efforts and she finally lost her tenuous control, throwing one of the dining chairs at the nearest wall with all of her considerable strength. It shattered on impact and she grabbed a sharp length of wooden chair leg from the floor. She felt more in control as soon as she held the primitive weapon in her hand even though she couldn't actually do anything to defend Bast while she was trapped there.

As if summoned by her temper tantrum, the door slid open silently as she watched. Her hand turned white-knuckled where she gripped the makeshift stake she'd scavenged. A moment later, the stake clattered to the floor from numb fingers as Sol's influence crashed over her. She froze in shock rather than picking it up as Bast's familiar form filed into the room behind Sol, half-hidden by the imposing silhouette of Sol's stardust wings.

"Bast!" she cried, running to him without thinking before pulling up short as Sol blocked her passage. "Move," she growled up at him.

"See, this is the problem. Even knowing I'm a threat, you can't hide your weakness for him," Sol said. "Go sit down on the couch so we can talk about this calmly."

Hel's whole body tensed as she fought the urge to punch the smug look from Sol's face. Pulling on her connection to Bast, she frowned as she realised she hadn't felt any of the thrill of recognition from him that her soul was thrumming with. Instead, he radiated a kind of dull confusion. It seeped into her, creating another point of contact with Sol's influence she had to fight. Fuck. Bast lacked the benefit of her natural resistance. He was fully under Sol's control.

"What did you do to him?" she hissed, trying and failing to push past Sol again.

Sol grabbed her throat and squeezed until she stopped pushing. "Don't start a fight you can't win, little star. I just made him a little more malleable. It wasn't hard when he recognises my power as his mate's. We are one and the same, after all."

Hel's mind and soul scrabbled at the barrier between her

and her power as she desperately tried to reach out to Bast with more than just their bond. Sol's fingers squeezed tighter still in response.

"Enough. Sit," he said, and a blast of his magic sent her flying across the room to collapse onto the couch cushions hard enough to knock what little of her breath was left in her lungs out of them.

Her wings crumpled awkwardly behind her as she fell and she winced in pain as she sat up and adjusted them to a more natural position. She was lucky she didn't have feathers that would crack and break from the impact. She would've jumped back to her feet, but Sol was moving toward her now with Bast trailing along behind like a lost puppy.

Her heart ached for her mate as she watched him pause in confusion as he looked between her and Sol, back and forth, until finally he seemed to settle on her with a tentative smile.

"You're my mate?" Bast said, half questioning and half explaining it to himself.

"Yes, love. I am. *Not* him," Hel said, glaring at Sol before holding a hand out to Bast for him to join her.

"He feels like you," Bast said, words slow as syrup.

"Does he, though? Can you feel his emotions? Can you feel his breath in your lungs when he inhales? Does his soul sing for you?" Hel asked, taking a deep breath and pushing her desperation and love for him through their connection.

Bast blinked in confusion and seemed to shake himself a little, frowning. "No, I can't. You're right?" he said, still sounding uncertain as he moved closer with hesitant steps.

Hel willed him to keep going, needing to touch him, but Sol's voice interrupted the moment and Bast paused to look over at him.

"We are the same person. If you love her, you love me," Sol said, cajoling.

"Shut the fuck up. Enough with the mind games. What are you even hoping to gain from this? If you want something, ask for it like a normal person so he can tell you to piss off to your face," Hel growled.

Sol smiled and it made Hel's heart skip a beat with fear. "I figured as long as he was here, I could try him out. Your bond has already established he and I would be compatible. I've always wondered what one would feel like."

"And you can keep wondering because you don't fucking have a bond with him and you never will. I swear if you touch him, I will find a way to kill you," Hel snarled, desperately willing Bast the strength to push through the mental fog and take the last few steps to her side.

"We could always skip straight to the part where I sever your connection and then use the damage to your psyche to take control of you and *make* you shift the contagion for me," Sol said, seeming to lose patience with the conversation.

Time seemed to slow as Hel tried to talk over her mate and stop the train wreck about to take place in front of her as Bast went to reply.

"Don't—" she cried out, but it was too late as his words tumbled over the top of her own.

"But we can only shift the contagion together," Bast said, looking even more confused as he gave away their secret and sealed his fate. "My power to contain it and hers to portal it away."

A slow smile spread across Sol's face. "Is that right? Thank you, Bastion. That is very helpful," he said, patting Bast's cheek in a way that made Hel growl again.

She would've jumped up at that point but Sol must have

realised she was at the end of her tether because his power was pinning her in place on the couch and her jaw was now clamped shut against her will.

"How *exactly* does that work? Your power and hers together?" Sol continued.

"The mating bond creates a shared resonance between them and twists them together. I can use a little of hers. She can use a little of mine. That's why it works," Bast said.

How could he string such articulate, revealing sentences together when he didn't even seem to be aware of where or who he was? Damn it!

"How *very* interesting. Maybe my little star was not so reckless after all. She used you to multiply the scraps of power that I gave her. And what else can you do with your power, Bastion?"

Hel let every shred of her terror at what Sol would do with Bast's ability to harvest the magic of the dead—the murder that would ensue—and shoved it down the connection to her mate in a reckless tsunami. His beautiful black wings went slack and he reeled back under the onslaught, collapsing to the floor unconscious.

Sol turned to her, frowning in annoyance. "That was rude. We were in the middle of a conversation."

The pressure on her jaw eased and Hel could finally speak her mind. "Fuck you," she spat back.

"You should be more grateful. He's earned you a respite from your mating bond being broken. I think I'll take him and see what his power can do for myself before we carry on this discussion," Sol said, scooping up Bast's muscled form in his arms like he weighed nothing. "He'll be sleeping in my bed while he's here where I can keep an eye on him. If you want me to keep my hands to myself, you *will* behave."

"You don't need him in your damn bed," Hel growled.

Sol tilted his head in acknowledgement. "Perhaps, and yet I find myself thoroughly intrigued by our power twining through his veins. Plus, you are too resourceful not to get out of your room and I wouldn't want to have to do something drastic if you managed to steal him away. He will stay by my side as insurance against whatever you're thinking about doing."

Hel seethed in place as Sol swept from the room carrying her mate, unable to move until the door closed behind them both and she was, once again, on her own and confined by the walls of her too comfortable prison cell.

HEL MIGHT'VE GONE mad with frustration if it wasn't for the whisper of souls she could hear again now that Bast was close enough. Sol had done something to control Bast's power; at least Hel assumed he had because she hadn't been able to use it to escape, but he couldn't block the innate ability to communicate with the dead. Many of the souls lingering in Travaris were not at all fond of him.

Where is Bastion? Is he safe? Hel asked them when a full day had passed since Sol had carried him from her room.

As the dead swirled closer, she said a silent thanks once again for the shielding Bast had fused into her wing structure that kept her safe from their torturous deaths. There was no way she could've dealt with that on top of everything else.

He tires. He's shifted three of the columns to the portal but he can't get them through it and his power can't mesh with Sol's like it does yours. He'll burn out if he continues.

Keep him safe, Hel pleaded. *Don't let him draw more power than he can safely use.*

She knew Bast couldn't shift the contagion alone. Back on the Melded Earths, it had only been possible with both of them and the vast release of power the second melding had released. Alone, Bast couldn't anchor his magic in the world beneath his feet, couldn't use its vast incomprehensible sentience to help defend against the rabid darkness of the contagion. And no matter how much Sol insisted they were the same person, the fact was that it was *her* magic that twined through Bast like a second nervous system, *not* his. There was no way Sol could work with Bast the way she did.

We can try and staunch the flow of power to him, but if he pulls hard we won't be able to stop him, the souls replied.

She would have to hope it was enough.

Their whispered voices kept her updated as time pushed on and she remained stuck where she was. Helpless to save her mate. Through their senses, she knew when Sol pushed too hard, asked too much, and Bast collapsed. She also saw when he made good on his promise and placed Bast in his own fucking bed until he came to twelve hours later. Neither of those things made her rage burn as bright as when he tried, and failed, to force their magics together in a dark parody of their mating bond. His power inserting itself in the twining rivers of their connection was a sickening violation even as it continually slipped clear, unable to bond. That was when she finally lost it, trashing her room as she let loose screams of frustration and pain. *No one touched her mate's power like that but her! No one touched her mate full stop!* Biting her lip hard enough to bleed, she pounded her fists into the couch.

With every failure, she knew it wouldn't be long before

Sol returned to her and demanded her compliance. He would be growing impatient and the risk of him resorting to torture or worse grew with every hour. At some point he would realise that if he simply started a melding here, he would get what he wanted without a fight. Hel would do anything to stop that kind of death and disorder, but once it happened it would be criminal to waste the power released when they could use it to save so many. Sol would know that. Would be counting on it.

She almost wished she had Sol's clinical, detached morality. He wasn't doing all this to gain power or territory. He was trying to save people. Multiple worlds' worth of people. In his mind, the sacrifice of one world for the many was more than justified. It made a sick mathematical sense, his pragmatic willingness to accept an immense loss for a greater gain. He was decisive and he had a solution he knew would work. Why would he waste time or energy on finding an alternative uncertain solution? Maybe she really was just like him, given she could understand his logic so well. Was there a part of her that had given up as well—resigned to what seemed the inevitable? How could she ever make up for her part in the loss of so many souls if he carried through on his threat?

Bast collapsed a second time the next day. The souls reported he was so close to the threshold of true death that they'd had to tether him to the land of the living, holding him in place while his pulse slowed and his skin grew grey. They sent her a vision of her mate lying in an enormous bed, his breaths slower than she'd ever seen them, even slower than her own breathing, which was so different to human and elemental. Sol had made her to be thrown into a void, after all. He'd ensured she wouldn't expire from lack of oxygen before she made it past the portal.

The snick of her door opening broke through her spiralling thoughts and she looked up from where she was pacing to see Aliya slipping into the room. It was the first time she'd ever seen the Air Lady walking in anything other than a prideful strut. Instead, her white-gold wings were cloaked in power that left her all but invisible as she checked the hallway behind her for anyone following and shut the door with exaggerated care.

"What do you want?" Hel snapped, not bothering to keep her voice down and taking great pleasure in Aliya's slight jump at the loud question.

"If you want to see your mate again, you'll shut up and come with me," Aliya hissed in response.

Hel crossed the room in an instant, getting right in Aliya's face. "You'll take me to him?"

Aliya nodded, already turning back to the door.

Hel grabbed her arm and held her still. "Why? Is this a trick? You've already killed him once. I will *never* trust you."

Aliya glared at her, but Hel could see the calculation and panic in her eyes as she tried to figure out the fastest way to get them out of there. "Bast is sleeping in his bed. In *my* bed. That's the last hold I have on him. If I'm not sleeping with him, there's no reason for him to keep me here. No reason for him to let me see our daughter. I need Bast gone. I need *you* gone. You're ruining everything. It can't all be for nothing."

Hel couldn't help the empathy that snuck into her gaze. Maybe Aliya had made her own problems, but also she'd never stood a chance against Sol's power. Whatever terrible decisions she'd made in the past, Aliya's present was a collapsing pile of shitty options.

She knew the feeling.

"Fuck you, Helaine. I don't need your pity. Are you coming or not?" Aliya spat.

Hel shook off the unfamiliar feelings and forced herself to focus. "I'm coming. What's the plan?" she asked.

"I will take you to Bast and keep Sol away for a few hours. No more. I can't risk any suspicion falling on me. You're on your own once you're there. If you betray me, I will make sure my people back on the Earths kill everyone you love. I mean *everyone*. That little girl. Mica's ridiculous human crush. All of them."

Hel ignored the threats. They were nothing new. "Where will you be?"

"There's a party he's taking our daughter to for the last shard being erected by the Avanthar. He wants to make a song and dance of it. He'll expect me to try and seduce him there. I can buy you time. You need to leave while I do."

"Bast's unconscious and fully under his thrall. How am I supposed to take him anywhere?"

"I'm sure you can figure something out," Aliya said, tugging her arm away and sweeping toward the door, clearly done with the conversation.

THEIR FURTIVE RUN through the circular, disorienting hallways of the building took them to the top of the building where Hel had never been. She guessed Sol had claimed the entire floor for his quarters. Aliya seemed to know exactly where she was going and when to pause to avoid sentries or servants. As they drew closer, she pulled off the cloak that had been hiding her appearance and Hel realised the garment itself was magical, an elemental weaving that turned eyes away and made the wearer all but invisible. Aliya draped it over Hel before striding toward a huge golden door as if she had every right to be there.

If she hadn't known how anxious Aliya was, she might've missed the slight tremble in her fingers as she waved her hand through the air to gain entrance. The door swung open without any trouble and Hel only just made it through behind her before it closed tight on her heels.

"Lady Aliya, this is a surprise. I thought you were staying elsewhere," a voice said from nearby.

Hel huddled under Aliya's cloak, certain they were about to be exposed.

"I need something from my dressing room before the party," Aliya said, barely glancing at whoever it was who'd dared interrupt her. They must've accepted the excuse because they didn't challenge her further.

Aliya strode ahead so fast Hel had to trot to keep up and she winced as she realised she was going to have to navigate back out of these rooms with a possibly incoherent Bast and no help.

They didn't stop until they'd reached a dressing room of women's clothing. Bending down to open a drawer, Aliya withdrew a glowing necklace.

"His chambers are through that door. I can't take you any further," she murmured.

And then she was gone in a flurry of white silk and cloyingly sensual scent.

Hel kept the cloak wrapped tight around herself as she stepped through the doorway Aliya had indicated and made her way through a series of smaller corridors and rooms, letting the pull of Bast's presence through their connection guide her. She could feel magic brushing over her skin at times, but once again her similarity to Sol seemed to work in her favour, confusing the protections into letting her through.

At last, she pushed through a doorway lined in what looked like black leather and fetched up in the huge bedroom the souls had shown her earlier. Her vision narrowed to Bast's shadow-black feathers contrasting against starkly golden linen sheets. She was oblivious to everything around her as she ran to the bed. The cloak drifted to the floor forgotten as she threw herself toward him and finally, finally, touched his skin with hers for the first time in what felt like an age. She got nothing back. He was deeply asleep, oblivious. Pressing her forehead to his, she breathed in the air from his all but unnoticeable exhale.

A distant noise recalled her to where she was and her head jerked up as she glanced around the room, but she was still alone. She suspected no one but Sol and those closest to him were allowed in here. And Bast. Her temporarily forgotten rage surged back as she remembered exactly why her mate was lying there.

Is he okay? Is he still near death? she asked the ever-present souls.

He is recovering and back firmly on your side of the veil, they replied and she breathed a silent sigh of relief.

Now all she needed to do was wake him, remove Sol's influence from his mind, escape the impenetrable building, figure out a way to save the worlds that didn't involve hundreds of thousands of people dying so Sol would leave them the fuck alone, and then go home.

Easy.

First step, wake up Bast.

Turning back to her mate—her love—she stroked a gentle finger down his wing surface. He was still wearing the button-up shirt he had been last time she'd seen him and she was grateful Sol seemed to have stuck to his hands-off promise for now at least. Reaching down, she unbuttoned the shirt with shaking hands, slowly revealing her mating mark over Bast's heart and the swathes of toned muscle and golden skin that would always leave her breathless and her mouth dry as long as they both lived.

A zap of shared sensation shot through her as she placed her palm on the place she'd marked him forever, focusing all her essence on their connection. Maybe neither of them could access their magic through the infuriating barriers Sol had erected to keep them under control, but he hadn't been able to block their mating bond. Even deep in Bast's confusion, he'd known who she was. He just hadn't been able to figure out who Sol was or why he felt so similar.

Closing her eyes, she drew in a deep breath and focused on happier memories. Some from the brief period after the second melding when they'd finally seemed to be becoming partners, and some from the heady days when they'd first met and everything was a burning conflagration of emotions and raw inexplicable need for each other. She hated the term 'fated mates', but for the two of them there was either this—being together—or they would have long since succumbed to death. There was nothing else. Would never be anything else.

The memories kept coming, brief moments of calm and of passion. Kawakawa tea at sunrise. A stolen kiss at a meeting of the city's ruling partnership interrupted by Ryker and Ra's catcalls. A shared smile as they helped stubborn little Kaia to train. She took all of it and used it to call him back to her with their bond.

A soft groan had her eyes flying open to the welcome view of the silver-ringed deepest black of Bast's pupils.

"Welcome back," she said, smiling as his firm hands lifted from the bed to skim up her sides and pull her closer. This was the Bast she knew.

"I feel like I've been dreaming forever," he whispered.

"Time to wake now. I need you," she said, voice breaking on those last words.

Bast pulled her closer until he could catch her lips in a kiss that went from soft to ravenous in less than second.

"Are you really here?" he asked when she finally pulled free to gasp in a breath. "I can't ... something's wrong with my brain, my thoughts," he said, that awful fucking confusion seeping back into his expression.

"He can't fucking have you," Hel said, bending forward and biting his lip hard as she initiated another burning hot kiss. "You're *mine*. *Not his*. Not ever."

She was ripping off the rest of Bast's clothes before she really thought it through, heedless of where they were and the danger they were in. She needed her mate back. Her touch seemed to be helping him overcome some of Sol's influence, but not enough. There was no way he'd be able to help get them clear in his current disoriented state.

Bast was weirdly passive for long moments, lying back and groaning as she traced her lips down his chest to circle one of his nipples with her tongue before sucking it hard into her mouth. His back arched beneath her and his grip shifted to hold her hair as she worked him over while focusing as much of her attention as she could spare on reinforcing the

connection between their souls the same way she was reinforcing the connection between their bodies.

"Need you," he moaned as she swapped sides to give his
other nipple the same attention.

He was hard as steel as she knelt over him and rocked
against his length, teasing them both as she reached up to
remove her shirt and bare herself to his gaze that was finally,
finally, hungry for her instead of confused.

"Beautiful," he whispered as she cast her shirt aside.

A gasp left her as he somehow flipped their positions and
she was flung onto her back and wings on the huge bed. Bast
trailed teasing bites and kisses down her torso as his hands
pulled at her waistband. Her memory cast back to that first
time they'd been together—the tension of something building
and building before the mating bond snapped into place
surprising them both. It felt a little like that again, that pressure building as she could sense their powers twining tight
through each other but she kept coming up against that
smooth barrier of Sol's block in her mind. She could feel it
weakening under the combined onslaught of their need for
each other, though. His block was designed to stop each of
them from accessing their own power, but with their physical connection and the mating bond amplifying everything,
it also needed to stop them from accessing each other's. With
just a little more pressure, she was confident it wouldn't be
able to stand up to the dual assault.

Her thoughts derailed as Bast tugged her pants off and
licked a path up her inner thigh as if he needed to taste every
inch of her skin, to devour her. Her head thrashed as his
mouth closed over her clit and his rhythmic suction made her
see stars.

Fuck. Stars. The echo of Sol's nickname for her was

enough to remind her they didn't have the luxury of time here. They were in his bed for fuck's sake. Tugging at Bast's hair, she tried to pull him back up her body, but it only made him more desperate for her. She groaned again as his tongue traced down lower, lapping at her wetness as he reached up and slid two fingers inside her down to the knuckle.

"Fuck," she gasped, pushing hard against his too talented mouth. "Fuck me. Now."

Pulled on his hair again, she twisted hard so he'd know she was serious. He growled in response, not wanting to be rushed, and the vibration sent another shock of pleasure through her. Finally, he let her drag him back up her body, every rock-hard muscle pushing just right against her and driving her crazy as he pressed a thousand kisses to her skin until he was pushing his tongue into her mouth and she could taste herself on him.

Tilting her hips up, she guided him to her entrance and wrapped her legs tight around him so she could leverage some control. His face dropped beside her and he nuzzled into her neck, sucking hard enough that she knew he was leaving a bruise. Moaning in pleasure, she drove herself onto his cock, pulling him into her in one smooth motion.

The barriers in their minds shattered at the same time as Bast's control. Hel bit back a scream of triumph and passion, bracing herself on the headboard as he gripped her tight and pistoned into her, each thrust driving them closer and closer to release.

"You feel so good, hellcat," Bast groaned, each word punctuated with a delicious driving force against that spot deep inside her that would send her flying.

"Don't you dare stop," she gasped back, giving back every bit as much as she was taking.

Her climax caught her by surprise, burning through her with life-giving fire and almost as much relief as being finally able to touch her power once more. She couldn't hold back her scream this time and the pleasure seemed to go on and on as Bast kept up his ruthless pace.

When her tense muscles finally started to relax, Bast bit down on her sensitive earlobe. His voice rasped beside her as he continued to rock inside her, somehow feeling even deeper than he had when he'd been pounding into her moments earlier.

"Again," he demanded, reaching down between them to stroke her oversensitive nerves.

She was powerless to resist his command, not that she wanted to. As he catapulted her into another peak, she clenched her muscles around him and concentrated on making him feel every part of the pleasure he was giving her until she dragged him right along with her. The throb of his release deep inside her set off even more ripples of satisfaction.

Silence fell as they both lay there panting with exertion in the aftermath until Bast looked around them with his usual bright intelligence for the first time since he'd arrived on the planet. His brow furrowed as his eyes took in the overstated opulence.

"Wait. Whose bedroom are we in?" he asked.

CHAPTER 11
BAST

"Yeah, about that..." his hellcat said, wincing as she disentangled them from each other and shifting her naked body to sit beside him as she reached for her clothes. "We're in Sol's bed."

Bast's hand froze as he reached for his pants. "We're in your father's bed?"

Fuck. He hated that the previous days were a clouded haze of half-there memory. He remembered enough to know roughly what had happened—Sol had turned him into a zombie and made him do his bidding—but he was lucid now and still hadn't even realised where he was. Breathing deep, he forced back his frustration. He could remember darkness closing in when he overextended himself. He must've been unconscious when he was brought here, which is why he hadn't realised where here was. It made sense, but it didn't make him feel any better.

Hel glanced at him as if searching for any hint of the confused fog he'd been operating under for days. He did his best to look fully cognisant, which he mostly was. Having access to his magic again was helping him fend off the drugging effect of Sol's influence, as did the constant brushes of her skin against his as they dressed.

"He's not my father. He made me with magic. Do you remember that?" Hel asked.

Bast fought through his sluggish recollection to find what she was talking about and his eyes widened as snippets of events and conversation started coming back to him. Shuddering in disgust, he clutched Hel close to him as he remembered the disturbing familiarity of Sol's magic and the way his own power had recognised it as it tried to force its way inside him. Sol had come so close to weaving his power through Bast's in a brutal magical assault that violated him on the most basic level. He'd tried to trick the mating bond into accepting Sol as a substitute for Hel and fully enslave Bast to him in the process.

Thank the Earths he'd failed.

Despite the surface similarity between Sol's power and Hel's and the vulnerability that had created, it was his mating bond with Hel that had kept him safe. His magic hadn't stretched back toward Sol's because it was already irrevocably entwined through the beautiful soul of the woman next to him. It had rejected Sol despite the vast pressure of his power on Bast's mind that had been all but broken at the time.

Drawing in a deep breath, he forced back the memories of being utterly helpless.

"Okay. We're in Sol's bed?"

"He was keeping you here to get to me. Aliya bought us a couple of hours to escape. We need to get moving."

"*Aliya* helped us? Our Aliya from the Earths? Lady of the Air Court? Murderous bitch?" Bast asked.

"Yup. She had a daughter with Sol and she doesn't want us usurping her place. Keep up," Hel teased, but he could sense the deep concern for his wellbeing as she strode toward a dressing room to rifle through the weapons stand there.

Bast's mind reeled, still struggling to kick back into gear after the days under Sol's influence. "So, what's the plan?"

"We can't leave the contagion here. It's putting people at risk and Sol will never stop coming after us while the threat remains," Hel said.

"He'll never stop coming after you regardless," Bast pointed out.

Hel tilted her head in acknowledgement as he joined her in picking out a collection of blades. "All the same, if he keeps coming after us while the contagion remains, he'll keep reinfecting the Melded Earths. We need to get rid of it at the root and then we can figure out the rest after."

"And how do we do that? I've spent days shifting the damage here and all it did was burn me out. Do you know when he plans to cause another melding?" Bast said.

"He's at some party celebrating the completion of the stasis shards, so probably not long, especially now he knows that together we can give him what he needs."

"So, what's the plan?" Bast asked again.

"We need to at least try and close the portal together. We don't know for sure we can't do it with normal power levels," Hel said.

"Even if we shut the portal, what's to stop the contagion coming back—maybe not in a year or even a hundred years, but someday?" Bast asked, regretting the words as soon as he spoke them because of the hopelessness that snuck into Hel's expression at his words.

"I don't know. So, what do we do, then?" Hel asked.

"We need time to figure that out. Let's do what you suggested and see what we can achieve at the source contagion site here. If we can't come up with a solution, we portal back home to buy some time so Sol doesn't force our hand with a melding. You can take us somewhere on the outskirts of the city and I'll shield the portal site so whatever contagion follows us through doesn't spread."

"That's a shit plan, but I don't have anything better to suggest," Hel said and Bast couldn't help but lean down to kiss her frown away, his fingers trailing down her cheek as he tilted her face up to his.

"We'll figure it out," he said.

"But how many people will die before we do?" Hel whispered.

WATCHING Hel wave her hand at the wall and have the whole thing fold into itself was a disturbing reminder that whatever protections Sol had in place recognised her as being the same as him. Bast did his best not to let his discomfort shine through in their connection. He didn't want to distract his mate with his lingering trauma.

Hel and Sol's power felt like two parts of a whole to his senses and it was disconcerting, but now that he'd finally thrown off the fog of confusion, there was no confusion about who Sol was to him—his enemy. His mate was her own entirely separate person. He had no connection to Sol. It might've felt wrong at first to feel Sol's too familiar power without it twisting through his veins, but that was down to Sol's compulsion on him.

Despite everything, there was a moment of pure joy as

he and Hel launched themselves out into the freedom of the air together. Indulging in a brief twisting spiral around each other as they flew, he revelled in the return of their connection. Their movements were perfectly, subconsciously synchronised as they angled toward the distant columns of light surrounding the portal through which the contagion had invaded this world and others. Unable to look away from Hel for fear she might disappear again, he admired the surging strength of her flight, grateful for the transformation of her form that had given them this ability to soar together.

By silent agreement, their powers merged and reinforced each other as he wove a shielding spell that would, hopefully, keep them hidden from Sol and his people. Hel was learning fast, but she'd spent her entire life avoiding using her magic, whereas he had many decades of experience. As defensive as she could be about some things, she'd never once protested his gentle direction of their magic. Instead, he felt her watching avidly and soaking in the knowledge she'd been denied by her ... by Sol. He wasn't her father and to call him her maker made her sound like a thing, which she wasn't.

Bast kept the shield as small as he could in the hope it would help them avoid notice. It forced them to fly so close to each other that their wingtips occasionally brushed together, sending a buzz of tingling energy through them both. He wasn't complaining. Each touch reminded him they were still alive—that they were still together.

Last time he'd travelled to the contagion, Sol had portalled them there and he'd been so out of it he hadn't even really noticed. This time, he looked on in interest as the strange city passed below them. A surge of guilt rippled from Hel as they passed over a group of homeless people in a park.

"Who are they?" he asked.

"They're Tir's people—the ceptae—displaced when we shifted the contagion from our Earths to theirs."

Bast winced. "We'll make it right," he promised, his guilt now echoing hers.

When they arrived at the nexus of contagion, Hel frowned beside him. "It's grown larger even just in the few days since I was last here. I think shifting the rest of the contagion closer has made it worse."

Bast warily inspected the barely contained writhing mass of darkness ahead of them and could only agree with her assessment. What had been a relatively tidy staging area ringed with the permanent portals Sol had established so long ago was now riddled by the columns of contagion Sol had made him shift there. Trails of absence like an apocalyptic slug had slid across the landscape showed where Bast had dragged them closer.

The portal itself now bulged like it was just waiting to burst free and tendrils of contagion were lashing out like whips at random before subsiding back into the seething mass. It was hard to estimate growth in such a barren space with nothing to compare it to. Bast guessed the contagion had probably doubled in height since he'd collapsed while moving it, powerless to resist Sol's compulsion to keep going past the limits of his strength.

If Sol hadn't already noticed this alarming acceleration, he soon would. It would only increase his urgency to complete the melding and have Hel and Bast expel the contagion from this world.

Reaching out, Bast twined his fingers through Hel's, squeezing reassuringly. "We need to hurry," he murmured.

Hel closed her eyes beside him and he followed suit, focusing inward to sink deep into their shared power until the two of them were so closely aligned they could operate as one. Stretching out their combined awareness, Bast tried to get a sense of what this portal was, how it stayed open against Sol's efforts, and, most importantly, how to shut it down. It was an almost impossible task. His power repelled the contagion, which was great for making containment spheres but meant he was trying to feel his way without being able to touch.

Sensing his frustration, Hel took over their efforts, abandoning their careful inspection to reach out to the vastness of the planet beneath their feet, instead—touching the essence of Travaris. A small smile ghosted across his face. His hellcat could be so impatient, but he loved her growing confidence in her power. Through it, he could feel Travaris's essence. It was so very different from when they'd communed with the Melded Earths. This planet was much older with a stronger and less damaged sense of personhood. It wasn't fractured and hurting like their world was from the meldings and it was far more practised at communicating with a creature on its surface courtesy of coexisting with Sol.

You are SolnotSol? Travaris' voice of rumbling tectonic plates and life-giving water sounded in his bones. He could hear it with Hel's power in the same way she could hear his souls.

I am myself. Helaine, she replied.

As if that moment of communication had released a floodgate, he felt a dozen other worlds pressing in against their awareness through the permanent portals that ringed them nearby. In among them was the familiar patchwork identity of the Melded Earths claiming them as its own in a way that reminded him of a cat possessively twining through their legs.

Responding to the flare in their joint magic, a tide of souls followed on the worlds' heels, countless voices creating a cacophony in their minds. Between the incomprehensible vastness of the worlds and the numerous dead, the sheer volume threatened to drown them.

Quiet, please, Bast's mind voice was a careful whisper, conscious he needed to protect Hel from anything that made the throbbing ache of their volume worse.

He was quiet, but firm and the souls subsided to a respectful calm, recognising his authority. Once they stopped crowding them, they started swirling and organising and he noticed with interest how they swarmed toward particular essences of the worlds who had turned their attention their way. Hel and Bast's combined powers had unwittingly opened up a channel of communication between the dead and their previous homes. Tenuous excitement filled him as he realised the possibilities. Surely, thirteen worlds and innumerable dead could come up with something useful between them.

We need to find a way to remove the contagion and stop it from coming back. No more worlds should die. Can you help us? he asked.

His body stiffened in place as the worlds insinuated themselves into their minds, their vast awareness picking through their memories and desires as if they were their own, which he guessed they were. What were living creatures if not an extension of the worlds that brought them into being after all? Distantly, he felt Hel falling to the ground right before he crumpled next to her, overwhelmed by the sheer vastness of the worlds.

Slowly, the chaos they'd made of their combined consciousnesses calmed and a more purposeful collection of memories formed in his mind's eye as the intangible voice of the Melded Earths said—*There.*

Souls encircled them like they were the eye of a storm as he picked out what the worlds were trying to tell them. They'd focused in on the shield he'd built for Hel to protect her from the soul taint of his power. Images formed around them showing them his memories of the scans Ra and Zee had completed and the way the technology had shown him how to construct the protection. At the time, it had reminded him of a vaccine anchored in their wings to create the magical antibodies Hel needed to withstand the soul taint. Overlaid on that message was an awareness of how his power warded off the contagion—like two similar polarities repelling each other.

The last memory they were shown was of when they'd expelled the contagion from the Melded Earths, except this time it was from the Earths' perspective. He could barely comprehend the emotions flooding him, riven as they were by the overwhelming sensation of three-become-one. Every experience of their Earths was filtered through the dual traumas of the meldings that had shifted its essence, its identity, fundamentally. Pushing aside the disorientation that threatened to derail him, he focused on the content of the images.

Do you understand what they're suggesting? Hel asked. He wasn't certain if she spoke the words aloud or not.

Almost? he replied, before directing his next words into the vastness of the beings around them. *What would we need to do?* he asked.

Shield us like you shielded her, so even when the contagion reaches us, it will not take hold, Travaris replied, the world best able to form coherent sentences.

Would it be enough just to shield the worlds linked by portal here or will it still be able to spread to others? Bast asked, putting aside the question of how the fuck they would manage even that for a moment.

There was a pregnant pause while the worlds seemed to converse with each other. *We think it will be enough. It needs the portals to spread. That's why it has spent so much energy keeping this one open.*

Is it conscious? Hel asked.

The question seemed to confuse the worlds. *Everything has a purpose,* Travaris finally responded, as if that explained it.

So we should leave it to destroy you? Hel snarked back at the planet, and Bast couldn't hide his amusement. Leave it to his Hellcat to try and start a fight with an entire fucking planet.

No. Its purpose is flawed. It needs to be isolated, Travaris responded, immune to her sarcasm.

There are so many worlds and no wings to anchor the magic. The power needed to do what you're talking about would be vast. We need a simpler option, Bast said.

You will find a way, the world replied. Possibly the least helpful response of any it had given yet.

What we need is some kind of chain reaction where the initial magical catalyst is smaller and the effects cascade out, renewing themselves as they go, Hel said, her voice thoughtful.

Yes. Like the way our stars function to give us life, Travaris said.

Right. So, all they had to do was figure out how to build a magical vaccine against the contagion that was powered by his and Hel's combined power somehow working like the fusion of a star so it could extend across thirteen worlds without killing them in the process, one of which—their own Melded Earths—was actually three realities combined.

I've never seen magic work that way. It needs a person to channel it and something to anchor it if you want it to last. Sol's not going to give us the time to figure this out, Bast replied, his frustration mounting as he tried and failed to come up with an option for how to make the construct work.

Sol could discover their absence at any moment and he couldn't handle the thought of succumbing to his influence again like a glorified fucking puppet. Hel's warm hand squeezed his shoulder in sympathy and he blinked his eyes open to a view of her achingly beautiful face.

"I won't let him take you from me again," she promised, but there wasn't a lot she'd be able to do about it in a face-off with the much more powerful Sol.

The pressure of the worlds' presence in their minds eased as they lost interest. Time was a tenuous concept to a world and, in their minds, the solution was found. Even though the way forward was one Bast had no idea how to implement.

"Nice of them to say goodbye," he murmured.

Hel smirked. "Worlds aren't great conversationalists. I'm surprised Travaris was so communicative. It must be used to conversing with Sol."

Bast frowned. "Do you think it will reveal our plans to him?"

He felt Hel reach out and try to connect with Travaris again, but the world ignored them. She winced. "I guess we'll just have to hope self-preservation keeps it silent. I don't imagine it's much fun being melded to another world. Especially when you have such a defined personhood like Travaris seems to."

The dead who'd observed their interaction with the worlds were still hovering on the edge of his awareness. *We will help you,* they said.

Thank you. We will need you once we figure out how to do this. The power you channel is what will keep the worlds safe. However this happens, we will need a base of souls in each world willing to make it work, Bast replied.

We will answer the call, countless souls said in unison, their combined ethereal voices sending a shiver through his essence.

Bast pushed aside the icy dread seeping into his mind at their words. Something told him a sacrifice would need to be made. The only question now was how big.

"I need space to think and I want to talk to Tir about how this could work. Can you portal us home now you have your magic back?" Bast asked.

Hel nodded, already reaching for her power. "We'll have to be quick," she said as the familiar searing heat of her star-like power surrounded them and a flash of plasma blue started swirling just ahead.

He'd barely taken a step toward her when the half-formed portal blinked out of existence.

"You really think you can use *my* power to portal away from *my* planet and I won't notice?" Sol drawled from behind them.

Bast reached for Hel in desperation as he felt the familiar brain fog descending on him, gripping her arm as if it was all that stood between him and destruction. Turning to face Sol, she wrapped one of her silver wings around him protectively and the contact paused the erosion of his free will, stabilising him enough to leave him a precarious grip on his thoughts.

Bast was distracted enough he barely noticed the slide of his feathers against her wings which usually would've driven him crazy. A young woman stood by Sol's side. She had feathered wings like an elemental that were the colour of the auroral lights playing above them, and delicate horns a little like Hel's, only they were a pure blinding white. Her face showed no expression as she watched on.

"Come," Sol said, turning his back on them.

An invisible force grabbed him and Hel, pinning their arms to their bodies before dragging them behind Sol and through a portal that tasted of a myriad of suns.

CHAPTER 12
HEL

Hel seethed as Sol forcefully pulled them back through to his study like they were recalcitrant children. He hadn't even bothered reinstating the block on their magic, so unconcerned about their power he didn't need to. The fact he was right and she couldn't hope to match him in a magical fight was infuriating. Bast was trying to calm her through their connection but she could feel his deep-rooted fear underneath. There was nothing worse than losing control of your own body and mind and he'd only just returned to his senses. She burned with the need to eliminate the threat to him, but they couldn't risk it. They weren't a match for Sol like this. Maybe if they had some backup they could, but not alone and not here on his home turf.

His daughter had parked herself on the edge of the room, leaning on a wall next to one of the huge framed scrying windows that showed a glimpse of the other worlds connected to Travaris. Hel froze as she saw the frame contained a familiar visage—Soul Tower at night, the nine lights of its crown shining brightly into the sky and making the twisting metal vines that encased the tower glow with reflected luminescence. The view expanded as she watched, zooming out to take in an aerial perspective of the entire City of Souls—from the Spiderhive to the north down to Wayland's forge to the south where everything had started all those months ago when she'd picked up the copper cuffs that had drawn Bast's attention to her.

"Don't," she whispered, remembering Sol's threats to her home.

"I warned you what would happen if you didn't comply," Sol said. "You obviously need a bit more motivation."

Bast stiffened beside her and she felt a new flash of sharp fear down their connection.

"Wait," Bast said, the desperation she could sense from him hidden in his firm tone. "We were out there figuring out how to do what you want. You can't hold that against us. We just need a bit more time. There's no point shifting the contagion through the portal and closing it if there's a chance it will come back again. Let us figure out how to protect your worlds."

Sol sat back against his desk, wings draping around him like a cascade of stardust made solid. "I'm listening."

The hold Sol had on their bodies loosened and Hel stepped closer to the framed view of the Melded Earths as Bast started explaining the construct they needed to create to protect the worlds. Her clever mate was stalling for time. Now that Sol had tried and failed to use Bast's power for himself, there was no reason to hold off on causing the melding and forcing them to act.

Hel was drawn across the room half by the need to drink in the view of their home, and half by the need to see Sol's daughter closer up. She looked about eighteen, still young enough that she might not understand her father's true nature. Especially if she'd grown up under his influence. What did she think was happening here? And what did she think her and Hel's relationship to each other was?

"Hi. I'm Helaine," she said softly, holding out a hand.

The girl looked at her in surprise, her eyes flicking to Sol for some sort of approval or guidance. He must've been okay with it because she reached out a moment later to return her offered handshake.

"Stella," she murmured in reply before quickly pulling back.

Hel cocked her head, watching the girl sharply enough that she shifted on her feet slightly, revealing her discomfort. "Do you know who I am?" Hel asked, curious.

"You're nothing but a piece of my father given separate life for a little while. One day he will take you back into himself," she said, taking after her mother as she let the disdain ring clear in her voice.

"Stella, that's enough," Sol said in warning at the same time as Hel let out an involuntary growl in response. The threat in Stella's words was enraging on top of their already precarious situation.

"Fuck that. I'm not a part of him and I never will be. Do I act anything like him? I've lived more years than you in the world. Do you think just because you contain some extra DNA that you are *more* than me? Better than me?" Hel snapped.

She didn't realise she was preparing to lunge at the girl until Bast came up behind her, wrapping a gentle arm around her chest and pressing himself against her wings as he kissed her neck. "You're getting mad at the wrong person, love."

Hel hissed in frustration and then let her body relax into his arms, turning her head to brush her lips to his as she let him calm her ragged edges. He was right, of course. But she didn't have to like it.

Stella watched their interaction with something like confusion. She'd probably never seen a healthy relationship in person. The thought made Hel snicker because at what point had their relationship built on blackmail and loathing become healthy? It had, though. Bast pressed another series of kisses to her neck as he felt the warmth of her feelings through their connection.

"If you're quite done, shall we finish this discussion?" Sol said drily from behind them. "Or I could let my general loose in your city if you're feeling like wasting some more time."

Bast spun them both around and Hel glared at Sol, but her comeback was interrupted by Aliya's sweeping entrance into the room.

"Stella, darling. There you are," Aliya said, crossing to her daughter and air-kissing both cheeks.

"Aliya, I didn't request your presence here," Sol warned.

"You told me I could spend the afternoon with our child. You brought her here, so naturally I assumed I was welcome," Aliya said, stepping closer to Sol and trying to kiss him in greeting until she came up against an invisible wall of his magic that stopped her from getting close.

"What's going on?" she asked, frowning.

"Your *boyfriend* was about to launch an attack on the Melded Earths because he doesn't like that we're trying to find a proper solution to the contagion," Hel said.

A sharp slapping sound echoed through the room as Sol's

fist hit the desk in annoyance. Pain stabbed through Hel's knees as she found herself harshly dropped to the stone floor alongside Bast, Sol moving their bodies like puppets with his power.

Fuck. She'd miscalculated.

"You will show me respect or this is going to get much more unpleasant than I planned very quickly," Sol growled.

Hel swallowed hard. Okay. She'd been trying to unbalance him, but she'd clearly tipped him over a limit. She could still backtrack, though.

"Fuck off. You're going to do what you want anyway," she snapped.

Or not.

"Look. We all want the contagion gone. With your help, I'm sure we can figure out the shielding I was talking about," Bast said, somehow sounding calm and sensible even though Hel could feel his heart rate rising like a skitter of rain across her skin.

"I don't have the luxury of time and the worlds will help figure it out once we get started anyway," Sol snapped back.

Hel frowned. She knew the contagion had expanded but was it really so urgent? "It's not the worlds who have the power we need, it's the dead. You need to listen to Bast," she said.

"Bast destabilised the portal when he shifted the contagion around. Like I said already, we don't have time. The contagion is collecting in on itself—condensing—and when it releases that gathering energy, it will break through the shielding and grow fast enough to consume Travaris in days, possibly even hours. We need to act now. We have centuries to figure out the rest before it will become a problem again," Sol said.

Hel winced. She was *not* spending centuries here. She didn't want to spend another minute here. Her knees throbbed where Sol's anger kept her pressed hard into the stone floor, a constant reminder of how outmatched they were.

"Even with your mind-control tricks, you can't force us to channel the level of power a melding would release. Your influence will wash free as soon as the magic flows," Hel said.

"You are viewing this like a child who can't understand trade-offs. Grow up," Sol said, frustrated. "This is a simple choice. A small sacrifice to ensure many more worlds stay safe."

"There's nothing small about it! Millions died in the meldings on our Earths. There has to be another way. We *will not* do what you want if you cause another one," she snarled.

The familiar guilt of not surrendering to him before the last melding returned as she seethed on her words. If she'd just given up earlier, all those people would still be alive. She couldn't face that second-hand guilt of being associated in any way with Sol's mass murder again. Her heart couldn't take it. A surge of love and acceptance washed through her as Bast sensed her turmoil and sought to reassure her. His guilt echoed her own, but together they could make sure this time was different. If she could just figure out how to get them out of here.

"Stop being so precious, Helaine. It's not even our world that will suffer unless you don't do what he says. His threat to the City of Souls is not idle and he has far more resources at his disposal than I did when I attacked. Your people won't stand a chance against him alone. You would do well to heed him," Aliya said, finally joining the conversation.

Hel glared at the Air Lady. Of course she had no compunction about so much destruction. "And what if your city here in Travaris, the seat of your empire, falls in the aftermath of this melding?" she asked Sol. "Are you willing to lose it all?"

Sol glanced over at Bast. "Your so-called mate seems able to stabilise cities during a melding. He won't let the city fall if you're in it. And you're both too principled to let that sacrifice go to waste," Sol said.

"Maybe. But I'm also too principled to let you manipulate us like this. If you cause a melding, I promise you we will destroy everything you've built here. It will be a 'small sacrifice' if it keeps you from causing another one," Hel said, echoing his earlier logic.

She was totally bluffing, but she could see it gave him pause because the move was something he would do and he still thought she was just another piece of him. His new insight into her personality was warring with what he thought he understood of her nature.

"I don't believe you," he said, but she'd planted a seed of doubt. He was hesitating.

"She doesn't have it in her," Aliya said, scorn dripping from her words. "There are children here. She wouldn't harm them," she added, her eyes flicking to Stella.

"Save my home. Please," Stella added, her star-filled eyes widening as her lip trembled.

The guilt wracked through Hel again before she clicked what was going on. Stella's expression was just a shade too contrived. "Really? *That's* why you brought her with you? To guilt-trip us?"

Sol shrugged. "You both have a weakness for the young. It was worth a shot. I'd prefer your willing help given the volume of power you'll be dealing with, but it's not essential."

Stella's face had relaxed back to idle contempt as soon as she realised they weren't buying what she was selling. Hel's thoughts were frantic as she tried to figure a way out of this. They needed to get home so they could protect the city from Sol's general and so he would have to delay the melding. There would be no point releasing that power if Hel and Bast weren't around to use it. The problem was that he'd been so quick to respond to her portal last time there was hardly any chance she could get the two of them out. Especially when Sol was in the same damn room.

Maybe if she formed it under their feet so they fell through the floor? He wouldn't be able to risk closing it if they might be caught falling through. She didn't know what would happen if a portal closed on you when you were partway through, but she was pretty sure it would be deadly. They needed a distraction. Something that would give her enough time to form the portal and start falling. Something big. World level big.

Travaris. Words formed in her mind before she'd even really thought them through. Talking like this was passive magic. Hard to sense, even for someone like Sol. All but impossible, even.

SolNotSol, the planet replied.

Hel resisted the urge to roll her eyes. *HELAINE,* she corrected. *I need your help. Sol is going to force a melding here like he did for the Melding Earths and break you. I need you to distract him so we can get clear. He won't do it if I'm not here.*

Her speech was only partly words, the rest of the message reinforced by a combination of memories and emotion. She focused on how disjointed her Earths had been after the last melding. Its personality and identity like three pieces of paper torn to shreds and only part of each clumsily taped back together to form something new. Its essence and purpose kaleidoscoping like it had some dissociative disorder.

Worlds were vast and unknowable. They were alive, but not in the same way that humans or elementals were. They worked to their own timeline and she often struggled to understand their messages clearly. In that moment, though, Travaris reacted instantly with a knee-jerk fearful defence against the threat she'd laid out. Their connection to the Melded Earths meant they knew exactly what was at stake.

Sol's eyes widened as he felt the effect of Travaris' panic —a volcano bursting forth within the city where none had been before, earth surging upward as buildings crashed down, seething magma and ash erupting into the air.

The second Sol turned from them to reach for his power and sooth the planet, she grabbed Bast's hand and wrenched a portal open beneath their feet faster than she'd ever attempted before. Raw power twisted between them, responding to her desperation. She had no idea how long this distraction would hold. They needed out.

Swirling blue fire filled her vision in an instant and the floor dropped away like a trapdoor, slingshotting them down to another room, another planet. Hel snapped the portal closed at the same time as her wings snapped out to try and catch their fall, becoming tangled with Bast's beside her. Her already aching knees jarred as they landed. Bast blinked in confusion and looked around them before a slow smile spread across his face despite the ominous space they'd arrived in.

"We're home," he said, surprise evident in his words as he took in the familiar view of the shadowy Spiderhive surrounding them.

Why did it always have to come back to the Spiderhive?

"You need to get a containment sphere up before the contagion follows us through and we need to get out of here before the arachdryn come hunting," Hel said, already pulling him toward the safety of the daylight shining through the triple-storey opening to the city ahead of them.

Bast frowned and nodded, quickly crafting the sphere that would hold the contagion at bay from where they'd emerged.

"We need to get to the tower and get the defences ready for attack," he said as soon as he finished, propelling them out to the concrete lip at the edge of the building and adjusting the shielding to let them through as they propelled themselves out into the sky.

Veering around the soaring cenotaph war memorial, they set a course for Soul Tower.

For home.

Her joy at that thought was short-lived. Barely two wing-beats away from the Spiderhive, an immense burst of power like the molten core of a sun radiated from nearby. Twisting mid-flight to search for the threat, a flash of movement caught Hel's eye below them. Glancing down, she saw a swarming mass of black fur and burning red eyes emerging in the middle of the road from the largest portal she'd ever laid eyes on. The gateway to Travaris was a white hot seething mass of power that had formed in the old human railway station where a huge circular window had once stood. Its searing form was framed by the remains of the eight doric columns at the brick building's entrance and capped by the now ominous seeming Roman clock that had stopped at ten minutes to two. As if even the remains of the non-magical human world knew they'd finally run out of time.

Dozens of slathering starhounds raced into the city as more strange forms emerged behind them.

"Stop," Hel cried, using a touch of power to make her voice echo in the space and channelling every bit of authority she could into her voice.

The hounds only paused for a single breath before carrying on to hunt out the city's vulnerable. Sol must've learned her trick with them and trained them out of it. They no longer reacted to her commands like they would his.

Another flash of light and the grinding crumble of bricks to the ground heralded an even bigger problem—a creature as tall as the multi-story building it was stepping through and straight out of a nightmare.

The monster looked like a living battering ram. Its three skulls were flattened and collapsed into themselves in a way that seemed like it should've given it irreparable brain damage but, sadly, didn't seem to be stopping it from functioning at all. Each head weaved on the end of a thick, long sinuous neck—poised to strike with a speed she didn't want to test. Its body was a Frankenstein mix of alien creatures stitched together, but the flesh was rotting and putrid, pieces flaking off as it brushed against the buildings it passed in huge strides. It didn't feel dead. She would've been able to tell with Bast's power if it was. It sure as fuck wasn't natural, though. It was a living weapon constructed by a power with no respect for life.

Wellington's ever-present wind chose that moment to change direction, wafting the stench of the monstrous creature toward them. She just about fell from the sky as she choked. Faltering mid-flight, she reeled for a second, dropping closer to the hounds surging below before she recovered.

Dull red flesh flashed at the edge of her vision—a squadron of those damn bat-winged soldiers arranged with military precision as they arrowed toward them. This general wasn't messing around. She really hoped they didn't all have the dangerous magic the one they'd dealt with months ago had or their scouts were going to be in serious trouble. The City of Souls wasn't defenceless, but it only had a handful of elemental mages with enough power to keep those around them safe.

"We need to get out of here and regroup," Bast said.

She almost missed the words in the thundering crash as one of the monster's colossal heads careened into the side of the Spiderhive where they'd just been, knocking a hole right through the wall. Arachdryn poured out of the space it had created, defending their nest from the threat despite the bright sunlight they usually avoided. Hopefully, they could slow it down. Somehow, the thing had smashed through Bast's shielding magic just as easily as it had the walls.

"Fuck," she whispered, as Bast pulled urgently on her hand and used his magic to weave a stronger protection around them.

It wouldn't be any use if that creature could smash through it. Dragging power to her, Hel opened a portal mid-air right ahead of them. They didn't have time to fly. They needed to get to their people and figure out how the fuck they were going to defend against this.

CHAPTER 13
BAST

Hel's portal took them to the roof of Soul Tower where Morrigan, Ra, Tir, Kairon, and Ryker were standing looking out over the city, most of them on comms to their various people organising a defence. The tower's shielding had kicked in automatically, one of several fail-safes Bast had arranged for when he was absent from the city. The silver of his magic encasing the building from its crown to the ground was a sparking haze across the horror show invading their city.

Copper power flashed in the distance—the defences Zee had built into the city's elemental architecture responding to the incoming threat as more strange creatures continued to emerge from the huge portal Sol's General had launched an attack through. At some point, he'd have to deal with the contagion the gateway would let into the city, but right now he was kind of wishing it would hurry up and infect the portal so it would stop their attackers.

"Where do you need me?" Bast asked, striding toward the others who hadn't noticed them arrive.

"Bro!" Ra cried, pulling him into a tight embrace. "Fuck, am I glad to see you."

"Helaine, can you portal that courier squadron into the middle of those bat-winged soldiers?" Ryker asked, gesturing to half a dozen of his couriers heading in their direction.

"On it," she said, for once not giving any grief to the man who'd raised her through her teens.

He didn't think Hel and Ryker had talked about the way he'd lied to her about her indenture yet—pretending she was indebted to the couriers just to keep her safely in the city. Bast, on the other hand, had railed at Ryker about it several times, deeply hurt by the way his friend had framed him as the worst kind of elemental lord through his deception. In the end, he'd still forgiven him. It *had* kept Hel safe, and if Ryker hadn't kept her in the city, Bast never would've met his mate—the love of his life. His heart ached at the thought. That didn't make what Ryker had done any more right, though. Shaking away the thoughts he didn't have time for, he revelled in the feel of the familiar fire of Hel's magic stroking along his soul as she let it loose to help Ryker's couriers.

Bast took in the scene before him for several breaths. It wasn't looking good for them. There were far too many attackers and creatures of unknown power coming through the portal.

"We can't win this as we are. Morrigan—start evacuating all our non-combatants. Get our children out of here. Hel can set up a series of portals to Ivy. Hopefully she's distant enough and powerful enough that they won't give chase. Ra —we need to call the Courts for reinforcements. All of them. If Sol takes over here, he'll use the city as a staging platform to take over the rest of the Melded Earths. Kairon, Tir—

anything you can do to assist will make the difference on whether we can hold out long enough for help to arrive. I'm going to release the dead on the streets to block those hounds while we get people to safety. Then I'll go keep those bat-winged assholes occupied," he said.

Someone's stifled gasp followed his announcement. He didn't know whose. They'd all hoped he'd never have to use the last ditch defences they'd planned for years ago, nor had any of them ever expected to call on the other rulers as allies.

"I will reach out to the separatists for help and transport them here if they agree," Tir said, a portal already half open beside them. "Then I can help transport the evacuees."

Hel, now finished helping the couriers, hurried closer to the Archivist, gripping their arm gently before they could leave. Bast caught just enough of their whispered conversation to get the gist. She was telling Tir about their people on Travaris—that they were homeless and the dual threat they faced from both the quickly expanding contagion and the new melding Sol was planning there.

Tir's tentacles thrashed in distress at her words and they looked out toward the huge portal to Travaris as if they wanted to step through it that second. "I will come with you when you return," they said, loud enough for both Bast and Hel to hear. "You owe me a life debt. I am claiming it. You will save my people."

Bast could only nod. He owed Tir everything. They'd saved Hel's life, given her back her true form. He'd always intended to do everything he could to save Tir's people, debt or no debt, and he was sure Hel had too. They just hadn't figured out how. Maybe Tir could help with that. The Archivist was far older than them and had travelled widely across worlds.

Tir disappeared through their portal without another word and Bast turned to Hel. Pulling her in close, he kissed the silver of her hair where one of her delicate horns twisted out from her scalp and breathed in her familiar scent.

"I'll need you to portal reinforcements from the courts if they respond as well, my love. Be careful not to burn yourself out with the evacuees," he said.

"Just worry about yourself. I'll take care of it," Hel said, pressing a kiss to his heart where her mating mark lay before launching out into the air with Morrigan to arrow towards one of the portal evacuation points they'd established after Aliya's attempted attack on the city months earlier.

His heart twisted in his chest as he watched her leave. Half his soul was flying into danger and all he could do was hope she stayed safe. Hel was tough and she had a thread of wild violence running through her he'd always loved. She wouldn't go down without a fight, and the General wouldn't allow her to be killed. Sol needed both of them back on Travaris, which meant separating from her and splitting their invader's focus was the best tactic. Even if it sucked and everything in him screamed to stay by her side.

Ra gripped his shoulder in support, sensing the conflict in him as he resisted the urge to follow his mate, and then handed him an earpiece to keep in contact with their forces.

"I'll call Nerida first. She's closest and first in line to be hit if we fail," Ra said.

"Leaving Mica til last?" Bast teased, only half paying attention as he began calling on the souls across the city.

Even among the danger they faced, he still smirked at the string of swearwords Ra let out under his breath in response. This wasn't the first time they'd faced death together and they'd never let it stop their snark before. He wasn't going to start now.

Kairon paused by his side on the way to the elevators. "My people and I will try to take out that three-headed creature, or at least slow it down. Our magic should be able to hasten whatever is making its flesh decay once we figure out how to attune to it."

"Thank you," Bast said.

Kairon nodded. "This is our home too, now. We won't let it fall."

Bast clasped the vampyr's shoulder briefly, his attention already refocusing on the cacophony of voices from the souls who guarded the city and had responded to his call. They'd held the city stable and acted as his sentries since the first day he'd come there, and they were fiercely determined to protect their family and their home. Bast drew in a deep trembling breath as he prepared to do what was needed. Would his people ever look at him the same way again?

We need to use the phoenix protocol, Bast told the souls.

Are you sure? a hundred souls sent back in various combinations of speech and flashes of emotive alarm.

Thanks to Ra's database and the tech interface to allocate the souls to their sectors, he'd been able to deploy them in the same way he would a living force. They had plans in place for several worst-case scenarios. He'd never thought he'd actually use the phoenix protocol, though. It may well damage his reputation irreparably. Even if it didn't, Niko would be kept busy long after this battle ended dealing with the rāhui prohibitions from accessing anywhere affected that would result. He just hoped the leader of the humans in the city survived to give him shit about it. Their people had already been forced to abandon their homes. If they had to stay away a little longer while the tapu was lifted afterwards, it was a small price to pay for their safety. And if his people turned away from him in the aftermath, at least they would be alive to do so.

"Shit. The hounds have cornered one of the human apartments and it's too close to Ryker and those bat-people to be evacuated from the roof," Morrigan said.

"What sector?" Bast asked.

"Three."

"I've got it." Luck was with them. That sector was adjacent to the Bolton Street Cemetery where the phoenix protocol was focused. There was no more time to delay.

Go! he told the souls, letting his power flood into the nearby graveyard like a torrent of water, urging it to seep into the earth around the cracked and lichen-ridden concrete of the resting places of the dead.

For the first time in his life, he wasn't an intricate soulweaver. He was the brute-force defiling necromancer that so disgusted the elementals who'd hunted him as a child. Murmurs of dissent came from the souls as they read his thoughts.

No. You are someone who will do anything to save his people, an old kaumātua replied. *Do you think thousands of the dead would linger here for decades to help you if you were that person you describe?*

As the first skeletal hand burst from the earth and the souls of their long-decayed bodies came to their defence, Bast hoped the city's still-living occupants would be as forgiving. He took just enough time to check the undead could hold their own against the hounds before looking away. He didn't need to watch as their bony fingers wrapped tight around the hound's necks or as teeth dripping with venom gnawed on long-dead femurs until they cracked. The walking dead swarmed to the apartment's entrance and created a skeletal tunnel for its inhabitants to escape through—a pathway lined with the reanimated bones of the dead. He could imagine the vacant eyes of the skulls in the tunnel's walls watching on as his people fled. As he turned his own gaze back to the skies, he could only hope the humans were brave enough to use it.

In the distance, Ryker's people were struggling against the winged attackers, blood and feathers dripping from the sky like raindrops as blades ripped open flesh. They wouldn't be able to hold for long without him, although portalling into their midst had been a stroke of genius because it both caught them by surprise and meant Sol's fighters risked hurting their own if they lashed out with the power they'd used to kill his scouts in the past.

Ra's voice was rising in anger behind him where he was still glued to his sat-phone, but he didn't have time to focus on it as magic surged in the distance. Three of Ryker's couriers were ripped in half mid-air, their bodies tumbling from the sky like winged seedpods helicoptering down to the pavement.

Rage filled him and he was launching himself from the rooftop before he could even think. He couldn't stay safe behind the shields while his people were dying. Souls flooded him with magic, driving him forward. As he drew his sword to slice through the first leathery wing, he sent his power slicing out at the same time—a scythe through a field of wheat. It was their attackers' bodies that fell this time, heads tumbling free as their wings collapsed in death. Ruthlessly tearing more power from the newly dead, Bast used them against their will to reinforce his attack against their brethren when they probably hadn't even realised yet they'd been killed.

He was forced to channel Hel's power to defend himself as the survivors rallied in response, their devastating power scraping at his shields as it tore at him. A sphere of all-too-familiar molten star power shot towards him and he twisted and dropped, shoulder tendons screaming in protest as he forced himself into a controlled fall before snapping his wings out and trying to shoot skyward. His path was blocked. More and more of those bat-winged forces were swarming close. The attacker who'd caught the brunt of the magical bomb Bast had just dodged froze in place mid-air, held paralysed by whatever it was.

"Bast! You were supposed to stay put on the Tower so they couldn't grab you!" Ra cried.

Dropping onto the roof of one of the city's causeways, Bast used a combination of his sword and power to clear a space around himself. For every creature he cut down, two more took their place.

"Fuck. Bast! Get out of there!" Hel joined in the calls in his earpiece.

"I can hold my own. Are the courts coming?" he asked.

"I'm about to open portals to the water and fire courts," Hel replied.

Bast's eyes widened in surprise at who had answered their call, and who had not. He hadn't been certain his half-brother would answer the call, but apparently their new truce was holding.

"Mica's not coming?" Bast checked.

"Apparently he's too busy to even answer," Ra almost spat, venom dripping from his words.

A deafening crash from his right put an end to their

conversation as the causeway Bast was standing on collapsed beneath his feet. As he spun to face the latest threat, he was met with the sight of a bloodshot eye the size of a dinner plate staring back at him. His wings caught the wind before he could fall and he searched the crowded airspace around him for a way free as the head undulated up to reveal the creature's gaping maw of fangs just as its other two heads came out to play.

His first strike at the monster bounced off its skull like his sword was rubber. There was no sign it had even felt it. The move cost him as one of the other heads slammed into his side while he was distracted, bulldozing through his shields just like it had at the Spiderhive. Bast winced as his body slammed against the side of an apartment building, holding himself in the air with only his magic and sheer force of will as his bruised wings struggled to function.

Just as one of the heads would've slammed into him again, blood-red magic formed a cloud around it, encasing it. The monster blinked in confusion, momentarily stunned until it reared its head into the next-door building in annoyance, thrashing in an attempt to clear the magic as it took out most of a wall and left the structure teetering dangerously over the street.

"We're struggling to hold it, sorry," Kairon said through his earpiece. "It's a chimera of so many pieces it's hard to attune to it and it has very little of the blood we can call to. We've slowed it down, but we're limited to taking pieces out of it with claws and weapons."

Bast took advantage of the creature's distraction to push a little higher through the swarms of attackers above him. At least his shielding was still holding against them, even if it was now ragged and strained from the abuse it had taken.

Even as he hovered searching for an opening to get clear, he knew he hadn't gained enough distance from the monster writhing nearby.

"Need a hand?" Nerida called from the other side of the beast, her form wreathed in the cool blue light of her ocean power.

With a flick of her wrist, she sent spears of ice thudding into the creature's necks, pinning it to the wall. A hoarse, nauseating scream like a thousand dentist drills burrowing into the delicate bones of his ears filled the air. Even the attackers surrounding him grasped their heads in pain. Fighting through his own visceral reaction, he took advantage of the holes opening in their ordered lines to gain some height.

Nerida's spears didn't hold the monster for long. With a shake of its necks, the ice piercing its body went flying. Bast frowned as he noticed the wounds it had taken were barely visible, not even bleeding. It hadn't slowed at all.

Nerida's shielding seemed to work slightly better against the monster, the sphere of her power keeping the heads clear from her body as the creature lashed itself at her over and over in its rage. Each time it struck her defences, elemental power scattered like mini maelstroms into the air.

"I can't hold this for long," Nerida said, her voice sounding strained.

Reaching out to the walking dead, Bast drew the nearest elemental skeletons airborne, using his power to let their featherless wings hold them in flight so they could fling themselves at the creature. He swallowed hard as the remains of his people, animated by their brave souls, lodged their bones into the monster's six eye sockets, blinding it. It only served to further enrage the creature that had now wrapped its necks around Nerida's shielding to squeeze her like a constrictor snake.

Bast watched in horror as the liquid blue of her magic pulsed ... once ... twice ... and then gave way. Her defences popped like a soap bubble, leaving her totally exposed and surrounded.

"No!" Kairon's cry sounded in stereo—both from somewhere below and in Bast's comms earpiece.

As the three monstrous heads converged on Nerida's exposed body, blood-red magic snuck up and around each neck faster than light. Bast watched in fascination as the lines of power wended their way around the scattered remains of Nerida's magic, weaving together much like his did with Hel's. When Kairon's magic reached the Lady of Water, it coated her skin in a thin film that seemed to pulse with suction. Drops of Nerida's blood seeped out through her pores to join the twisting magics and coalesced into three impossibly thin spinning blades that ripped out from her body, beheading the creature in the time it took Bast to blink.

The creature's death throes fell into one of those eerie silences that will sometimes float over a battlefield. The clash of metal on metal paused along with the noise of the explosives and buildings the city had been using to defend itself. Into the quiet thumped the sound of three giant heads smashing into the tar seal like wrecking balls. Nerida's dazed form fluttered in translucent blues and greens down into Kairon's arms where he was waiting on the ground.

Bast would've been worried for the Lady of Water, but her voice rang clear only moments later. "Don't you dare touch me! You stole the blood from my veins!"

He winced in sympathy for the vampyr who had saved her life, but there wasn't time to play peacemaker. Nerida's words had sparked a return to the fight. With another wave of power, Nerida called to the wyrms beneath the city and the earth dragons erupted from the street to drag the remains of the monster into the earth's depths. Nearby somewhere, Bast could feel his half-brother calling to the local dragon and griffin population, recruiting them to help.

As he scanned the skies in vain for a clear path back to the tower, a bundle of electric blue and cream dive-bombed through the enemy fighters toward him in an explosion of power.

Fuck. Kaia.

Bast wasted no time, shooting straight up through the path she'd cleared in the still regrouping attackers to catch her in his arms as he flew far faster than she was capable back to Soul Tower. Her power was so much stronger than it had been before she'd been taken and it was still leaking out of her like a jetstream as they shot clear. She was like a magic bomb waiting to detonate until she had the training she needed to use it safely.

"You're supposed to have evacuated! You could kill yourself using your power like that," he chided gently, clutching the girl tight to his chest in his fear.

"If I don't use it, it'll kill me faster," she shot back, uncharacteristic bitterness in her voice and a dullness to her expression that Bast would do anything to take away.

He hadn't been there since they'd rescued her. Hadn't been able to hold her close and figure out what her cruel treatment and the constant drain on her power had done to her.

"We'll fix it," he whispered, kissing her hair as he shot raw power around them in a sparking cascade to make it back to safety.

"Will you fix me, too?" she asked, the words choking off partway through.

Bast's heart ached and all he could do was hold her closer for a moment as they landed on the rooftop. "You're not broken. You saved me. Now, you need to stay clear of the fighting. You're our future. We can't lose you, baby girl. I love you."

Kaia's shoulders were slumped as she walked away toward the doors leading inside. He only just caught her final words to him—"I'm already lost."

Another explosion forced him to turn away and refocus on their defence. He wished the world would pause for even a second and give him the time to help heal her. Ana had raised her to be strong. He'd just have to hope she could hold on a little longer. And that one of them would still be around to help when the dust settled.

Looking out over his city, he was reminded of the devastation when he'd first arrived there mere hours after the original melding. Buildings that had crumbled beneath the monster's onslaught sent clouds of concrete dust into the air. Elsewhere, thick plumes of black smoke were rising, whether from the city's defences or from the attackers he couldn't say. Screams and booms carried on the ubiquitous winds and the shrieking cries of the souls animating the corpses from the old cemetery formed an eerie backing chorus only he and Hel could hear. The rancid scent of the wreck of a monster had somehow reached even his high perch, settling over the buildings in a stomach-churning miasma.

The latest explosion had come from where he could sense his mate in the distance, nearer to the portal that was still open to Travaris, but he knew Hel wasn't injured. Yet. The skies were chaotic with wings that now included flashes of Water Court blue-green and Fire Court yellow-orange among the more familiar colours of the City of Soul's citizens.

"What's going on, Hel?" he asked.

"Nerida's people are circling in from the south, trying to drive them back toward the portal. Ty's are closing here to ambush them as they come out," she said, the clang of metal on metal following her words.

"Quite the mess you've made here, brother," Ty's voice sounded in his ear. Someone must've given him a comms device.

He opened his mouth to shoot back an insult like they had their whole lives and then forced himself to pause. Ty had come halfway across the world to help and his taunting words seemed more habit than anything truly malicious. He had turned up. As Bast's city was succumbing against odds they couldn't possibly fight. As his people lay dying. Ty was here. Helping. Maybe they would never love each other like brothers should. Maybe they would never even like each other. But if Ty helped save his people, he could forgive him just about anything.

"Thank you for answering our call," Bast said.

"Yes, well. Even I'm not stubborn enough to ignore an entire invading force no matter what Aliya might've said. I thought I understood her motives and how far she would go, but this I never expected," Ty said.

"Less talking, more killing," Nerida cut into their conversation.

"A woman after my own heart," Kairon replied.

Nerida didn't even bother to respond.

The invading force had stayed clear of the tower at first, wary of the vast store of power in its shielding and the offensive strikes that launched from the building's crown when any of them got too close. That hadn't lasted long. Starhounds were now throwing themselves at its base to the point that some of them were snapping their own necks as they tried to force their way through. The three-headed monster might be dead, but there were plenty more strange and murderous species stalking the streets that his people were struggling to contain.

Desperate fear shot through their mating bond from Hel and he was launching himself out into the air again before he could even think, driving himself so fast to reach her that he was a blur of shadow in the sky. He was halfway to her location before he realised her fear hadn't been for herself, but for the elemental who was once her guardian.

Ryker's familiar burgundy wings were flailing awkwardly as he intercepted another of those blue spheres someone had lobbed at Hel's back while she wasn't looking, placing himself between her and the danger. His old friend was already locked in combat with an assailant, holding his attacker at bay as he dragged them both into the sphere's path with gravity and sheer strength. Ryker caught the globe of Sol's burning power straight to his face and instantly went stiff as a corpse as it rendered him unconscious. The bat-winged man he'd been fighting—the General Bast noticed with a sinking sensation in his stomach—took full advantage. His long deadly glaive arced through the air, slicing one of Ryker's wings off at the shoulder. The strike was followed by a burst of magic that sent Ryker hurtling to the ground two storeys below them. It was too great a wound. Too fast a descent. There was no way to cushion his fall as he plummeted to the ground.

Hel's comm wasn't connected, but he could hear her scream on the wind, echoing his own—"Ryker! No!"

Hel tore to where Ryker had fallen without a care for her own safety and Bast's heart raced as he fought to put on the extra speed he needed to get close enough to protect her.

With eyes only for Hel, he didn't even see the magic trap he careened into.

An invisible net strung across his path yanked him gracelessly through the air, interfering with his power in that infuriating way only Sol could to leave him utterly vulnerable. He couldn't even get a warning out on the comms.

All he could do was watch the world turn into a grey blur as magic crushed his wings tight to his body while he was spun into the searing heat of Sol's portal.

CHAPTER 14
HEL

Fear for her mate threatened to undo her the moment Hel felt Bast pass through the portal back to Travaris. Although he was still a matter of wing-beats away while it remained open, the distance between them on such distant worlds was vast and their connection was stretching thin once more. Letting out a scream of frustration, she pressed her hands to the gaping wound where Ryker's wing used to be, desperately trying to staunch the blood flow that was spreading on the concrete beneath him in a sinister parody of his missing burgundy feathers.

"Don't you dare fucking die," she hissed at him, half her attention on his face that was still frozen and unmovable from Sol's magic, the rest of her firmly focused on the portal her mate had just been taken through.

Seeing Ryker's eyeballs flicking back and forth rapidly, she shook off her panic and used her power to blast away the effects of the magic holding him so he could communicate.

His words gurgled as he spoke, his ribs now piercing a lung from the fall. "Go. Save him," he gasped.

"I'm not leaving you here," Hel said, cutting off the rest of the sentence—*to die alone.*

"Allow me," one of Kairon's people said from near her shoulder, gently pushing her clear and letting her blood-red healing magic flow into Ryker.

Hel stared down at her hands stained red with blood and watched helplessly as the vampyr tried to stabilise the closest thing to a real father she'd ever had. The elemental who'd insisted she get medical help whenever she did something stupid on a courier run and got injured. The elemental who'd turned a blind eye when she'd snuck weapons out of the armoury to practise late at night. The elemental who was no doubt responsible for her favourite meal turning up in the shared kitchen every Friday night even when she refused to eat it with him. Why had she let her anger at him keep burning so long? Life was too fleeting.

"Thank you," Hel whispered. Too little, too late. "For everything."

Ryker winced as he tried to breathe deep and failed. "Love you, too, hot stuff," he said, using the name he used to tease her with when she was chasing a bonus. "Always have. Always will. Now, go. The city will fall without him. Bring him home."

Hel reached down and clasped his hand. Warrior to warrior. Family to family. "Don't let him give up," she ordered the vampyr who was working too frantically to respond.

With one last squeeze of Ryker's hand, she launched herself into the sky. The bat-winged asshole who'd taken him out was looming overhead. His power had been raining down on her shielding the whole time she'd been kneeling next to Ryker's broken body.

"You wanted my attention? You've got it," she said, letting her voice travel over the skirmishing fighters surrounding them.

Reaching for her magic, she let loose in a way she'd never been able to with the threat of Sol's hounds on her trail. *No one* was ever coming between her and Bast again. Instead of trying to breach the nearby portal swarming with attackers, she opened her own portal to Travaris.

Right in the middle of the General's chest.

She might have only a fraction of Sol's power, but it was still more than these attackers could muster. She over-whelmed him with sheer anguished determination. As the familiar burning plasma blue of her portal swirled into place above her, the General's body was seared from existence, torn apart as his shredded remains were sucked into the vortex she'd opened. She wished she could've made him suffer longer, made him gasp for his final breaths like Ryker. But she didn't have time.

Shooting through the narrow portal, she snapped it closed before the General's squadron, swarming closer at his choked-off death rattle, could launch a retaliatory ambush. She could only hope the attackers lost momentum without their leader and the city could hold on a little longer while she brought Bast home. She'd have to trust Nerida and Ty to hold them at bay. And wasn't that one of life's great ironies? If someone had told her even a few weeks ago that she would leave the city in the hands of the Fire Lord for safekeeping, she would've laughed her ass off.

THE DRY PLAIN of the staging area on Travaris stretched out below her, glinting gold specks of some mineral in the earth reflecting the auroral light-play of the sky where Sol's power enveloped the planet. Scents of aggressive battle magic drifted everywhere and, strangely, cries of agony broke the stillness of the air. The huge portal to the Melded Earths was centre stage before her—the jewel in the crown of the twelve shielded permanent portals to the other worlds of Sol's empire circling the bare plain.

As impressive as the crossroads between planets was, the black taint of the contagion looming on the far side of the battleground overshadowed everything. It no longer looked like a portal. It looked like an immense wave of dark absence growing above them as it threatened to break upon the worlds to wash them away. Already it stretched as high as the auroral lights above them.

It wasn't the contagion causing the screams she'd heard. The contagion was a silent killer, instantly snuffing those it touched from existence like they'd never been. Wrapping her power protectively around herself as she hovered, she scanned the chaos around her for Bast and the source of those cries.

Ground troops waiting to storm the City of Souls through the huge portal were scattered haphazardly across the landscape. She soon realised where both the cries and that lack of military discipline were coming from. People were toppling to the ground like bowling pins as the earth shook beneath their feet before splitting open and swallowing them into the depths of its ragged maw of rock and jagged crystalline teeth.

Travaris was a world betrayed. It was angry.

So was she.

Opening another portal before any more flying attackers could swarm her, she focused on the presence of her mate somewhere nearby and used the familiar feel of his magic through her soul as a target. She emerged mid-air behind the attacker who'd dragged Bast away from her. Her mate was an unnaturally rigid form dangling from his grasp as his wing-beats carried them closer and closer to the threat she needed to stop them from reaching. Not giving the guy time to process her presence, she drew her twin blades and sliced deep into his carotid arteries from behind, raining his lifeblood down onto the surface of Travaris below—a sacrifice, and a promise.

Like she had with Ryker, she smashed the magic around Bast away with her own, catching him as he fell from the soldier's now slack grasp and gripping his biceps tight to hold him aloft. Reaching out with her soul and her power, she used physical contact to reinforce their connection as she worked to erase any trace of Sol's influence from his mind, burning it away like the disease it was.

They dipped closer and closer to the dangers of the enraged earth for three strained wingbeats before Bast's glassy eyes finally blinked slowly and his facial muscles lost their slack visage. Hel sighed in relief as she felt his familiar soulweaving power wrap around them to keep them airborne and reinforce their shielding while he forced his sluggish wings to function again.

"Oh good. You came," Sol said. As if he hadn't launched a full-on invasion of their world to drag them back.

That voice too close behind them destroyed any semblance of reassurance from Bast's recovery before it had a chance to form and Hel's heart skipped a beat as despair threatened to set in. Fuck that. She wasn't giving Sol one more ounce of her fear. Taking strength from Bast's presence beside her, she dug deep into a lifetime of the rage that was her strength and used it to hold strong against the vast and overwhelming presence of her maker.

They spun as one to face him.

Hel smiled grimly as she took Sol in. He'd seemed weary from withstanding the contagion when she first arrived. That was nothing to how he looked now as he was forced to defend against not just the accelerated darkness but also the planet itself that was both his home and part of the source of his magic. The inner light he shone with had dulled and his eyes had shadows of fatigue beneath them. Despite that, she could still feel the seemingly bottomless well of his power. He'd called himself a living star and he felt like that to her senses, especially now he was too tired to hide his nature. It was like they had strayed too close to a searing fusion of raw energy.

In contrast to Sol's struggles, Travaris was willingly feeding Hel power from the connection points with the other worlds to replenish her reserves. The world knew she was its best hope of freeing itself from the contagion eating it alive and of losing its selfhood to Sol's apocalyptic manipulations. She drew deep on the magic it channelled to her, feeling Bast do the same from the ever-growing swarm of the dead, their powers twisting around each other like a double helix. Two essential halves of a whole.

A glimpse of metallic reflection below caught her eye, drawing her attention away from the threat before them for a moment as she took in the all-too-familiar silhouette of one of Sol's shards of stasis looming out of the ground. This one was even taller than the ones he'd erected on their Melded Earths. Its pointed tip leaned toward them like a sinister proboscis waiting to suck some other reality into the surrounding space.

The shard throbbed like a pulse with Sol's power as she watched and Hel realised they were fast running out of time. Throwing herself between Sol and the structure like her physical presence could somehow block his connection to it, she sent out a shot of searing heat threaded with pure death, blue and silver sparking together as she and her mate synchronised their willpower.

Sol batted their magic aside like it was nothing and Hel burned with frustration. She *would not* stand by while he killed millions again. Drawing her blades once more, she arrowed her flight straight at Sol, ignoring the spike of Bast's fear at her recklessness. She was intercepted by more of those bat-winged assholes before she even got close, barely able to move fast enough to hold them at bay. Bast somehow got through to join her before she was overwhelmed. Placing his back and wings firmly against hers, he spun their power around them to keep the attackers at bay and held their flight stable while Hel parried and thrust with her blades. A grim inevitability burrowed inside her each time she felt their sharp lengths slide home through flesh and sinew.

It wasn't going to be enough. *They* weren't going to be enough.

Hel could feel Travaris' frustration that Sol was blocking its efforts to eject the shard piercing its skin. The world surrounding her trembled in her consciousness. It was afraid. The darkness of the contagion pulsed now barely contained across the battlefield, erasing more of the planet's essence every second as the sky darkened with its absence, and Travaris was powerless to save itself.

Sol's words from his study played again in her mind—

once the destabilised contagion burst free, they might only have hours. But he'd said that before he opened such a huge portal to the Melded Earths to attack them. She doubted they'd have even that long now. She could already see the first threads of black absence wending through the portal's edges like an event horizon growing around it, its tendrils stretching skyward and drifting overhead toward the source of the larger coalescence of darkness in the distance. If they didn't do something soon, they'd be surrounded.

Travaris' growing panic fed her own. There was something fundamentally wrong about as ageless a being as a planet showing such mortal distress. But Travaris was unlike any other world. It had learned to converse with Sol, had become a little more person-like each time they spoke. Now, that personhood was being eroded by the contagion like it had been eaten away by acid.

Hel could hear the world's memories of their conversations surrounding her as the planet's fear threatened to wash her own consciousness clear. Is this how Sol had transformed himself from a star to the being he was now? Had someone else shaped his desire to be a different kind of person through communication, through connection, like he had with Travaris? Had the world been seduced by the ability to touch the life around them instead of passively receiving their footsteps? Would the elemental strongholds one day seek to walk or fly among their chosen family in the way Sol did?

Hel blinked and forced her mind free of the whirling influence of the planet as she ducked a violent slashing strike from a figure who should have been trying to capture her, not kill her. Sol's need for their power should've held their attackers back. It wasn't. Sol was losing control of his soldiers, the planet, and the contagion. That did not bode well for the worlds.

"I really hope you have a plan. Because I'm all out of ideas," Bast said as he wove a deadly mist into the air around them and watched flying soldiers slam to the earth like hail only to have more take their place. Sol's resources here were too great and he didn't care how many people he had to sacrifice for the greater good.

Hel took advantage of the momentary break in attack to turn into Bast's arms and wrap a portal around them that took them outside the immediate ring of fighters who'd been ambushing them and right next to the looming shard of stasis. Reaching down to the dirt beneath her feet where it met the alien metal of the shard, she opened another portal, swaying from the amount of power she was expending.

Travaris roared in her mind as the planet realised what she'd done. Hel slumped in Bast's arms as he flung them clear of the world's vengeance, catapulting them into the sky and away with his magic. The portal she'd opened at the shard's base led straight into the planet's molten core. Travaris took full advantage of the momentary opening to let forth a torrent of high-pressure magma at the shard like a fire hose seeking to extinguish the cross-dimensional threat embedded in the planet's skin.

The shard's surface blistered and cracked, but the fiery stream was quickly cut off by Sol erasing her portal as if it had never been.

"Enough!" Sol's voice echoed across the wide open plane and every being around them froze in place.

Silence fell, even Travaris held in thrall to the living star's command.

Hel reached out and gripped tight to Bast's hand a

second before both their bodies went rigid as Sol took hold of them with his power. She'd have to hope the contact would be enough to keep Bast's mind safe. She could feel his laboured breaths in her own lungs as he fought to stay calm. Their power twined so tight around each other it was impossible to tell where one started and the other ended. She could sense Bast calculating beside her, trying to find a weakness to exploit. Only there wasn't one.

"Stay!" Sol snapped as if they were errant pets in need of reining in.

He seemed to grow even taller as he spun mid-air to face the shard and reached a hand out toward it. Raw power rushed to his command, forcing Travaris to submit—forcing all the worlds linked through his portals to submit. This was it. Another melding. They'd failed. Again.

Right before the Shard could let his power loose, liquid shadow flickered in Hel's awareness and hope stuttered back to life in her heart as Sol's forehead creased in surprise. As half a dozen portals formed across the landscape, scattered seemingly at random, all hell broke loose.

Tir had joined the fight.

A giant wyrm from the Melded Earths reared up through one of the portals and snapped its jaws around four of Sol's fighters at once. Ripples of heat haze emerged from its skin as projectiles rained down on it. Fire exploded from its length, incinerating everything within a twenty-foot radius.

A flash of blue wings was followed by ice raining down in deadly spikes of hail as Nerida joined the fight.

Blood-red power washed across the ground, turning it into a lake of horror as hearts stopped and lungs perforated at Kairon's behest.

Sinuous tentacles carried more of Tir's people across the plane, their feet barely touching the ground as they joined the fight in their defence. Not all of them. Not even most. But those who had chosen to switch their allegiance more than made up for their low numbers with those portals and their vicious fangs as they flashed in and out of the world.

Ahead of her, a tentacled form appeared mid-air, tri-hinged jaws gaping as it ripped into an attacker's throat before disappearing in liquid shadow before gravity could have its way with the otherwise flightless beings.

The power holding Hel and Bast snapped and they tore toward Sol as he let loose a swathe of death, uncaring whether he took out friend or foe. With his attention split, he couldn't hold Travaris stable in the way he had before and geysers of rock started shooting up at random as the planet rejoined the fray. Travaris seemed just as uncaring of who it took out and Hel cried out in warning as a stone the size of a grapefruit tore into one of Nerida's men. His feathers were iridescent like a blue morpho butterfly, and the speeding missile tore through him like he was as delicate as one.

Stop! You're hurting our people! Hel shouted to the planet, but Travaris didn't listen, half-mad from fear and the effects of the contagion eroding its mind.

She didn't have time to calm it. Sol was already gathering himself for another salvo of destruction. Bast's fingers were still woven with hers and they clung to each other as they took in the scene before them.

"Our people can't take another hit like that. Not enough have come through and Sol is closing off Tir's portals," Bast said.

Hel watched in frustration as the swirling liquid shadow of Tir's constructs faded before her eyes.

"We at least need to distract him," Hel replied.

"Brute force it is, my love," Bast said, raising her hand to his lips and kissing her knuckles before he drew deep on their combined power to fire bolts of raw energy at Sol's form from all directions.

Sol dissipated them as easily as he had their first attack, but Bast was sending them from so many angles that it was at least preventing him from letting loose his counter-attack. The only problem was there was no way they could keep this up. Even with the dead and Travaris feeding them power, the effort of channelling so much magic, so fast, for so long, was catching up on them.

With no melding to draw power from, they were fading. Fast. And so were the forces who'd followed them here from the City of Souls.

Even as she watched, the majestic wyrm let loose a blood-curdling scream and took out another half dozen attackers as it writhed in its death throes, half its face blasted clear off and its brain matter oozing onto the barren soil of a planet impossibly far from its home. Her throat ached with sympathy as a voice that sounded like Nerida's let loose a mournful howl across the chaos of the battlefield.

At some point, Sol's starhounds had joined the fight and four of them had clamped onto the limbs of one of Tir's people, tearing at them until their limbs fell clear. The ceptae sacrificed its appendages like Tir had sacrificed their hand to avoid death from the venom the hounds' fangs would've been pumping into their bloodstream, but the move left them all but defenceless on the ground. Fuck, she hoped it wasn't Tir. She couldn't see well enough to tell. As the hounds swarmed onto the body, whose only defences were now its lashing tentacles and fangs, she turned her face away.

Tears streamed down her cheeks unchecked.

"Are you ready to put a stop to this?" Sol asked, his voice carrying clearly once more.

He'd landed on the ground, the rise and fall of his chest the only sign of the effort he'd spent. Hel could feel Travaris straining beneath his feet, murderous and not-so-slowly losing its mind.

"This could all have been avoided if you'd just done as I asked," Sol said.

"And you would have killed more people even faster," Hel snapped back.

A flash of white and gold behind Sol heralded Aliya's arrival. He barely acknowledged her presence at his back as Hel and Bast landed nearby. They didn't have the resources to fight this battle here. Her mind spun, thoughts frantic, as she tried to think of a way clear.

Kairon emerged from a cloud of dust nearby, limping slightly as blood dripped from his mouth—whether it was his or one of his victims, she couldn't tell. Nerida hovered in the air to their left. All of them waiting for something neither she nor Bast could give them—a victory.

Tir portalled into the space between them, missing an arm and with half their tentacles burned to a crisp, but still alive. Hel breathed a silent thank you that it hadn't been them who'd succumbed to the hounds and then felt guilty for whoever it was who'd died.

"I feel your essence. You are a life-giver. Why are you taking so many?" Kairon asked Sol, head cocked to the side in question.

Sol's gaze flicked over the vampyr. "It's the only way to save them," he said.

"Are you sure about that?" Nerida asked, her voice

sounding colder than she ever had before, like the deepest parts of the ocean she ruled. Grief was written in every line of her.

"I am older than you can fathom. I know the universe in a way you never will. You know nothing, elemental," Sol said.

His voice was calm, as if he had complete control and all the time in the world. Hel felt him reach for the damaged but still functioning shard and knew history was about to repeat itself. Millions would die. Again.

Before Sol could follow through, the air pressure plummeted and darkness cascaded around them in an instant as the contagion broke loose of its bindings. The wave had finally crashed, stretching over them to reach for the matching taint in the portal to the Melded Earths.

Sound became muffled and all sensation dulled.

The contagion pulsed everywhere she looked, surrounding them under a dome of its annihilation until there was only darkness and the absence of everything in all directions but for the last vestiges of the earth beneath their feet. The glow from Sol's body, and from her own, was the only light in that darkness—two parts of a single living star.

It wasn't their light that bought them this fleeting moment to contemplate their destruction, though. The final barrier that held back the darkness was the fading threadbare winds of the gathered souls swirling to protect her and Bast— the loyal dead flocking to protect the soulwoven bond of the Lord and Lady Soul, refusing to let them go.

You honour us. We thank you. Hel and Bast's voices twined together as one as they spoke to the dead.

We will hold you safe. You can still save them. All of them. Hurry, they said.

Hel was so distracted by the actions beyond the veil of the living, she almost forgot they weren't alone in the eye of this apocalyptic storm until Nerida spoke in response to Sol's words.

"Perhaps. But I know vengeance. My family died today. I may not be a match for your power, but I will be sure to take yours with me before I go," Nerida said, and a tornado of water surrounded Sol's daughter Stella where she stood behind her mother. Hel hadn't even noticed her there.

Chaos reigned as the move broke their shared paralysis and everyone seemed to act at once. Sol's focus, for once, was on his only daughter, his brow furrowed as if the magic threatening to drown her was merely an inconvenience. He was surrounded by predators and, even as powerful as he was, he shouldn't have shifted his attention for even a second.

Kairon was beside him in a split second, his eerily fast movements bringing him close enough to touch a single finger to his skin. Blood beaded on the surface of Sol's neck as Kairon drew it from his veins in far greater quantities than when he'd used this trick on Nerida in the earlier battle. Tir portalled to Sol's other side, tentacles wrapping tight around his throat to divert him from killing the brave vampyr jumping to Nerida's aid. Aliya screamed and the water around Stella dispersed as the two elemental ladies went head to head—water magic versus air.

Hel and Bast added their power to the assault against Sol, but they both knew it was a losing battle and a distraction they couldn't afford with the contagion looming close threatening to destroy them all. They needed to portal everyone clear before it was too late. As much as she hated Sol for everything he'd done, she knew his vast power might prove vital to the worlds' defence. No one was expendable in this fight against the devouring darkness. Not that any of them had the power to kill him, anyway.

"Stop!" Hel called.

No one was more surprised than her when everyone paused in their dance of death. It was Aliya's voice that replied.

"No."

Sol's eyes widened in shock as the tip of a golden blade emerged from his chest. He looked down in surprise as his own sword pierced his heart from behind—Starkiller. Aliya, standing right behind him, looked almost as surprised to be holding its hilt.

As Sol twisted to face her, Hel could see her hands were trembling where she held the weapon. Was that a tear tracking down her face? She hadn't thought the ruthless Lady of Air had it in her to feel remorse. Veins of searing starlight radiated up Sol's neck and face from the wound in his chest, cracking open with flashes of blinding light before resealing and opening again.

"You said sacrifice was necessary, my love. You have the power they need. And you are only one person. No one else needs to die. Our daughter doesn't need to die," Aliya whispered.

"You don't have the power to kill me, Aliya. Even with Starkiller," Sol said.

"No. But you have the power to let me succeed and save them all," she whispered. "End this. For your daughter. Or, if not for her, then for yourself and the part of you that will live on in Hel."

Sol's eyes turned to Hel's and she drowned in the galaxy of their depths.

"I will return for you, little star," he said, and then that searing light that had been flashing in bursts from the cracks in his skin became impossibly brighter. Everything else faded from view but for that and the black hole of absence that surrounded them swallowing even Sol's vast light as his true essence slipped free from the body that had contained it.

It was a death of sorts. And it was a new connection between Sol's star-self, the myriad portals he maintained across the multiverse, and the planet beneath their feet to whom he was sacrificing himself to save.

The rush of power inside their last remaining bubble of reality was immense for both Hel and Bast. Far greater than a melding and like nothing they'd ever felt before. They would never find a source of magic more perfectly tailored to them. Never have such an exquisite moment of all-consuming transcendence.

Hel drew that power into herself like she was bringing it home, gorging on the light that would make her complete. That would make her whole again.

She was a star. A ruler. An Empress.

With this power weaving so close with Bast's, she could save everyone and ascend the throne that was rightfully hers.

Blinking in confusion, terror filled her as her sense of self was cast adrift in an ocean of starlight and Sol's essence flooded through her in an inevitable tide.

No. No no no no no. I'm NOT HIM, she silently screamed.

CHAPTER 15

BAST

Bast clung to his mate's presence in his soul as he felt her dissipate in a way that should not have been possible, like everything that made her his was fading away. Like everything that made her *her* was dissolving.

"We'll never overcome the contagion if you destroy her," he growled into the surrounding starlight that would've blinded him if it wasn't being consumed by the contagion he was now finally able to push back a little with the power of Sol's 'death' flooding through him.

Sol's corporeal form had died and, with it, the thinly veiled constraints on his vast energy. Bast didn't really understand how he could have died so spectacularly and yet still be causing fucking havoc around them, but who knew what a living star was capable of. Apparently, he'd seized the opportunity to try and recombine the two parts of his essence. Was he a dying star now, or was he reverting to his natural state? It didn't matter. What mattered was his mate clinging tight to him as the pressure forcing its way inside

225

her finally abated. Sol seemed to have realised the truth of Bast's statement and abandoned his bombardment of her identity.

"Fuck *off*, Sol!" Hel screamed into the void.

The murderous rage buzzing through his veins was all the reassurance he needed that his mate was still herself. He turned his attention back to the black hole of contagion surrounding them and their people. They needed a solution. Now.

"Still with me, Hellcat?" he whispered in Hel's ear, kissing her skin and drawing her scent into his lungs to reassure himself.

"Yeah." Hel sounded dazed, her essence in shock from whatever Sol had done to her. Bast wrapped his soul around hers even tighter, holding her safe and present through their mating bond.

"I'm going to try and construct a shield against the contagion around Travaris. I need your help, my love."

Hel's response was a gift. Her trust in him, her belief in him, shone strong through their connection as she placed herself between him and the vast power of the dying star that threatened to consume them, filtering it with her essence so he could weave it into something that might hold.

Her mind's voice rang through him as she spoke to Travaris and all those planets linked to it through the portals that still stood just inside the fast-contracting dome of dark contagion surrounding them. He wished he had time to marvel at Hel's power because it was a thing of beauty to watch her speak to the very earth beneath their feet and all the worlds countless lightyears beyond.

Help us, she begged, and the thirteen worlds connected there answered her call, anchoring them against the dual pressure of the tides of darkness and light that threatened to wash them away.

The release of a star's worth of power around them was the missing piece of the puzzle they'd been solving. The magic instinctually formed itself into the strands he needed, still controlled by Sol's consciousness even with the death of his physical form, or perhaps *because* of the death of his physical form. Now Sol wasn't trying to force his way into Hel's body, all their focus was on constructing a shield through Travaris in the same way Bast had shielded Hel from his soulweaving.

The scale was so much larger than anything he'd ever attempted, but it was a relief to have somewhere to channel so much power despite the pain searing at their souls as he clung tight to Hel.

The first step was to push the contagion threatening to consume them back to the breach through which it had first entered this world. Bast's power channelled from the souls beyond had always repelled the contagion and the starlight of Sol's death seemed to revel in its newfound power over the dark threat. Its light forced the contagion to give ground, confined into a tighter and tighter space. As the contagion ebbed, the starlight surrounding them grew ever brighter and hotter, becoming a threat itself to the world around them. Hel was the only thing standing between them and instant annihilation as she fought to keep that part of Sol, of herself, from harming their people.

"We're spread too thin. Bring the portals closer," Bast said through gritted teeth as he fought to hold his focus through the torrent of power. If they wavered for even a second, it would consume them.

As Hel called Sol's twelve portals to them, Bast called to

the dead. The souls who answered came from every single one of those worlds, united in their need to help them overcome the threat to the families they'd left behind. Even the dead of Sol's loyal armies supported them, sensing their emperor's residual power flowing through and around them.

When Bast had saved Hel from the soul taint of his power, he'd used the scans Ra and Zee had made of his protections to construct a kind of magical antibody anchored in the structure of her wings. Planets didn't have wings, but as he stretched his awareness out through his power, he found something that would work just as well—the stars that created the planets' orbits, their mass directing their flight through their solar system. The network of the souls they'd been home to guided him like a memory of its lifeblood.

Each star would anchor their magic, keep it self-sustaining, and the souls would carry it to every shadowed corner of the worlds. The dead would protect the planets that had once sustained them just like they protected the City of Souls, holding reality safe with their willpower and using the power they channelled to eject the contagion from their presence.

Reality faded away from him as he worked except for the power he was weaving and Hel's presence in his every cell. She'd done as he asked, the comforting burn of her power drawing the twelve permanent portals of Travaris closer until they framed the black hole that was the source of the contagion like a guard of honour, like vultures waiting for the threat to finally die, like a shrine to the stars who had died and to those that would give them back their life.

Bast and Hel were tiny compared to the scale on which they worked their magic. They were nothing but two specks of dust trying to shift shadow and encircle solar systems in their arms. As Sol's essence and his death tore through them, Bast lost control of the construct, becoming nothing more than a channel as the stars and planets used him and his mate to protect themselves from the reality contagion that had threatened them for so many years.

Bast watched, unable to cry out as Hel stepped forward in a daze, footsteps not her own, and stood in the centre of the portal that led to the contagion. Too close. Too far past its threshold. Through her skin, he could feel the absence tearing at her soul, at both their souls because they were two halves of a whole. Her breathing stopped and his own lungs halted in sympathy. She could go without oxygen longer than anyone he knew, but how long could she hold on with the contagion licking a mere atom-width from her body. He focused everything he had on holding her to this world, wreathing her skin in his power's protection as her hand drifted out, dreamlike, and started pinching the portal closed.

The searing heat of Hel's power felt like no more than a flickering match against the darkness and he could sense the depth of the contagion's reach stretching out beyond the portal. So many worlds lost. So much darkness. So much death that was more final than death should ever be. Souls rushed to his aid as his mind slipped closer to the portal, closer to Hel, closer to the end. Each one was a tiny light against that endless void. A million lives lived. A billion whispers against the silence. The hope to his rising despair.

Their strength let him stagger forward to his mate, bolstering his arms as they wrapped tight around her wings from behind to pull her back to his chest. And all the time, the stars and worlds were pulling from them, pulling through them, to create the constructs that would keep them safe.

Tugging Hel back the half-step needed to clear the portal's edge, he slid his hands through hers, twining their fingers as he twined their power even tighter and helped her pull the rift in reality closed. If this was the end for them, he knew they would both go down fighting. Fighting, and loving. They would get this fucking thing closed if it was the last thing they did and then they could let go wrapped around each other in every way they could be—physically, magically, and emotionally. Soul mates. Always.

Maybe he should've felt something about the fact that their unique bond had turned out to be the answer to what the worlds needed, but this close to the end all he could care about was that Hel was the answer to *his* need, his everything, just like he was hers.

I love you. Hel's mind voice was barely more than a fading whisper in his mind.

I love you, too. Forever, Bast replied.

The closing of the portal ricocheted through reality, its event horizon collapsing into itself with a backlash of explosive power that ripped through them, tearing at everything they were. And still they weren't finished, couldn't let go, because the stars and worlds were still dragging the endless power released by Sol's death through their bodies to wrap around them like a cloak of protection.

The dead swarmed from the place beyond, answering the call of those who'd stayed behind in a way Bast hadn't even known was possible as they stretched themselves around their earthly homes, cocooning them in their protection. If he survived this, he would never be without power again because in every world they were connected to, the souls of the dead now stood as a satellite guard against the darkness.

Through Hel's connection to the worlds he felt the last spots of contagion being rejected by the Melded Earths and he breathed a sigh of relief. The portals in the City of Souls had reintroduced the darkness to their world and he'd worried what would happen if they didn't make it home to contain it.

Kaia, Ana, Ra, and everyone they loved were safe. The city was safe. The Melded Earths were safe. The contagion had retreated into itself, hemmed on all sides by worlds now immune to its dark absence—an impenetrable wall of protection between it and the rest of the universe.

They could let go now.

Hel's beautiful eyes staring back at him were the last thing he saw as his own slipped closed. Eyes the colour of home. Her essence still burned bright despite their bone-deep exhaustion. As their bodies hit the ground, they went down in flames—burning for each other.

Just like they'd started.

CHAPTER 16
HEL

Everything hurt.

Every. Fucking. Thing.

Even the damn horns emerging from her skull she still hadn't gotten used to even after over a month. Her skin felt like it had been stretched three sizes larger than it needed to be and then left to snap back onto her bones like it was a rubber band pulled tight and lined with shards of broken glass. Her soul ached. Her magic was like acid against her awareness, but also against itself? Did magic even have nerves? It did now.

Her groan of pain made it worse. Strained vocal cords scratched like gravel in her dry throat. Someone pressed something cold to her lips and she was so out of it that all she did was open them and accept whatever it was.

Ice melted on her tongue and trickled welcome relief through her insides as she finally managed to swallow on her fourth attempt. A minute later, soft fingers touched her own and that same coolness radiated from them throughout the rest of her, taking the worst of the pain away. Some of the fog lifted from her brain and her heartrate picked up in sudden panic. What happened? Where was she?

"Bast!" she croaked out, trying and failing to scramble upright and search for her mate.

"Relax," a familiar male voice she couldn't quite place said. "He's right there beside you. The bed's just really big for all that extra wing you folk carry around."

Hel flung a trembling arm out until it connected with the familiar feathers of Bast's wing somewhere beside her. She'd know them anywhere. If she was a little more with it and a little less raw, she would've realised she could feel his presence so close through their connection. Taking a breath now she knew he was alive and safe, she dragged her eyelids open and blinked until the world came into focus. A pale face framed by jet-black hair was leaning over her, the light teasing of his earlier words belied by the concern in his eyes.

"Kairon?" she asked.

"I wondered if you'd remember me. We met so briefly and so very far away," the vampyr said, smoothing out the covers she'd twisted around herself in her panic.

"You made the pain better," she said.

"I did."

Hel could see the strain on his face. As if he hadn't just made the pain abate but had taken some of it into himself to spare her. "Thank you."

Kairon inclined his head and shifted to give her some space. "It's the least I can do when your efforts saved my people and so many more."

"How long?"

"The days do not pass the same here as on our world. A week since you exploded the portal. Give or take."

A flash of energy through their bond was followed by a low moan from Bast beside her as he finally woke.

"Let's get some food in you both. There is much to do and we need to get you home," Kairon said.

Hel almost whimpered at his words. She was so tired. They both were. She didn't want to do anything but shuffle across the bed and into Bast's arms. But her endlessly responsible mate was already struggling upright, concern for her and for their home ringing clear in the connection between them.

Sighing, she let Kairon support her until she was leaning against the headboard.

A solid meal and a hot shower later, Hel felt vaguely more alive although her energy levels were still shot. They managed to limp over to the couch at least instead of going back to bed. With her head leaning on Bast's shoulder as their wings brushed against each other, she finally processed her surroundings just as a door opened across the room. Her spine stiffened as Aliya entered.

"Relax. I'm not going to kill you. I need you to get home. Kairon called me to say we'd be heading out as soon as you're ready," the Air Lady said. She looked wrecked, for once too exhausted and grief-ridden for the arrogance and ruthlessness that epitomised her.

"Why are we in Sol's room?" Hel asked Kairon, too tired to even swear despite wanting to ask him what the fuck he was thinking to let them rest there.

"Your connection to the planet here was all that was keeping you alive. We couldn't risk removing you from this world and you needed medical treatment. This was the safest place to take you and once Sol's people realised he was gone and you'd saved the worlds together, they insisted you take his room. Apparently, he'd named you as his successor in the event of his death."

"I'm not even sure he really died," Bast said, voice as croaky as her own. Kairon handed him a glass of water and sat down with them. It didn't escape Hel's notice that he kept himself between them and the Lady of Air, guarding them.

Hel frowned. "What? Of course he did."

Bast shook his head. "He released a huge amount of power, but it didn't feel right. I don't think stars live and die the way we do..." his worlds trailed off as he looked at Hel and they both realised that meant she wouldn't live and die the same way either. She wasn't Sol, but she was something similar. She'd have to figure it out later. A lot later.

A throat cleared from nearby and Sol's daughter Stella appeared in the doorway. Great. Just what she needed. An even larger audience to the fact she was so weak she could barely sit upright. Bast threaded their fingers together and squeezed gently.

"You're correct. We don't," Stella said.

"Stella! Where have you been? I had people out searching," Aliya cried, striding towards her daughter with the closest thing to caring Hel had ever seen on her face.

Hel watched Sol's child warily as she side-stepped around Aliya to move closer to them. Even in the few times they'd met, she could sense something had changed about the young woman. She was holding herself differently, her gait heavier. As she stared into Stella's eyes, the slightest flash of a galaxy stirred in their depths that hadn't been there before. Was she coming into her power? Or had Sol found easier prey after Hel had resisted his efforts to turn them back into one being? Reaching out with her magical senses, she ignored the burn of pain from her overextended mind and scanned Stella's power signature.

Horror filled her at what she found and a strangled gasp escaped her. Bast's grip on her hand grew tighter as he processed the information her power fed to them both.

"Interesting," Stella said. No. Not Stella. Sol. "I didn't think you would notice. I was hoping you wouldn't, given how drained we all are."

"What the fuck? She was your daughter! And you've just taken her body over like some kind of fucking puppet?" Hel yelled.

"This way I can still protect my empire and guard the crossroads. I couldn't abandon them. The alternative was you staying here to rule in my place. Which would you prefer?" Sol said.

A scream of pure despair rang through the room—Aliya. The Lady of Air lunged toward her daughter, to do what Hel had no idea. If there was one thing the bitch was, it was loyal to her offspring and she didn't think Aliya would risk damaging Stella's body in case she was still buried somewhere deep inside.

The world slowed.

Aliya's progress paused, her body leaning forward mid stride and her wings flared wide behind her in a flash of brilliant white and gold. The blood in Hel's veins turned sluggish and her breath stayed trapped in her lungs. Bast's fingers tightened infinitesimally on hers, but they were both incapable of doing anything about what was happening in front of them. Kairon jumped to his feet, but even his usually impossibly fast movements looked like he was swimming through treacle.

Something was deeply wrong with the passage of time.

Something that felt like the familiar searing heat of a thousand suns.

The only one who seemed unaffected by the shift in how time passed was Sol in Stella's body. Taking the final step closer to Aliya, he drew the delicate sword hanging at what was once his daughter's waist and stabbed up through Aliya's solar plexus. The same strike she'd used to kill his last body, only this time she was facing him, forced to watch his every movement as death came for her.

A trickle of blood formed at the corner of Aliya's mouth and dripped down her chin as he twisted his wrist and dragged the blade higher, right up through her heart, cutting through bone like it was butter. The move seemed to break the magic's effect on the Lady of Air and she dropped to her knees before him.

"How could you? She was your daughter," Aliya gasped, the blood foaming in bubbles as she bled out into her lungs.

"You betrayed me. It was always going to end this way, Aliya."

The Lady of Air toppled forward, the pommel of the sword thumping against the wooden floor and pushing even further into her chest as Sol released its hilt.

Pushing her body aside with his foot, Sol met Hel's horrified gaze, seemingly unfazed by killing his lover. "You did us proud, little star. Perhaps you're right and you have become your own person. If anyone could do that with the start you had, it's a part of me. One day, we will sit down and chat about your future. But I can see that might take a few centuries. I will let you leave for now. I'm curious how your power will develop with this mating. Until next time, little star. Don't stay too long or I might change my mind about letting you go."

And with that, Sol took off out of the balcony at full speed as the rest of them remained stuck in slow motion.

Hel wasn't sure how long time crawled around them. Eventually, Kairon became a blur of motion as the lunge he'd started to face Sol's threat coalesced and was then aborted in favour of pressing slender fingers to the pulse point at Aliya's neck. She was already gone. They'd all seen the light leave her eyes as they were forced to watch, motionless and soundless.

"Fuck," Hel said.

"Yeah. Fuck," Bast agreed.

"We need to get out of here," Kairon said, much more sensibly.

In their defence, they'd just woken up after a week so close to death Hel could still feel the concerned souls forcefully holding them back from the place beyond.

"I don't think I could form a portal to save my life right now," Hel said, her mind still spinning with what it all meant.

Bast shot upright beside her and she felt his fear as her own as he asked the question she was too overwhelmed to even think of. "Is the portal the army came through still open? Is our home at risk?"

"Tir closed it after Nerida and the others went back through. Sol's army retreated here as soon as the dust settled and we didn't want anyone sneaking out. Tir said they'll get us home. They've been busy meeting with their people and trying to figure out where they're going to go," Kairon said.

"They don't want to stay here?" Hel asked.

Kairon seemed to be deciding how much they could handle in their current state, but he didn't hold back when he finally answered. "Half the planet was destroyed, either during the fighting or when you expelled the contagion. They were already homeless, but now there's nowhere to rebuild."

Hel blinked back frustrated tears. It was their decisions that had made the ceptae homeless. Turning her head up to Bast, she drew his scent into her lungs that somehow still smelled like the winds of home over the harbour even though they were lightyears away.

"We owe Tir. And we owe them," she said.

"Some of them may still be loyal to your ... to Sol," Bast said in answer to the unspoken question hanging between them, but there was nothing but acceptance in his voice.

"Taking in more strays?" Kairon asked, a self-deprecating smirk on his face.

Bast held Hel's gaze for another breath and they had an entire silent conversation in those seconds. A conversation of responsibility and of honour. A conversation of partnership in the truest sense of the word. One would not decide without the other. And both were absolutely certain they would have the backing of the city's other leaders. It was who they were after all.

THEY FOUND Tir and their people in the charred remains of the refugee camp she'd only ever seen from above. As they walked through the gathered ceptae, Hel swallowed hard, holding back the tide of grief and guilt washing over her. Everywhere she looked, she could see signs of the battle they'd fought—bloody bandages, missing limbs, and the scared faces of children whose tentacles trembled as they passed. Did they fear them?

Pausing next to an uprooted tree, Hel crouched down before a child only as high as her hip, letting her silver wings drape in the soot and dust behind her.

"Thank you for saving us," the child said, their voice soft and sibilant as their parent came and placed a comforting hand on their shoulder.

The words broke Hel's heart.

"It's you who saved us," she said.

"So what are you going to do about it?" Tir called from nearby.

The noise of the crowd around them quieted and Hel straightened, standing shoulder to shoulder with her mate as Kairon watched on.

"We will forever be grateful to the ceptae for rallying to our side when we'd lost hope. And to Tir for their friendship, their generosity, and for saving our asses more times than I can count. Our actions hurt your people and we are so fucking sorry for that," Hel's voice cracked on the words and she fought the urge to stare down at her scuffed combat boots. She wouldn't hide from her responsibility to the ceptae. "We can't take that pain away. We can't bring back your homes here. But we can promise to help you rebuild your lives if that's what you choose. Together. We'd be honoured to welcome you to the City of Souls."

"How do we know we'll be safe there?" someone called.

It was Bast who replied. "The City of Souls took us in and became our refuge. Even though my own people despised me for what I was. Even though Hel is so unique they couldn't hope to understand the beauty and courage of who she is. The greatest strength of our people is in our differences. It's in the respect we hold for each other and the willingness to listen and truly hear the needs and contributions of each person who lives there. That may not always make for the easiest road. We will all make mistakes, but we will never stop trying. Never stop listening. The Soul Court will *always* protect those who need a place to call home."

"Always," Hel affirmed.

"Well, that is just as well. Because we already voted to accompany you home," Tir said.

Hel snorted softly, lips twisting up in a grin Tir returned in a flash of sharp teeth as their dry humour eased the ache of guilt in her chest the tiniest bit.

"We accept your apology. Without your actions, everything would've been lost. That doesn't make what happened okay, but intent matters. As does taking responsibility. We will be proud to walk into the future with you," the other ceptae added, and Hel made a point of memorising their features. She suspected they'd be dealing with this elder a lot in the future.

As the familiar liquid shadow of Tir's power coalesced to their left and the ceptae gathered with what was left of their belongings, Hel took one last look around the beautiful, broken, scarred battleground that was Travaris. The auroral lights of the shielding overhead brightened for a moment, a farewell from Sol that she ignored. Reaching out to the earth beneath her feet, she connected with the ravaged awareness of the planet. Despite the damage done, it felt more stable than it ever had before now the constant threat of the contagion eating away at its surface was gone and the souls of the dead formed a protective cocoon around its vast essence.

Farewell Travaris. Heal. Live.

The planet's response was wordless, its consciousness all but dormant while it recovered. Beneath the lingering scents of magma and death, the zephyr of wind that wafted between them in reply smelled of growing things and hope.

Bast pulled her close and pressed a kiss to her temple, wrapping an impossibly black wing around her as they stepped up to Tir's portal together, the ceptae gathering at their back.

"Come on, Hellcat. It's time to go home."

CHAPTER 17
BAST

One month later

Bast's eyes rolled back in his head and his groan echoed off the elevator walls in Soul Tower as he clenched a fist around one of Hel's horns, restraining himself from doing anything more than holding her close and using that extra touch as an anchor against the sheer pleasure rushing through them both.

"Fuck. I'm so close. What are you doing to me, Hellkitten?"

Hel's eyes glittered as she stared up at him from where she knelt before him, his cock in her mouth. The Lady of Souls. On her knees. Because she wanted to be. Who was he kidding? She was still totally in control of this and he was loving every second of it. As was she judging by the endorphin high he was getting down their bond. He had no idea how their fucked up relationship and worlds had brought

243

them here, but he was grateful every day. There was no sweeter feeling in the world. Even if it was going to make them very, very late for the worldwide multi-species summit they were about to portal their people to.

Hel pulled back, drawing another long groan from him as she responded to the thoughts he hadn't bothered verbalising. It wasn't uncommon for them to communicate without words, their connection deeper than ever after everything they'd been through.

"Better hurry up then. Wouldn't want to keep them waiting," Hel teased, before swallowing him down to the hilt, her nose nuzzling into his groin as she did something criminal with her tongue that had him seeing literal stars.

A teasing voice crackled over the elevator intercom—Ra. "You two planning on joining us anytime soon or shall I go find Tir to get this party started?"

Hel's mouth curved in a smile, humming around Bast's length in the way she knew drove him crazy, and he smashed his hand onto the alarm button to cover his cries of pleasure as he lost control and thrust into her with abandon until his orgasm rocked through him.

Panting like he'd flown halfway across the world, he pulled Hel to her feet by her muscled biceps as soon as he could manage and spun them so she was pinned to the wall. Their kiss was pure passion and dirty enough to threaten to set them going again despite the fact they'd both just had their way with each other. His knees still ached where he'd worshipped her before she'd gotten her revenge. His cock tried to rally as he tasted himself on her lips.

"Fuck. We really are late," Hel moaned, as he bit his way down her throat, his fingers running over and over the subtle bump where her birth control implant sat on her arm.

"Don't even think about it, necromancer," Hel warned, as she felt the turn of his thoughts.

He grinned and bit her harder, making her curse and reach for her baton.

The alarm he'd been ignoring shut off and Ra's voice filled the elevator again. "For real, though. We do actually need you to get down here, bro. Hel, stop tormenting the man."

"Never!" Hel said, laughing.

It was a month since they'd returned from Travaris and the core of his mate was the same gloriously prickly, challenging woman she'd always been, but the eternal weight of being hunted, of holding the future of their world on their shoulders, was finally gone. Not forgotten, but firmly and purposefully set aside so they could live. Truly live.

He knew just how much of her thoughts and emotions had been tied up in running from her father. He'd experienced it himself running from his brother's assassins. But it was one thing to know it, and another to watch her realise she was truly free. To see her portal to Matiu to help the native griffins without worrying about discovery. To see her playing in the skies with the city's elemental children as they taught her the aerial acrobatics she hadn't had time to learn.

The only black lining to their silver cloud was Kaia. Where the events of the last year had finally set Hel free, it had come at a heavy price. So many lives lost. So much destruction. Nothing wrenched quite so painfully as the effect on the niece of their hearts. Kaia's power was dangerously unstable after the days she'd spent being drained by her captors. She needed training from the best elemental mages, and she needed it yesterday. But she was so fragile, so traumatised.

She'd been a ball of sunshine just like Ra but with the innocence and trust that only the young can sustain. All that was gone now. She barely spoke to them. Spent long hours in her room. She was in so much danger every day from her own power, but none of them could face making her leave. Sending her away alone to one of the other courts when she was barely hanging on seemed like the worst kind of neglect. That thought reminded him of the other neglect he needed to make sure never happened again—the soulweaving infants like the one he'd helped while he was searching for Hel who now resided in the Tower.

"We'll figure it out and keep her safe. We'll keep them all safe," Hel whispered in his ear, once again sensing the direction his thoughts had gone. "One wingbeat at a time."

He sighed and held her tighter, kissing her temple. "Guess we'd better get flying then," he said, pushing the button on the elevator that would set them moving again.

They were only two floors from their destination. It wasn't enough time to avoid the good-natured teasing from their people as they emerged from the elevator too dishevelled for polite society. Oh well. It's not like anyone would be surprised. They were ravenous for one another and always would be.

Hel raised her middle finger at Ra as he catcalled them, striding past him toward the council chamber where everyone had gathered. With a succession battle still playing out in the Air Court, the other courts had finally acknowledged his and Hel's power with a formal invitation to the Soul Court to attend all future council sessions. They'd declined, stating they were only interested in attending if there were representatives from all the peoples now resident on the Melded Earths—humans, vampyr, and ceptae alike, including the separatist organisations around the world.

They'd both been pleasantly surprised when the other rulers had agreed. The first summit of the Melded Earths was being held in the Antarctic, as neutral a territory as anyone could find, with the ceptae acting as transportation for those who needed it, mostly via Tir. It turned out that portalling was as rare a power in their people as it was everywhere else with only a handful who were capable, and of those most were limited to portalling within the world they occupied, not between worlds like Tir.

The thirteen vampyr voices, five of the ceptae, and seven human leaders had accepted the invitation to attend along with Bast and Hel, and the other three elemental court rulers. They were probably missing some groups, but it was a start at least. A lower-level Air Court member was attending as well to report back to whoever came to power. It was either that or invite every contender for the Air Court leadership and no one could be bothered with the shitshow that would be.

Bast pulled Hel aside before she could set up the portal and combed his fingers through her silver hair, brushing her sensitive horns as he set it to rights before smoothing the creases from the linen of her shirt with a touch of his power. He couldn't help ducking his head to claim a kiss while he was at it and as she opened her mouth to let his tongue gain entrance, he lost track of their surroundings until a chorus of wolf whistles reminded him they had an audience.

They pulled apart reluctantly, Hel smirking at him as she returned the attention he'd just given her and straightened his suit as she tried to make it look a little less like they'd just blown each other in an elevator on the way there.

Ra's arms looped around both their necks when she was done. "Finished primping?" he asked.

Bast shoved his friend's shoulder before grabbing the back of his neck and pulling him into a hug, resting their foreheads together. He was so fucking proud of the man he called brother. Ra had worked tirelessly over the previous weeks, wrangling and cajoling the courts into accepting this summit, and doing everything needed to set them up for success. Bast and Hel's power might be what made the rulers listen, but it was the vision of the city's ruling partnership and Ra's raw determination and fierce drive for equity that had pulled it all together.

"You did so good, brother. First you saved me, now you're going to save the whole fucking world."

Ra's deep familiar laugh filled the space. "Nah, bro. World saving's your gig. I'm just nagging you all until you remember to talk to each other. Besides, there's a better than average chance this thing will end in bloodshed. Don't jinx it before we even get there."

Bast smiled and let his friend go. "Everyone ready?" he asked, addressing the gathered people in the room—Kairon, Tir, and Niko, who were coming with them, and Ana, Morrigan, and a still wan-looking Ryker who would hold the fort at home.

Kairon's people had somehow kept the chief executive of the couriers alive, but losing one of his wings had hit him hard. He was healing slowly for an elemental. Ryker must've seen the look of concern on his face because he waved him off, straightening his shoulders and letting his remaining burgundy wing rustle out before pulling it in tight to his back.

"No Kaia today?" Bast whispered to Ana as she hugged him farewell.

The older woman shook her head as she dropped it to his shoulder, hiding her face. "I don't know how to help her."

Bast kissed Ana's forehead softly as Hel wrapped an arm around her other side.

"We've got her. We won't let her down. Kia kaha. Kia māia," his mate murmured to her. Stay strong. Be brave. Words his mate lived by.

THEY EMERGED from Hel's portal into a world of cold and white. Nerida had taken responsibility for constructing the space in which they would discuss the future of the Melded Earths. She was probably the only one with enough spare power to do so. Ty had almost burned himself out when he'd single-handedly held their defences in the City of Souls after Nerida and Kairon joined them in Travaris. The Air Court was a write-off until they had a ruler again. Bast and Hel had been totally caught up in repairing damage from the attack and finding homes for the influx of vampyr and ceptae in the city when they weren't trying to figure out how to help Kaia and the others injured in the battle recover. And Mica looked worse each time they saw him, still struggling with the catastrophic damage to his living home, his stronghold. Bast hadn't truly understood the symbiotic relationship the court rulers had with their sentient homes until he'd seen how rough these months had been for the Earth Lord. When the contagion had destroyed the core of the caves that made up the earth stronghold, it hadn't just damaged limestone and rock. It had fundamentally damaged the psyches of everyone who lived there, the Earth Lord most of all.

The Water Lady had done a stunning job with the venue. It wasn't surprising, given the medium of her construction was snow and ice. She was well-suited to the task. In a rare moment of diplomacy, she'd avoided the kind of ostentatious display the elementals were known for that would've driven the human separatists to distraction. Instead, she'd created simple elegance, the sweeping wave-like lines of the main chamber soothing to the eye. The only concession to the usual ostentatious elemental style was the soaring ceiling height and the balconies higher up that would allow the winged among them to take off from inside the building if needed.

They'd picked the location to be near the old human South Pole Research Station, fixing it up so they had func-tioning facilities to use. The boxy building was somehow complemented by Nerida's construct rather than over-whelmed by it, the human and elemental architecture seam-lessly integrating just like they did in the City of Souls.

It was a start anyway. A new beginning. They would not solve the world's problems in these three days, but the dialogue and connection between their peoples would be given a chance to form. It's always easier to hate a nameless, faceless person than one who passed you the jam for your scone over morning tea.

Other than paving the way for a more equitable power balance, there was only one other thing Bast needed to achieve from this meeting. He'd returned to Bolivia shortly after they arrived home and ensured the soulweaver baby whose mother he'd helped would be safe from his powers as he grew up, but he'd seen the way the infant's own family looked on with fear. His grandparents refused to even touch the baby when his mother stepped away for a moment and he started crying. That was no way to live.

Hel squeezed his leg under the table as he prepared to rise and speak on the last day, her support now the foundation that held him steady. When he stood, so did she. Right alongside him. In some ways, it would be harder to gain the courts' acceptance of soulweaving than it was to integrate the two new species into their world. Kairon and Tir didn't have to overcome generations of prejudice and fear. Soulweaving would always be an incredibly rare magic, but in a people who lived forever, that still meant there would be many more babies over the years ahead. Or at least there could be now he could shield them from the dangerous taint that would've killed them.

The gathered leaders quieted where they sat as he cleared his throat to speak, turning to him with slight frowns. He hadn't put this item on the agenda because it wasn't up for debate.

"Hel and I have an announcement," he started.

Hel snorted softly beside him as several faces softened with smiles. "We're not fucking pregnant," she sniped.

He grinned down at her. She could be diplomatic when she wanted, but he doubted she'd want very often.

Turning back to the gathered peoples, he continued. "No, we're not pregnant. But we *are* welcoming the soulweavers of the world into our home. This is your notice that if a child is born in your territory with my power, we will be there to protect them and they will always have a safe place with us if they want it. The dead are watching and they will tell us all. We will not tolerate persecution, and you cannot hide them from us."

Unsurprisingly, it was the elementals who looked most discomfited at his words.

"Will you build an army of necromancers then, Bastion?" Ty asked.

His brother's voice was still full of disdain, but he was using Bast's actual name, which was a pretty huge step forward. It was Hel who answered him, head held high and her stunning silver wings flared out to catch the morning sunlight through the ice walls.

"No. We will build a sanctuary of soulweavers," she said.

"Are there even any children like you in the world? It's so rare," Nerida said, her face giving nothing away about how she felt about the announcement.

"We've transferred two children from the Air Court already. One born there recently and one taken from the Fire Court and kept in Caelus' cells for research." Bast's voice cracked with rage on those last words.

A fortnight earlier, they'd finally tracked down the reason the Air Court mages had become so adept at countering his power. They'd been practising with an all but feral ten-year-old soulweaver. Who knew how long they'd held the child captive and forced to perform. He'd figured out some protection from the soul taint instinctively like Bast had, but he hadn't been as successful. He was alive, but his mind was ... different. Broken. He might always be different. That was okay though, so long as he was safe. So long as they were all safe.

"You're stealing our children now, necromancer?" the representative from the Air Court spat.

Her name was Violette and she'd been more trouble than she was worth these last few days. Her wings were a dusky cream rather than the white and gold of the court's powerful mages. She knew she was only there because she didn't have enough power to be a threat to any of the contenders for ruler of the Air Court and she had an inferiority complex about it. It wasn't her fault. Her life had probably been miserable growing up in the most power-hungry of spaces. But at this point, Bast didn't give a shit. She needed to shut up and show some respect.

"Watch yourself," Hel snarled at the woman, jumping to his defence as she echoed his feelings.

"To be fair, you did trespass on Air Court lands and take two of their people. If Aliya were still here, this conversation would likely be much more violent," Nerida said, voice still calm. "Your ability to portal needs some controls around it, Helaine."

Bast exhaled in frustration. He should've anticipated Nerida's angle on this. He couldn't see her objecting to him saving children. Most elementals held them as precious, given how rarely they conceived. But he could see her getting anxious about their ability to invade their territories at will.

"Helaine is not the only one with that power. Would you hamstring my people?" Tir asked.

Nerida glanced over at the Archivist. "Helaine is different. She is the only one with that power who has inserted herself into elemental politics. Or is she giving up the title of Lady Soul?"

Bast growled in response, pulling Hel closer as possessiveness roared through him.

"I don't have time for this. I need to get back home," Mica said, surprising everyone as he broke his days-long silence from where he'd slumped in the corner with dark circles beneath his eyes and fatigue in every line of his body.

"The girl will act as insurance against Helaine's behaviour when I take her to train her."

Relief and anger warred inside Bast as he glared at the Earth Lord and tried to figure out his play. This was the first time he'd confirmed he would take Kaia, but was he really suggesting she be held for ransom? Before he had time to respond, Ra stormed into the chamber. He'd joined them for the last day to work through some logistics and must've been listening in.

"You bastard! She's a child! Not a pawn in your fucking games!"

"Bastion. Get your human under control," Mica snapped.

"Oh, you fucking didn't," Ra snarled in response to the derogatory words.

Bast lunged for his friend before he could ratchet the tension any higher and gripped his shoulder tight. They couldn't risk anything jeopardising Kaia's training. Even if Mica's words had him fuming as well.

"Calm down, brother. Take a breath. We can't risk messing this up for Kaia," Bast whispered.

He'd never seen his easy-going friend so mad. Never seen such loathing in his eyes as he glared at the Earth Lord across the table of ice.

"If you're going to speak that way about humanity, I'm not sure we will come back to this table," Niko cut in, the separatist leaders already rising to their feet and looking like they were about to walk out in solidarity.

Fuck. This wasn't how this needed to go. Peace was more important than anything. Mica seemed to regain something of his old diplomatic demeanour as he realised he'd gone too far. The Mica Bast knew would never have let his emotions get away from him like that, would never have been anything but calculating in how he operated in discussions like these. The Earth Lord was hurting more than any of them had realised from the damage to his stronghold.

"I apologise for my poorly chosen words. They were not a reflection on humanity. Just on him," he said, gesturing toward Ra and adding salt to the wound.

Bast pulled Ra's face into his shoulder so no one could see him hold a hand over his mouth to keep the vitriol he could sense in his best friend from spilling free. "Not here, brother. Not now," he whispered.

Ra spun on his heel and stalked from the room, not bothering to answer him. Bast watched him leave, knowing his concern was too visible before putting his poker face back on and turning back to the table. Ra may hate him for what he said next, but he couldn't let this summit fail.

"I believe Mica speaks the truth. His words were ill-thought and insulting, but he meant no disrespect to humanity. The two of them have a ... history ... with each other," Bast said, swallowing back bile at what felt like a betrayal of his friend.

It was cold comfort that his words and his willingness to stay were the only reason the separatists resumed their places at the table. They were following his lead, and he couldn't in good conscience lead them to anything but peace even if he wanted to slap Mica back to his senses.

"It is not unusual for the courts to secure relationships by fostering children. Kaia was heading to Mica's court anyway. I'm happy with this solution so long as it is understood that portalling into a stronghold without prior permission will be considered an invasion and will be responded to as such," Nerida said. "As will any other unauthorised entry," her eyes flashed at Kairon on those words and the usually inscrutable vampyr glared at her.

Something had happened between the two of them but Kairon had refused to answer any question about it when asked.

"Noted," Hel answered, inclining her head at the same time as Tir and the other ceptae.

"Then we're done here," Mica said, striding out of the room with his huge copper wings sweeping behind him.

It might not be the note on which he'd wanted to end the summit, but they'd achieved more than Bast had thought possible. He had hope for their future.

CHAPTER 18
HEL

Hel blinked open her eyes and rolled over in bed, her gaze caught by the beauty and peace of her sleeping mate's face. He looked so calm like this. His breaths deep and even. She could feel them both brushing over her wing surface and inside her own chest, just like his heartbeat. Reaching out, she traced a gentle finger across his cheekbones and down to his soft lips, licking her own subconsciously as she remembered what they'd done to her last night and throughout the early hours of the morning. They were still insatiable for each other. She suspected they always would be.

Shifting closer to him, she nuzzled into his neck and traced a trail of butterfly kisses up to his ear. His breath caught and a strong hand wrapped around the back of her neck to keep her in place when she started to pull away. Her smile brushed across his skin as she sucked it into her mouth hard enough to bruise. Bast's moan filled the bedroom.

"What time is it?" he asked, as his hands stroked down her folded wings to find her waist.

257

Hel's whole body shivered at his touch and then she sighed. "Late. I was just waking you up. We need to get moving."

"Such a fucking tease," he said, voice still gravelly as he pulled her into another kiss and they lost themselves in each other again.

A sharp knock on their door reminded them they really didn't have time for this. They both groaned in frustration and then obediently slipped out of bed.

"We'll be out in a minute!" Hel called.

"You'd better be!" Ana called back.

Hel shared a pained look with Bast. They could both hear the grief she was trying to hide in her voice. Today was the day she was losing her little girl. It wouldn't be forever, but it was the first time they'd ever been parted. When Kaia returned, she'd be a young woman secure in her power. Or so they hoped.

They didn't waste any more time getting ready. When they emerged into the living space, they found a table laden down with waffles, bacon, and fresh orange juice and a very pale, very quiet Kaia sitting waiting for them. They were all her favourite foods, but she hadn't made any move to take them. Ana was still bustling around in the kitchen making kawakawa tea. Hel suspected she was doing it more to hide her tears from her daughter than for any genuine desire for the magically enhanced stimulant.

"Hey, baby girl. Got space for me there?" Hel asked, gesturing to the seat beside her.

Kaia nodded, her fingers gripped tight to the pounamu pendant hanging around her neck, stroking the smooth jade surface over and over—a piece of home her mother had given her to take with her.

Bast started serving everyone food and Ra stepped through the door a moment later. Hel frowned a little at the stilted hug he gave Bast in greeting. Things hadn't been the same since they got back from the Antarctic. She knew they'd get over it. They loved each other too much not to. But it was one more thing for everyone to deal with in the meantime.

"I got a present for you," Hel said to Kaia.

The girl's eyes welled with tears as she looked up at her and she wondered if she should've left it.

"Can't have my best girl out in the world without a decent blade," she said, and for the first time in months, she saw a spark of excitement in Kaia's eyes.

"Helaine. You better not be arming my barely teenage daughter with a lethal weapon," Ana called.

"No comment," Hel called back, winking at Kaia as she passed her a wrapped box.

The girl tore into the package and her eyes widened as she stared down at Hel's gift.

"It's just like yours," she whispered, stroking the metal baton that could be twisted out to form two long blades.

Hel watched as she took it out of the case reverently and turned it until the words she had engraved on it caught the girl's attention—Kia kaha. Kia māia.—the same words she'd said to her mother not so long ago. Stay strong. Be brave.

"Thank you, Auntie Hellkitten," Kaia said, throwing herself into her arms with a sob. It was the first time she'd used the teasing name since she'd been taken.

"You're welcome, sweetheart. Use it well. We'll be right here waiting for you when you're ready to come back home."

"You'll rescue a whole gaggle of baby soulweavers while

I'm gone and forget all about me," Kaia said, swiping at her tears.

"Never. You're burrowed too deep in our hearts for that. We will always be there for you, baby girl," Bast said.

Ana's sobbing grew louder. She was one of the strongest women Hel had ever met and it broke her heart to watch her run from the room, setting off Kaia as well. Bast went to follow her, but Hel pulled him back.

"You three eat. I'll go."

She found Ana in her old bedroom with a duster attacking imaginary cobwebs.

"We have to let her go to save her," Hel said.

Ana looked back with red-rimmed eyes. "I know. That doesn't mean I have to like it."

"You need to hold it together until she leaves, then. She needs to see this as a good thing, a positive thing. She won't be able to heal and learn otherwise."

Ana turned away and stared out the floor-to-ceiling windows with the panoramic view over the City of Souls. "Haven't I lost enough? First her father, now this?"

Hel pulled the older woman into a hug. "If I could save you from this pain I would. She's not leaving forever."

Ana sighed and patted her hand. "I know, dear. I *can* do this. I just needed to break for a minute."

The two women returned to the table to find Lord Mica had joined them while they were gone. She'd known he'd arrived as soon as she walked in and saw Ra sitting stiff as a board in his seat. No one else made him react that way. Despite his earlier words, she couldn't fault the Earth Lord's commitment now he'd agreed to take in Kaia. He'd even agreed to come and spend the day with them to ease the transition for the girl. They had one last surprise for Kaia before she left. She just hoped the animosity between Mica and Ra didn't make things worse.

Hel nodded a greeting to the Earth Lord, heaping some waffles onto his plate for him because he was sitting just as awkwardly as Ra, and then went and draped herself over Bast's lap, not caring about Mica's raised eyebrows. She needed a hug too, dammit. Bast pressed a kiss to her cheek with a low chuckle, wrapping his muscular arms around her.

Kaia's wide eyes flicked back and forth between the adults at the table, but at least she was finally eating something. Ana went and sat next to her daughter, the two of them whispering quietly to each other as they said the things that needed saying before she left.

Bast was sending Ra worried looks as they ate and the rest of the table was stuck in an awkward static silence that seemed to grow tighter and tighter with invisible tension. Hel jerked in surprise when Ra's voice cut across the table like a whip.

"I'm coming with her," he said, glaring at Mica in challenge as if he could force his way into the Earth Court by sheer willpower.

Bast's hand stilled on the inside of Hel's wrist where he'd been tracing a soft pattern. They hadn't discussed raising this again. Mica had refused the request repeatedly. They'd wanted to send someone with Kaia but the politics had been too fraught and they'd decided to wait and see how she fared. After months of trying everything they could to help her out of the darkness she'd fallen into, they'd realised she might need this trip away for more than just getting her errant power under control. Sometimes strangers could help when family could not. Mica knew she needed support and was providing a therapist as well as promising to keep a close eye on her personally. He might've betrayed them when he agreed to hand Hel over to Sol, but he treated all children as precious and no one could accuse him of not having a moral compass even if it sometimes put them at odds. Hel could understand his reasons for his past actions, even if she hated them.

Watching the hope form on Kaia's face at Ra's words, she thought maybe they'd miscalculated when they'd decided to let her go alone. Fuck. Kaia was going to be crushed when Mica turned down Ra again.

Mica's eyes flicked to Kaia and Hel was grateful for the control he seemed to have regained since the awful end to the summit. He was back to his staid, diplomatic self even if he still looked tense and drawn.

"Why would I let you do that?" he asked.

Hel held her breath as she waited for Ra's reply. She'd expected an outright refusal.

"Because I might be able to help with the stronghold. We use technology and magic together here in a way you don't." Ra's conciliatory offer sounded like it had been dragged from him unwillingly, like it was the last thing he wanted to do. His eyes were on Kaia as he spoke. He'd do anything for her. Even work with the man he now despised.

"Ra was the one who came up with the system I use to manage the souls and his tech was what let me design the shielding for the soulweavers. There is no one more qualified to find a technological solution to a magical problem," Bast said, sensing the crack in Mica's defences and jumping in to support Ra's argument.

"You think I would expose my stronghold to someone like him after what he did?" Mica asked.

"I think you don't have a choice. It's not getting any

better. It's been months. You look like a crack addict who's—"

"Ra!" Bast cut over the top of him before he could finish whatever insult would guarantee he failed.

Ra swallowed and then clenched his jaw, eyes back on Kaia. "I apologise," he said through gritted teeth.

Mica stared at him for a long moment and then tipped his head in acknowledgement infinitesimally. "Fine," he said, probably surprising himself more than anyone else at the table, and that was saying a lot.

"What?" Ra croaked.

"I said fine. You may accompany Kaia. Bring your technology. But you can't work for Bastion at the same time. If you insist on coming to my court, you are *mine* until you leave and this disrespect ends now. I won't tolerate you undermining me in my own court."

"Respect goes both ways," Ra shot back.

Hel's eyes bounced back and forth between the two men. They'd always had a fire between them. It had started as lust and nothing was darker than when that kind of passion turned to hate. What the fuck were they doing?

"Fine," Ra said, finally. "I agree to your terms."

Bast shifted beneath her. "Brother..." he said.

Ra looked up at him and a silent understanding passed between them. Hel could feel the stab of pain in Bast as he realised he was losing the first friend he'd ever had.

"Thank you," Bast finished, even though Hel knew that wasn't what he'd started to say.

The two of them had been inseparable for a quarter of a century. Ra was his right hand. They both looked shocked at the sudden knowledge that they would be on opposite sides of an ocean, unable to talk freely.

"I'm counting on you to look after him for me, Hellcat," Ra said.

"Always," she promised. "Just like you'll take care of Kaia for us."

Kaia, bless her, chose that moment to let a little of her sunshine back into the room. "Now that's sorted, I wanna know what my surprise is, Uncle Ra."

The strained smile Ra was wearing stretched into something more genuine as he watched Kaia bounce in her seat.

"You weren't even supposed to know there was a surprise, K-bear," he teased. "You're too sneaky for your own good."

Kaia jumped to her feet and started pulling on his arm. "Come *on*."

"How do you know your surprise isn't up here already?" Ra asked, laughing.

Hel and Bast shared a look as Mica's face softened a touch at the exchange. Maybe they wouldn't kill each other after all.

"Māmā, make Uncle show me," she said.

Ana surreptitiously swiped at her eyes and then stood, starting to clear the table. Hel and Bast jumped in to help and before long the six of them were heading to the elevators.

"Close your eyes, scamp," Ra said as they stepped into the small space.

It got awkward quickly as four sets of wings jostled for space and Ra ended up reaching around Mica to press the button. Both men froze at the unintended intimacy.

"Are we going to The Crypt?!" Kaia squealed, breaking the moment.

Hel laughed and put her arm around the girl. Kaia had

never been allowed in the nightclub for obvious reasons, but she'd tried to sneak in there a dozen times throughout her childhood. They'd decided it was the perfect place to host her farewell.

"Happy moving day, sweetness," she said.

Kaia glanced up at her, surprise and then determination showing on her face. "Happy?" she asked.

"We're going to make it happy. You are so loved, darling girl. This is just the next exciting chapter in your story," Hel said.

Kaia glanced to her mum for reassurance and Ana pulled it together enough to smile. "Hel's right, sweetheart. Show Lord Mica how we party here."

"I'm familiar," Mica said, eyes meeting Ra's before he turned away. Hel wondered, not for the first time, how far things had progressed between them when Mica had stayed with them all those months ago.

"Do you have parties in the Earth Court?" Kaia asked as the elevator doors opened.

Mica smiled. "We're planning one of the biggest parties ever in a few months."

"Can I come?" Kaia asked.

"Of course. I'd be honoured," Mica said, inclining his head before stepping aside to let them lead the way under the bronze plaque at the club's entrance and onto the dancefloor.

"Surprise!" a cascade of voices called out, and Kaia froze in place at the door, the electric blue of her wings trembling as she took it all in.

Everyone who cared for the girl was there—her friends from school, her teachers, the couriers she used to tease and harass. It was a mark of how special the girl was that the room was also filled with the entire ruling partnership and mix of all the peoples they'd welcomed into the city. Kaia might be hurting and broken, but that hadn't stopped her from checking in on the children of both the vampyr and the ceptae and easing their transition into living with them. She may have lost her joy for now, but she'd never lost her empathy. Now, it would be her turn to start her life somewhere new with strangers. They could only hope the residents of the Earth Court were as welcoming to Kaia as she had been to the City of Souls' new residents.

Ra made his way to the DJ turntables and as Kaia's favourite songs filled the space and colourful lights flashed across the room, the girl found her footing and greeted her friends with hug after hug.

Leaving her for now, Hel and Bast made their way by silent agreement to the bar where the bartender Dee handed them two glasses of whiskey. It was only early afternoon, but sometimes you needed to steal a moment of familiarity wherever it could be found.

As Bast pulled her into his arms and wrapped his wings tight around her, they swayed in time to the thumping beat of the music.

"Are you going to bite me if I kiss you?" Bast whispered in her ear.

Hel smirked at the reminder of the words he'd spoken the first time they'd stood like this in The Crypt. There had been so much lust between them. So much hate.

"Only if you ask nicely," she said, her lips curling into a smile against his skin where the top buttons of his shirt were open.

Bast gasped and then threw back his head in laughter as

she pressed the tip of her dagger to his thigh teasingly, just like she had that night.

"You're a fucking menace," he said, kissing her neck as he wrapped her tighter in the black of his wings to hide them from view, sparks of their silver and blue magic thrumming between them and twining tight.

"Just kiss me already, necromancer," Hel smirked.

And he did. Soft and full of love. A promise of forever.

The familiar first thrumming strains of a remixed 'Wicked Game' sounded across the club, perfectly in time with their shared heartbeat, and they both glanced over and smiled at Ra across the room. Mica had drifted closer to him, as if unable to fight the draw to the irreverent brightness that was their friend and brother.

Kaia came over to join them by the bar a moment later, wrapping her small arms around them both and leaning her head on Hel's arm as they pulled her into an embrace.

"I'm going to miss you," she said, almost too quiet to hear.

"We're going to miss you, too, sweetheart. More than you know. We love you," Hel said.

"Uncle Ra's going to drive Lord Mica crazy isn't he?" she asked.

Hel glanced in the direction Kaia was looking and saw Ra had joined the dancefloor, a crowd of men and women around him although much more G-rated than he usually would've been. Mica was heading their way.

"We need to get going," he said, glaring at the people surrounding Ra.

"One more dance?" Kaia asked, holding out her arm to Mica in invitation.

The Earth Lord looked surprised, but he took her arm and

led her out to the dancefloor before bowing like the courtier he was and sweeping Kaia into a formal elemental dance that he somehow made work despite the modern human music.

The cheeky girl manoeuvred them so they were dancing right alongside Ra and the two men studiously ignored each other.

"She's going to be alright, isn't she?" Hel asked, smiling at the girl's antics.

"Yeah. I think so. Eventually," Bast replied.

"And Ra?"

"It's anyone's guess how that's going to play out."

She didn't really need to move anywhere in particular to portal the three of them to the Earth Court, but when the song finished, they made their way to the roof of Soul Tower anyway.

The cool wind tugged at their clothes as they stood under the bright sunshine and said their final farewells.

"Stay safe, baby girl. We'll be here waiting when you're ready to come home," Bast said.

Hel pulled Kaia into a tight embrace and whispered her love. Ana had said her goodbyes just outside the nightclub, unable to face watching the moment her only child left her for distant shores.

"Thank you for taking her. Please keep her safe. You have our heart in your hands," Bast said, turning to Mica.

"I give you my word," Mica said.

"Is it too much to ask you to keep Ra safe, too?" Hel asked.

Ra rolled his eyes. "I don't need a damn thing from him."

Mica ignored the angry words. "Like I said, while he's in my court, he's mine. I will protect him the same way I protect all my people. And if he betrays me again, I will punish him the same way I would one of my own."

Hel winced. The Courts were ruthless about loyalty. Ra looked like he'd swallowed something sharp. Mica stepped away to help collect Ra's cases of tech to carry through, and Bast turned to his closest friend.

"Don't do anything stupid while you're there. I can live without you here every day, but I can't live in a world where you don't exist."

"I can still help—" Ra started to say.

"No, brother. If you can't abide by his rules to keep *yourself* safe, do it to keep Kaia safe. No touching base with your old team here. No checking in with Morrigan. No communications with any of us you wouldn't be happy with Mica reading."

Hel's heart ached for the two of them.

"Fuck," Ra said, the gravity of his situation hitting him.

"I love you, brother."

"Love you too, bro."

Bast and Hel worked together to form the portal that would take their family away from them, careful to keep smiles on their faces as first Mica, then Kaia, then Ra stepped through. As they let the rift collapse closed, Bast pulled Hel in tight to his chest. She gripped tight to his arms where they wrapped around her waist. Together, they looked out on the glittering cerulean of the harbour shining in the distance framed by the silhouettes of the nesting griffins circling in the air. Magic thrummed on the breeze and the noise of distant construction filled the air as their people worked to restore the cityscape to what it had been.

"Don't ever leave me," Bast whispered into her hair, his words almost lost to the breeze.

Hel tilted her head back and pulled him down into a kiss.

"I'm yours forever, Bast. Just like you're mine. Even death couldn't keep us apart."

LATER THAT NIGHT in a Soul Tower that felt strangely empty with the loss of two of their closest family, Hel and Bast were once again wrapped around each other in their bed. The sheets were twisted and their bodies sweaty with the release they'd tried to lose themselves in. Kaia and Ra hadn't lived in the penthouse with them, but somehow it still felt unnaturally quieter with their absence.

Bast was stroking Hel's hair and tracing his fingers along her horns as she rested her cheek on his chest where her mark was branded into the skin over his heart.

"I love you," she whispered. "Thank you for finding me. Thank you for giving me the family I didn't know I needed. It might hurt sometimes, but it's everything."

Bast tilted her chin up and kissed her lips softly, his power reaching out to stroke along hers as her body tingled everywhere they touched. "*You* are everything," he replied. "My body. My heart. My soul. It's all yours. Forever."

The distant sound of the front door crashing open interrupted them before they could continue.

"Lord Bastion, help!" a woman shrieked.

The two of them stumbled out into the living area, silk sheets clutched tight around their naked bodies to face whatever threat was behind those words.

Bast had shoved her behind the sweeping sensuality of his black wings despite the fact she didn't need him to protect her. She would've pushed him aside, but he'd stopped in his tracks and was bent over wheezing. She might've been concerned if she couldn't feel his amusement through the connection before his laugh rang out in the space.

Peering around him, she saw the baby soulweaver they'd saved from the Air Court in the arms of his mother ... juggling glowing balls of memories of the dead like it was nothing. The kid could barely get his thumb in his mouth and yet his twitching fingers were making the silver bubbles dance around him and his terrified mother. Hel peered closer to see what the shifting images in the spheres contained, but thankfully they were only happy memories from the dead. The shield they'd embedded in his young body was holding strong. She could feel the indignation from the souls around her that she'd even had to check.

Through Bast's connection to them, she heard them speak. *He couldn't sleep and his mother was so tired. We were just keeping him quiet.*

Hel and Bast's eyes met and they shared a wry smile. This was their life now. Adopting the outcasts of their world into their weird little family and taking midnight calls when the dead got a little too playful with their charges.

It was perfect.

Ana knocked softly on the door a moment later and took the mother in hand, gently directing her to the couch while Bast went to the kitchen to make some calming tea for her. Ana had always had an uncanny way of being there when she was needed and that wouldn't ever change.

Hel reached out and gently scooped up the infant from the overwhelmed woman, cuddling him to her chest as she walked to the nearby windows to look out over the City of

Souls. Bast joined her a minute later, wrapping her in the warmth of his wings and arms as she softly sang the only lullaby she knew from her childhood while they rocked the baby back to sleep together. It was the song she'd sung to Bast as he flew with her in his arms on a night that seemed so long ago now. Before she had wings. Before he'd become her whole world and opened up the whole world to her in return —*a breath of home.*

THANK YOU FOR READING! *The next book in the Melded Earths world will be ECHOES OF EARTHSHINE, a stand-alone novel about Mica and Ra set immediately after the events of the Soul Court Ascension trilogy.*

If you'd like to hear about my new releases and read the prequel short story of how Bast came to the City of Souls during the Melding and met Ra, sign up to my newsletter through my website.

ACKNOWLEDGMENTS

We did it!

Thank you so much to everyone who has helped me on my journey to publishing my first novel series!

Special thank yous, in no particular order, go to: my wonderfully supportive family, Bex who has read everything right from the start, my awesome proofreader and cheerleader Madeleine Collinge, Amber and Marie who resparked my joy in reading and writing and answer my million neurotic publishing questions, Cassie who gives so much and always has my back, Toni for her friendship and thoughtful responses, my beta reader Priscilla and my ARC reviewers, my brother Dave for sharing his travels in Bolivia and sending me a photo of that perfectly spiky sculpture for Chapter Five, my workmates for enthusiastically listening and supporting, and to all my wonderful writing friends and communities who encourage and build me up every day.

And, most of all, thank you to my readers! You rock! I hope we go on many more sexy-winged adventures together.

ABOUT THE AUTHOR

Mel Harding-Shaw is a paranormal romance and urban fantasy writer from Wellington, Aotearoa New Zealand. Her debut novel *City of Souls* won Agent's Choice in the RWNZ Great Beginnings Contest.

She's also a widely published award-winning writer of short speculative fiction as Melanie Harding-Shaw and has published five books under that name: a trilogy of near-future novelettes, a story collection *Alt-ernate*, and a witchy urban fantasy novella *Against the Grain*.

Mel won the award for Services to Science Fiction, Fantasy and Horror in the 2020 Sir Julius Vogel Awards. You can find her at www.melaniehardingshaw.com and on social media.

Printed in Great Britain
by Amazon